Search for the RED NAPOLEON

Ukraine, Spring of 1919 and Aftermath

War Journal

Norm Mitchell

 Oakheart Scriptorium

Paperback: 979-8-218-13681-9
eBook: 979-8-218-13682-6

Cover and book design by Mayfly Design

Library of Congress Catalog Number: 2023901429

"The only thing new in the world is the history you do not know."

—President Harry S. Truman

"Should random fate discover something for you, hold it dear, for it shall become most valuable."

—Madame Daria, The Fifth Day of August,
Eighteen Hundred and Ninety-Two

Norm's Note

This may be the last remaining account of the challenging events leading up to a pivotal battle during the Russian Civil War of 1917 to 1923 and its terrifying aftermath. Lieutenant Colonel Mikhail Antonovich Baron Markov, a cavalry squadron leader of the White Guard, documented it in the ninth volume of his war journals. I have no idea where the other eight volumes are located. The White Army's struggle against the Bolshevik Red Army was a bloody conflict largely unknown in the West, and you will discover why. You will also learn why it should be known today. The struggle he faced, far from being ancient history, is like the struggle we face today.

The original war journal is in my safety deposit box. It was written in French, because, like other members of his class, the colonel, a Russian aristocrat, spoke French with his family, his equals and his superiors. He reserved Russian for his troops. I found the journal after the death of my mother in December 2007. It was a surprise to me, as she had never mentioned it. I began my translation in September 2020 after submitting my latest manuscript, *Prisoner of Hope*, to the publisher, and this new project kept me busy during the remainder of the pandemic lockdowns. It required a good deal of editing. For example, I have slightly tightened up his leisurely style and removed irrelevant asides that slowed down the text. I have preserved the few Russian terms he used—*Muzhik* for the Russian peasant and *Zhidy* for Jew, plus *shtetl,* Yiddish for a Jewish village in eastern Europe. I have also retained the old Russian "ii" suffix to indicate the plural, as in "bolshevikii." Also retained is his idiosyncratic capitalization. He refused to capitalize "Bolshevik" or "Cheka" because he found both so despicable. To avoid confusion, I've used the American equivalents for Russian military ranks and Westernized place names (Kiev rather than Kyyiv). Editorial additions or explanations are enclosed in brackets. Mikhail's asides are in parentheses.

Mikhail's journal ends abruptly, and what I found particularly fascinating follows: entries by two other individuals that take the story further.

Now let's turn to the journal. Tucked in the front flap is a preface, which is undated. The paper is yellowed and wrinkled from water damage, and it retains the faint odors of tobacco, gunpowder and sweat.

War Journal IX Preface

I am Lieutenant Colonel Mikhail Antonovich Baron Markov of the White Guard Cavalry, formerly of the Tsar's Imperial Horse Guards Regiment. We are at war with the Red Army, and my squadron is assigned to Lieutenant General Anton Ivanovich Deniken, the White Army Commander-South.

As an amateur historian, I hope my son and his sons may gain crucial insights into my time and even theirs. Therefore, I shall endeavor to present these events and myself as honestly as possible. Had I been free to choose my own path in life, I would have preferred to be a professor of history at the great University of Kiev. The life of a scholar still holds great appeal for me, and one day, God willing, when this wretched business is done, I should like to resign my commission to follow that course. For the present, however, I must continue to wage war so that my sons and daughters will know peace.

I began to write about my life as a soldier in the spring of 1904, just prior to the Japanese War. It was a brief letter, just my credo and biography. But as time passed, my accounts have become longer and more complicated, until now, in 1919, that first account seems almost like child's play. I began the Up-to-Date in Volume VII in late 1916, during the Great War. Each time I begin a new journal, I transfer these pages to the front flap so that I can reread them for inspiration and peace, and add events to the Up-to-Date.

MY CREDO OF WHAT I BELIEVE AND WHY I SERVE

A good warrior is not just a man
who does not lose his head
at the crucial moment.
A good warrior is a man
who does not fall into boredom
when there is nothing to do,
but endures everything.
Try as you might to sway such a man,
he will stand his ground.

These are the words of Ukrainian folk hero Taras Bulba, telling his sons what makes a good Zaporozhian Cossack, from the eponymous book written by Mr. Nicholai Gogol. I am pure Zaporozhian—The Host from beyond the Dnieper Rapids—descended from countless generations. Our fiercely independent Cossack ancestors bravely defended their homeland in central Ukraine, which means "border regions"—part of the steppes, vast plains of rich agricultural land that has long been a buffer against invasions. From the west, the Roman

Catholics from the Polish-Lithuanian Commonwealth. From the northeast, the Russian Orthodox Muscovites [later Tsarist Russia]. From the south, the heathen Moslem from the Crimean Khanate bordering the Sea of Azov.

The Cossacks were ferocious warriors, but they lacked discipline and order. Ukraine was eventually bested in the late eighteenth century and forcibly incorporated into the Russias. In time, the proud Cossacks were subsumed into the Imperial Russian Army. But even today, the wild, free heart of a Ukrainian Zaporizhian Cossack beats in my breast. It has been the struggle of a lifetime to reconcile being Ukrainian with living in a Russian world of order.

A Brief History and Biography

The Markovs are an ancient and honorable family. Beginning some millennium and a half ago, we were allies of the ruling family of Ukraine, the Amal Ostrogoths, and at one time, we held extensive lands north of Kiev, near Chernobyl. I am the second son of Count Anton. When my father went to his reward, my older brother stood to inherit the land and title of count. I was expected to enter the military, although this was not my inclination. But my father was a very wise man, whom I admired and respected. Thus, when he told me there was no future for me in Ukraine and I should go to St. Petersburg and become a good Russian, I did so, at least externally. I was ten when I entered St. Petersburg's Imperial Page Corps School for the sons of the nobility and high-ranking officers to prepare for military careers, although I knew from a young age that I wanted to be a cavalryman. The curriculum was encompassing, and we even had the opportunity to be pages at the Imperial Court. When I was older, I was a page for a time to one of the Grand Duchesses, on whom I had a secret crush. (Of course, I did not dare tell her.) Upon graduation, I had a choice of regiments where I would, as cornet, the lowest officer rank, carry the regiment's standard [flag]. And I was made strong at the school by corporal punishment as well as bullying by the older cadets. Thus, I was well prepared for all that lay ahead.

My Ukrainian pride stems from the powerful and civilized Kievan State, where the east-west Great Amber Road intersects the Dnieper, then the main north-south trade route to and from the Byzantines. Kiev was founded in the ninth century, many centuries before Moscow, which was originally little more than an obscure northern outpost. You may well ask, then, am I anti-Russian? No, I respect and treasure the imperial order the Russians have bestowed on us. That is why I did as my father asked. I think the peoples of the Russias fear anarchy and chaos more than anything because of our tumultuous history.

The Up-to-Date

As I recounted in Volume VIII, the council in St. Petersburg overthrew Emperor Nicholai in March 1917 to establish a republic. But this grand enterprise was violently overthrown in October 1917 by the bolshevikii, a faction of ruthless partisans led by Vladimir Lenin.

By 1917, the Eastern Front war ended, and my troops and I were sent from Anatolia [Turkey] to Ukraine. After a brief interlude, we fought the Red Army there. Our battles continued even after the Armistice. The situation was like the American Civil War in 1863 when either side could still win—decisive battles lay in the future. Although surrounded by the Whites, the bolshevikii were firmly in control in Moscow and Petrograd, as St. Petersburg was now called. The Reds had unified leadership and strong supply lines. The Whites outnumbered the Reds and were better trained, but they were not unified. Our leadership was divided, fighting on four different fronts. For both sides, though, Ukraine—the Breadbasket of Europe—was the ultimate prize.

The situation here is complex and chaotic, not least because the Great War made over six million Russians homeless, and with this ongoing war in the Russias, even more. European and foreign correspondents report in their newspapers about a civil war. Were it so simple. White Russians such as I remain loyal to the former government and the memory of the Emperors. [Mikhail refers to the Tsar as "Emperor"]. The Reds, or bolshevikii, are trying to establish their communist rule over all the Earth. Also fighting for control of Ukraine are the Nationalists, led by Simon Petluria's socialist forces, and the Green Army, the peasants or common people of Nestor Makhno's Muzhik forces, officially known as the Revolutionary Insurrectionary Army of Ukraine. Other contenders in the fray are the Germans and the Austro-Hungarians, who again want to seize this rich territory. The Nationalists and the Greens have each declared Ukraine an independent country, and each of these parties hopes to rule it. The bolshevikii, on the other hand, declare that Ukraine remains part of the Russias. This may be the only point on which the White Russians and the bolshevikii agree.

What really muddies things is that this is a war of ideas, not of territory. There are no true front lines, as in the Great War when the struggle was for land. This is a war of dogma, and we are fighting among sects, as we did in the past against the Poles and Lithuanians, or in the wars over Russian Orthodoxy, or even as the German states did in the seventeenth century in the Thirty Years War. It is a religious war, in effect, such as our three-hundred-year war with the Mohammedan Turk. The "fronts" are inside the heads of men, and they can be here, or there, or nowhere. Not all combatants wear uniforms. Since we cannot peer into a man's mind, how can you tell if he is friend or foe? The seemingly peaceful Muzhik you pass today may turn out to be a Red partisan tonight, or an anarchist saboteur, or nothing more than some apolitical peasant concerned only with working his fields.

My father and older brother always made certain the shtetl villages of the Zhidy under their control were never subject to the vicious pogroms that have occurred in Ukraine for as long as anyone is able to remember. Such pogroms are why so many Zhidy have joined the Red Army, in particular the cheka. The devil Felix Dzerzhinski has placed many Zhidy chekists in Ukraine, and they have exacted a steep revenge on our people.

My father, older brother, and their families were killed last year defending their land. I do not know the exact circumstances. I suppose I am now the Count, but of what? Our estates have probably been confiscated by some army—who knows which. I have heard rumors that my mother and sister-in-law escaped the violence but have not been able to find out more. I pray for their immortal souls that they were not captured by the bolshevikii, as that would be a fate too ghastly to contemplate. I have seen the results of bolshevik rule in areas we have won back from them. Ah, yes, evil does indeed exist.

We <u>must</u> prevail. We know that Pravoslavni, the Christian Orthodox faith—the true faith—is what holds Ukraine together. The godless bolshevikii are ultimately doomed. That is why I must continue to serve.

PART ONE

Tuesday, 1 April 1919, outside Odessa, Ukraine / 0615 hrs. [6:15 am]

I now begin the latest installment of my wartime journals. We have completed our fighting retreat from Kiev. I have deployed half my squadron to protect our front, rear, and flanks, with the rest here in the center for rapid support. Thus, I have a few moments to write here as we await daylight for safely transiting our defensive lines before Odessa. Warm by my fire in my great-coat and fur hat with flaps, I take pen to paper and hope the ink does not freeze.

About a week ago in Kiev, Lieutenant General Anton Ivanovich Deniken, Commander-South of the White Army, summoned twelve of his most experienced cavalry officers. At first, our meeting was the expected assessment of the retreat and what would come next. Per routine, no note-taking was allowed. But afterwards, the general distributed prime Cuban cigars and VSOP brandy from his private stock. To our surprise, he now urged us to take careful notes.

[He resumed in French.] "You're reputed to be soldiers," he said. "Are you realistic and practical men, or are you fanatics and politicians?"

"Realists, practical men," we answered, stiffening our backs.

"We fight for a reformed republic, General Deniken," I said, raising my glass. The other officers raised theirs. ("Here, here!")

"Do any of you want to conquer the world?" he asked.

"No!" we thundered.

"Where is this leading, sir?" Major Nubtelni asked.

General Deniken smiled. "I just wanted to confirm that my senior officers don't have a messianic complex."

The general then told us of a new threat we must defeat: the Red Napoleon. The similarities between the bolshevik coup in fall 1917 and the French Revolution of 1789 were disturbing, he said. He went on to review events we knew well. After the revolution in France, there was a moderate National Assembly responsive to the will of the people until 1792, when it was overthrown by the Jacobins. The ruthless Jacobins had killed King Louis XVI and Queen Marie Antoinette, warning the people that there would be no going back to the old regime. The Jacobin Reign of Terror devastated the aristocracy and, ultimately, turned in on itself to purge its own leadership. The weak Directory that followed ended on 9 November 1799, when Napoleon Bonaparte, the leader of the French army, launched a coup. Napoleon proclaimed himself First Consul and, after bending the government to his will, Emperor. He subsequently waged a terrible war against Europe for almost sixteen years.

The Russian Revolution was following a similar pattern, General Deniken said. In October 1917, the bolshevikii overthrew the Russian Provisional Government. They killed our Imperial Emperor and his immediate family. The bolshevikii were now at the Reign of Terror stage: the Red Terror. Our best intelligence reports agree that there is already fighting within the bolshevikii regime. Their leader Lenin was seriously wounded by several assassination attempts last year, and his health is questionable, but he is holding on to his power.

The time appears ripe for a military coup. Like most of the bolshevikii, Lenin is an intellectual and no match for a coup by a charismatic commander. What we fear, General Deniken told us, is a strong Red Army commander with a messianic complex who does want to change the world through war. First, he would restore the Russian Empire and then, like Napoleon, move across Europe. With artillery, tanks, cavalry, aero-planes and legions of troops at his command, he could destroy a Russia and Europe already devastated by the Great War, the Spanish Influenza and the tribal conflicts still raging in Central and Eastern Europe. There are at least six senior Red officers more fanatical than their fellow bolshevikii. Of course, there may be equally fanatical junior officers, but it is doubtful they could succeed—senior officers have a much better chance of convincing an army to follow them. No commissars were being considered, he said: they were too loyal to the bolshevik regime. Even if this messianic leader merely wanted to restore our former empire, the war would exact a terrible price. Far better to restore the empire through diplomatic meetings among all the newly independent Russian states.

Who was this Red Napoleon we were to pursue and destroy? The general asked us for our candidates.

"We will pursue the most plausible one first," he said. "Think this over carefully and inform me who you believe this Red Napoleon to be. I shall make the decision and choose the officer to lead the mission to find and destroy him. It is not lost on any of us that when we do this, we are de facto protecting the current bolshevik regime from its worst enemy. A classic case of the lesser of two evils.

"But the White Army shall prevail in the end, even if a Red Napoleon does succeed. When we take Moscow, we shall show no mercy to whatever regime is in power."

I had no hesitation about my choice and informed the general right away. It is Nicholai Janovich Sabantsevski, who is bringing terror, chaos and death to Ukraine. But I have my own reasons for wanting him dead. General Deniken knows that, and I think that makes me a strong contender to lead the search. I have also had experience in such search-and-destroy missions. I trailed a number of Austro-Hungarian and German commanders and killed them all. My biggest regret is Karl Graf (Count) Huyn, commander of XVII Corps and military governor of Galicia. Finding him was simple enough, but his security was unexpectedly strong. I was still devising strategy when we were ordered elsewhere, and Huyn is still alive.

The light is coming, and it is time to move on to Odessa, my third home.

Thursday, 3 April 1919, Odessa, 2200 hrs. [10:00 pm]

Two days ago, after seeing the ladies of the squadron and our refugees safely transited through our lines, my White Guard Cavalry squadron arrived in Odessa at 0721 hrs. We are here to regroup and have our numbers reinforced before our next mission. I hope that mission shall be the search for the Red Napoleon, which shall be made easier because the weather is slowly becoming warmer.

Several disturbing things have happened to interfere with my pressing duties. This morning Corporal Stantuski barged into my office, disheveled and unshaven. He was one of my troopers who went missing during our retreat from Kiev, but before I could discipline him, he drew a pistol on me. Despite my commands to stand down, he proceeded to accuse me of being a coward and a Capitalist exploiter—and that I shall not repeat, except for the key word—oppressor. His vocabulary betrayed him—he had clearly gone over to the enemy and wanted to collect the cheka bounty on my head. This was a shock. He has been in my command for five years, with a good record. I had even considered promoting him.

He moved closer and cocked his pistol. I eyed my sidearm, about two and a half meters [8 feet] away on my desk. I needed to talk him down.

"Tell me what has angered you," I said.

"We should have fought to the last man in Kiev."

"Do you have a death wish?" I asked. "I do not." I thought that such a romantic notion made perfect sense for a novice radical. "But if you want to kill me, fire now."

I moved closer to him. The corporal is a small, wiry man, and I looked down at his twisted face. He did not fire, and I moved toward him, close enough to smell his foul breath.

"You shall not collect that bounty, you know. Usually, only chekists collect it."

He shook his head. "My commissar promised me that if I kill you and return with proof, such as your bloody tunic with bullet holes, it will be mine."

"Do not be a fool," I said. "You take my tunic back, and you shall only be rewarded with a quick death."

"No," he said, wagging his head back and forth, "no, Comrade Commissar Lourissa has promised me the bounty, and she is an enlightened woman of her word. We are friends, and we are going to be better friends."

As he pressed the pistol against my heart, I said, "You left the door open, Corporal. You shall be heard. If you shoot me, someone will come running and shoot you dead. You shall never leave the compound alive."

A pistol fired.

Thank God I was still alive, and the corporal was not. Sergeant Rupok Kapolski had also put a second bullet into the corporal's head. I had sent Kapolski on a search for supplies an hour or so earlier. Had he come back sooner, we could both be dead.

Rupok has been my Under-Prime scout for many years. To thank him for saving my life, I promoted him on the spot to First Sergeant and Prime Scout. He will replace the former Prime, who was killed on our retreat. Rupok is now in charge of all ten of our scouts. I have great faith in his abilities. He is tall, which is unusual for an Oriental-looking Khazaks, but, like all their men, a natural horseman. Most important, he is bold and daring. The former Prime had become too cautious, which I believe contributed to a number of our losses.

"I'll take care of the body," Rupok said, and I knew I had made a good choice.

I left him to it and decided to go to the military hospital to visit our wounded. Outside, I realized I was shaking with terror. A Guardsman had betrayed me. After all our campaigns together, our squadron had become a fraternity of trust and mutual respect, or so I believed. Are there other Reds in our midst? The corporal was a good trooper, but his defection erased all that. He shall not be buried with his fallen comrades. Indeed, he shall not be buried anywhere except perhaps in a refuse dump. Bolshevism is a seductive plague. There is no cure except death.

I am surrounded by death in Odessa. This is not the same city I have known most of my life. These days it stinks of filth and sewage, and the air is filled with disease. Typhus and the Spanish influenza are rife here. Everyone except the very poor wears a face mask.

I am also surrounded by refugees, whose numbers seem to multiply daily. I hear explosions now and then, a reminder that the Reds have been shelling the city, which is more annoying than lethal. Thus life goes on in a besieged city.

At the military hospital, I visited with our many wounded. There should not have been so many dead and wounded. Part of the responsibility belongs to one of my lieutenants, Vladimir Antonovich Tomsk, who was derelict in his duties when he failed to bolster our right flank during a fierce fight on our retreat. I must record something very painful here. I summoned the lieutenant to my office. Our interview was brief. I offered him a choice: face court martial, or take a pistol shot to the head. He understood that I was allowing him the choice of dying honorably as a casualty of war rather than dishonorably by firing squad. Nor would he be damning himself by suicide. He would have an honorable burial. I allowed this because he had been a proper officer until his fatal blunder.

I shot Lieutenant Tomsk. I shall miss him and really cannot afford his loss. But I had no choice. Seeing the suffering of the many wounded in the hospital reinforced that hard decision.

My next destination today was headquarters. I had been summoned earlier by Regimental Colonel Kamaranski. He praised my conduct in the fighting retreat, then handed me a sealed dispatch from General Deniken. To my delight, the dispatch ordered my squadron to go in search of Nicholai Janovich Sabantsevski, the most likely "Red Napoleon." The whole future of the Ukrainian campaign depends on our mission, the general stated. That is how important Sabantsevski is.

Others are searching for the Red Napoleon, especially two intertwined organizations: La Revanche [Revenge] and La Mort [Death]. They are merciless, as their names imply. They have the same goals, and sometimes they work together. Then their names are linked—La Revanche et La Mort—and called simply La ReM.

Both are secret organizations, but this is what I know thus far. La Revanche is a group of women—rumor says they are modern-day Amazons—headed by Baroness Lucine. Her title is Mother of Revenge on the Turk. Everyone knows her as "Mayr," the Armenian word for mother. She has been of great assistance to us because of her extraordinary network of agents throughout the Caucuses and, recently, Ukraine. Little is known about her, but there is a multitude of rumors. She shall send a contact to meet us in Kiev to give us details on the mission, even though Kiev is dangerous during the Red occupation. We know only that our contact's name is Aishna (Persian?) and that she has startlingly blue eyes.

La Mort seems to be more conventional—a cadre of soldiers— led by Mayr's husband, Baron Jacques Charbonnet. He is a former French captain. He is also hunting Sabantsevski, but rumor says his real target is one Comrade Koba, a man known for his brutality and sadism. Koba is reported to be Sabantsevski's commissar.

Some bad news: I shall not receive any new men for the mission. Kamaranski said that even though my orders are high priority, the defense of Odessa is an even higher priority; every man is needed here to hold the lines.

"Which direction will you go?" he asked me.

When I said I had not decided, he said, "Red forces seem to be weaker to the west. You should be able to exfiltrate through the lines at that point on the night of the fifth—the last moonless night this month."

"What about our other troops and the civilians if evacuation is necessary?"

"I am negotiating with the French now. Their ships will evacuate us if we must."

My expression no doubt betrayed my low opinion of the French.

"I agree. I had rather not ask the French, but they are our only chance. I can not count on our Black Sea flotilla, and that is the only fleet within reach."

"Once I have left, I shall not be able to protect my wife and daughter, Colonel Kamaranski. They must be aboard the first ship to leave. Their trunks are packed."

"Agreed, Colonel Markov. You have my word. Your wife and daughter are far too charming to be left behind."

"Where will the evacuees go?" I asked.

"I do not yet know," he said. And even though I kept pressing him about how I could contact my family in the future, he would not tell me, urging me not to be concerned. Besides, he expected the status quo in Odessa to hold until late spring, when White forces planned a major offensive against the Reds in Kiev. By that time, I should have completed my mission—Kiev would be liberated, and I would be informed of my family's whereabouts.

I was not satisfied with that response but knew it was futile to pursue it further. I have known Kamaranski for a long time. At one time I outranked him in the regiment, and because of that, he holds a grudge against me. I do not trust his word. He will do whatever benefits himself first. Nevertheless, I saluted and took my leave of him after burning the dispatch and scattering the ashes in the fireplace.

Sabantsevksi is a much more formidable rival than Kamaranski. I have known Nicholai Janovich Sabantsevski for thirteen years and he is charming, brilliant, and heroic. But underneath, he is a ruthless schemer devoid of conscience or decency. He is Lenin's guarantor, and without him, Lenin would soon be dead at our hands. But protecting Lenin is only a ruse for Sabantsevski. When the Red Terror reaches its zenith, the present leaders shall fall. Feliks Dzerzhinski, master of the cheka, shall, like Robespierre, fall victim to his own terror, and Sabantsevski will make his move against Lenin. The revolution always eats its own in the end.

I had luncheon in the Officer's Mess with my old friend Captain Grigori Sergeyovich Orlov, who is my medical officer and field surgeon. It's good to get Grigori's perspective. He's a non-combatant and, thus, not directly in my chain of command. I am able to frankly confide in him—his discretion is absolute. He confirmed that thirty-four died in the retreat—twelve due to Tomsk's blunder—and thirteen were wounded. I am deeply saddened that the squadron started out last year with two hundred men but now has only fifty-two fit for further operations. I had hoped the medical facilities here would be better. But we are almost out of medicine and have no anesthetics. Grigori has little hope for survivors with shrapnel wounds. He wants to receive drugs and medicines this afternoon from our long-time supplier, and I gave him two hundred roubles. Let us hope that is enough and that he is able to avoid the black marketeering scoundrels who have doubtless inflated their prices, as they tend to do. They should be honored to give up their supply for those who protect them, but they care for nothing but their own hides—the parasites. Bolshevikii abhor the black market and shoot those suspected of being involved. I think we would be well advised to borrow that page from our adversaries.

After Grigori returned to his duties, I drank coffee and thought of my family. I am proud of their roles in this fight against the bolshevikii.

My lovely wife, Baroness Ekaterina Ivanovna Markov—Katarin—is pregnant, yet she is still the senior surgical nurse at the military hospital, as well as unofficial leader of the squadron's wives and children. Our daughter Marianne is now eighteen and has also been a nurse for the last two years. They both know the fate of White Russian women captured by the bolshevikii, and that is why they are always armed when on the streets, where their beauty—shining blonde hair, blue eyes—always attracts attention. I must remove them both to safety. Our son Vitali is nineteen now and serving with distinction in another White Guard Cavalry squadron at the siege of Tsaritsyn in the Don River Valley. Tsaritsyn controls traffic on that vital river.

The five years of war have been devastating for Marianne. She was always sociable and cheerful, in keeping with her namesake, the Spirit of France, but all the horrible things she has seen in the grim operations of the military hospital have made her taciturn and withdrawn. Even so, she has had some happiness. For several months now, she was in love with Lieutenant Leonid Sobelovich Barinskov of my command, and recently he had asked for her hand in marriage. I gave my approval, as he was a fine officer with a brilliant future. Plans had begun for their wedding at St. Uspenski Cathedral here in Odessa. But he was seriously wounded in the recent campaign. His condition worsened, and despite our shortages of supplies, including the lack of anesthetic, surgery could not be delayed. The poor fellow was given only shots of vodka. After dreadful agony, he perished on the operating table. Marianne was distraught. Katarin and I spent some time trying to calm her. Thank God we had brandy to help soothe her to sleep.

The ladies of the squadron are a heavy responsibility. It is a blessing that most of their children are no longer in our care. When the Great War broke out in the summer of 1914, all the children of the regiment were sent to schools in Switzerland, and some stayed in Europe. By the end of 1917, the squadron had twenty-five ladies and only a few unmarried children. Now the number of ladies has been reduced by various factors—death, disease, decisions to return home—to six, with no children. Three of the ladies are widows who wish to remain with their friends. Lt. Barinskov was supposed to escort them to safety, but what now? It would be unseemly for them to travel without a gentleman officer whom they know (it would be a scandal to have a stranger escort them)—and I cannot spare a single man. As a young single woman, Marianne is especially vulnerable. I shall have to appeal to Colonel Kamaranski for help with the ladies. Perhaps Katarin will have some advice for me.

Post Scriptum 2330 hrs. [11:30 pm]

As I was about to retire, Katarin came home from a day at the hospital. She was clearly exhausted, yet warm and cheerful as ever for my benefit. I try to be the same for her. She had news about Vitali. His colonel has written in dispatches about Vitali's grasp of tactics and his initiative and courage. How proud we are of him.

She expressed her pride in me when I told her about my secret mission. "If anyone can accomplish this, it will be you, Misha," she said to me.

Knowing my beloved wife as I do after twenty years of marriage, I understood the pain behind her words. But Katarin is a baroness and the wife of a senior White Guard officer, and she knows her duty all too well. I am weary after five long years of war because I see no end to fighting the Reds. But, like Katarin, I must do my duty without complaint. We must treasure the time together that this war allows us. I think often of a few months ago in Sofia, Bulgaria, when we had a rare week's leave. After the privations of war, our hotel seemed wildly luxurious. I remember Katarin in the hotel bed, wearing, then discarding, her Parisian negligée. Her fair beauty is so much greater than when she was a bride of eighteen. "You are the tsaritsa of my life," I told her. "I shall never leave you until my last breath." One of those nights, she became with child. What a joy! If the child is a girl, Sofia shall be her name.

Katarin and I have been separated for much of the last five years, so when we have time together, it is as though we are newly wedded. We made love even tonight, in our exhaustion. Her ardor has grown over the years, as has mine. I have never been loved like that by any woman. Her love will be a beacon to me in the dark loneliness of my mission when we will be apart for who knows how long.

I thank God for this inner light at a time when the world is so dark. The Great War has sundered the fabric of both European and Russian society. In the so-called peace talks at Versailles, Britain, France, Italy and the United States are at cross-purposes as they try to establish a new international order out of the defeated empires of the Hapsburgs and the Ottomans but also restore a semblance of the old order. Meanwhile, our Slav brothers are making their own states out of the Hapsburg dominions. Yet bolshevikii are struggling for dominance. German workers infected with bolshevism attempted to seize power from the socialist governments in Berlin last year, and there are rumors of a coup against the weak government in Bavaria. In Hungary, Bela Kun has inaugurated a Soviet state. If he succeeds, our task will be even harder. May God watch over my family in the coming days and months.

Friday, 4 April 1919, Odessa, 1530 hrs. [3:30 pm]

Marianne joined Katarin and me in bed last night because the infernal shelling had begun again. I now understand it is more to deprive us of slumber than to destroy or kill. I was pleased the shelling did not darken my ladies' spirits. They left for their early call at the hospital with firm determination. I breakfasted alone at the Mess.

This morning Grigori reported on his efforts to get drugs and medicine on the black market. Unfortunately, our long-time provisioner has left for safer climes, and Grigori had to deal with Boris Samsonovich Sandikoff, a notorious scoundrel. Grigori was able to purchase only a minute quantity of what we need with the two hundred roubles. I examined his bottle of anesthetic and thought, had we had this for Lt. Barinskov, he would still be alive today. We needed much, much more from Sandikoff. This was a case for Sergeant-Major Vladimir Bagrov and Staff Sergeant Baadur Tshavthavadse—Vlad and Shav—and I sent for them at once.

I shall record here just who they are since who knows whether my previous journals shall survive. Vlad is Ukrainian and has served with me faithfully for over twenty years. He is wiser than his thirty-eight years would suggest. He is also a tall, strong soldier, and brave. He saved my life at Port Arthur, Manchuria, during the Japanese siege of 1904 and served with me during the Japanese War. He is like a younger brother, and I often consult with him. Shav is more the muscle man, and his body bears the scars of many battle wounds. He is a huge Georgian—almost two meters in height [6.5 ft.] and ninety-five kilograms [209 lbs.] in weight. He is about ten years younger than Vlad and holds strong to his traditional beliefs. He shaves his head and sports a black handlebar mustache. While new to my command, he proved his courage and loyalty during our retreat from Kiev so well that I promoted him from sergeant.

Within the hour Vlad and Shav were with Grigori and me, and we walked together through Odessa to confront the black marketeer. (As petrol is rationed, I try not to use my staff car.) Conditions in the city are terrible. We had to step around dead bodies from the winter that lay still uncollected in the streets. Sidewalks are clogged with the pitiful refugees, the destitute, the starving and the desperate. We have to be vigilant, sidearms chambered but ready to draw. Most of these hollow-eyed roamers give us a wide berth because of our uniforms, but the children—some of whom are feral, surviving any way they can—theft, robbery, even prostitution. Some of the girls are indecently young. One little girl seized my arm and would not let go. She demanded money, and I finally gave her two roubles to prevent a scene. Bless me, but I have become numb to the victims of war.

Grigori guided us through the alleys and byways until we came to an unremarkable storage building on an unfamiliar street. There was a long queue, and we pushed our way to the front, although I felt some shame in doing so. The door was manned by a stout man who didn't mind being rude to Russian officers

At the front of the long queue, I asked for Boris Samsonovich Sandikoff. I was told disdainfully, "Monsieur is presently occupied right now and can't be disturbed."

Without speaking, Shav lifted the fellow by his neck with one hand and held him aloft until he motioned us inside.

Sandikoff was sitting behind a massive desk in his office down a hall. He was a well-fed, middle-aged man with slicked black hair and an absurd little mustache under a thick nose. He wore a red silk robe more suitable for a Parisian dandy.

"I'm a busy man. Just get in the queue like everybody else."

"I'm not like everybody else," I said. "The White Guard Cavalry is putting a stop to your dealings as of now."

Vlad and Shav took positions on either side of him.

"Your time is up, anyway," I added. I have been at the front. The Red Army is headed for Odessa. They will make a full assault. And they shall succeed, thanks to the weapons they captured from us at Tiraspol and Nikolaev."

I flung a hundred rouble note on his desk. "This is for your entire inventory. If you refuse this offer, we'll hang you from a lamppost. You have sixty seconds."

I took out my pocket watch. Sandikoff looked fearfully from Vlad to Shad.

"I need weapons for my troops. Right now," I said.

"I have not had weapons for months," he claimed with quavering voice. "Bolshie agents bought all I had."

Shav pulled Sandikoff up by his collar and punched him in the ribs. Sandikoff crumpled back into his chair.

I threw another hundred rouble note on his desk. "Weapons, now. That is my final offer."

"All right," Sandikoff said. "My secretary will take you around the warehouse."

When Grigori and I left Sandikoff's office, Vlad and Shav stayed behind—Vlad clearly anxious to have his turn with Sandikoff. The secretary took us through several rooms, one of which was most disturbing. It was a bedroom—at least it had a bed with black satin sheets and piles of cheap-looking fringed pillows. The walls were red, the carpet some dirty white furry-looking material. Sitting in the rumpled sheets was a naked woman. Her hair was cut short in that modern style, like a black cap, and I winced at her heavy black eyeliner and dark lipstick. She was studying her fingernails, painted black, and did not even look at us.

"Madame Alexander, visitors," the secretary said.

"Why hello," she said, falling back and spreading her legs. She must have been drugged to behave in this way. I was shocked when I realized that she was flat-chested—as Katarin would remark, "her rosebuds had not yet blossomed." She was only a child—surely no more than twelve. It was both sad and disgusting. We quickly left. We could not let Sandikoff go. I swore then I would hang him, if only for being a seducer of young girls. That crime brings back a terrible memory. I have no time to write about that now. Maybe in the future.

Sandikoff had more of everything than we needed in his accursed warehouse. Plenty of weapons, though no German Mausers, unfortunately. And plenty of civilian supplies too, including two elegant hats I took on impulse as presents for my wife and daughter. We spent the rest of the day choosing supplies and arranging transport by truck back to headquarters. Then people still in the queue were invited to take what they needed from all that was left. Vlad and Shav kept them in order.

Before we left on the last truck, I went to rescue "Madame" Alexandra, poor little wretch. Grigori and I waved farewell to the people still waiting their turn to enter the warehouse, and they cheered us, wishing us long life and good health. As we drove away, I saw Sandikoff hanging from a lamppost. Vlad had made a sign for his chest— "War Profiteer and Seducer of Young Girls." All the bodies hanging along the streets have these signs. People need to see that crime is punished. Otherwise, chaos.

I went to the hospital with Grigori to deliver Alexandra for medical care. I was able to find Marianne to ask her to help this poor girl. To my joy, I saw sweet Marianne's face light up in a smile for the first time since the death of her beloved lieutenant as she put an arm around the girl and led her away.

Back at our billet, I received a telephone call from Kamaranski. I was exultant at the day's work and expected at least a thank you. Instead, he reprimanded me for allowing precious supplies into the hands of civilians.

"I am acting on direct orders from General Deniken and have great discretion to ensure the success of my mission," I told him. Having seen the conditions of most civilians, I determined they need the supplies as much as we do, especially the canned goods, I went on.

Kamaranski did not even answer. He just hung up. The White Army has not treated Ukrainian civilians very well, which is a great blunder, in my view. But I created some goodwill today.

Katarin and Marianne were delighted with their new hats— wide-brimmed, with feathers and ribbons and whatnot, and they modeled them for me, linking arms as if they were promenading down a boulevard in Petersburg. I was grateful to have provided them a brief respite from their otherwise miserable existence here. May God protect them in my coming absence.

At 2100 hrs. [9:00 pm], Vlad reported that he and Shav had captured several bolshevik agents trying to start a riot at Sandikoff's warehouse. Under interrogation, they admitted they knew about our mission, although not the specific target. They also revealed there are more of them in the city than we knew. I called Kamaranski to relay this information, and he actually thanked me. He even allowed that perhaps he had been hasty in condemning me in our earlier conversation. I reluctantly accepted his apology and told him my squadron will leave tomorrow night.

PART TWO

Saturday, 5 April 1919, Odessa / 2030 hrs. [8:30]

The repercussions from L'Affaire Sandikoff continued all day. People talk of little else—the unheard-of distribution of black-market goods, the swift punishment of that evil scoundrel.

Medals for the battle of Kiev were given at a regimental ceremony today on orders from General Deniken. Little as he might like to, Kamaranski presented me with my third Order of Saint George First Class. It's a fine gold medal with three black stripes on an orange background. Vlad received the Cross of Saint George First Class, an important non-officer's award (his fourth). Shav had a Saint George Second Class (his third). Their medals are also gold.

As Sandikoff was a Zhidy, Muzhiks just outside the city started to attack other Zhidy, but a group called the Zhidy Association of Armed Combatants resisted fiercely and prevented a pogrom. I have mixed emotions about such a development. While it is past time for the Zhidy to defend themselves, they might harm our cause by helping our enemies and even instigating insurrection in Ukraine.

Katarin does not care for the bizarre clothing and rituals of the Zhidy, but she is appalled at the violence and berates all involved as barbarians. She does not blame me for executing this Zhidy Sandikoff, but now I am not so certain it was the right thing to do. The aftermath of his death has been alarming, and a man must be held responsible for the consequences of his actions, even ones unforeseen. To excuse him would lead to anarchy and chaos.

This evening we attended services at Saint Uspenski Cathedral, along with the staff, to pray for the success of our mission. The bishop spoke of sharing with one's neighbors and the sinfulness of hoarding goods and talents. He urged the faithful to follow the example set by the White Guard Calvary in closing down black markets. And to honor the sacred purity of young girls. Katarin turned to me and whispered, "We must adopt Alexandra before Marianne and I leave Odessa." Of course, I approve. It would a sin to abandon this small, desperate girl.

As we left the cathedral, Yuri Igorevich, the Principal Assistant to the Bishop and my father's younger brother, approached us. I had not seen him in quite some time. It was a surprise—in truth, he was never terribly close to my father, and I had lost track of his whereabouts. He bade Katarin, Marianne and me to follow him into the Bishop's office, and I dismissed my staff.

Like the cathedral itself, this room was ornately furnished and overstocked with icons and gold objects, such as candlesticks and bowls redolent of incense. The room was warmed by a fireplace. My uncle fit right into this setting with his black vestments that gleamed like silk and the jeweled cross that hung from his neck. He invited the three of us to sit in overstuffed chairs, and then the pompous ass sat himself at the bishop's desk.

"Closing Sandikoff down was a great public service," he said. "His rival profiteers are happy too. The Bolsheviks are obviously not pleased, however. They have placed another price on your head. This time they want not only you killed but your entire family as well."

I was dumbstruck. "Who told you this?"

"The Bishop knows everything that goes on in this city, and I have his complete confidence," my uncle said with a smug smile. "He knows all about your secret mission, as do I." He proceeded to describe it in some detail. I was speechless, as the ramifications of what he had told me made me feel ill and scared to the pit of my being.

"But I can offer assistance," he said, rising to unlock an intricately carved cabinet, withdrawing a map. "This map shows the latest positions of the Red army. There is a break in the lines east of Odessa. You can exfiltrate through there."

This contradicted Kamaranski's information on a break to the west. We would have to reconsider our strategy.

"My first priority is to get the ladies of the squadron to safety," I said. "Especially after what you have just told us about the new bounties."

"I can help there too," he said. "There is a yacht in the harbor. It belongs to a princess—a great benefactor of this cathedral—who can take all the ladies at least as far as Constantinople. There's a large White Russian colony there, and it is relatively safe."

"Why would this princess do that? It is bound to put her in danger."

"To be frank, she does some trading on the black market herself. She just sold her inventory at great profit. With Sandikoff out of business, it was worth ten times as much. She's grateful to you, Mikhail, and she's ready to leave Odessa now."

"A generous black marketer, whether aristocrat or not, is still a scoundrel," I said. "And a scoundrel can never really be trusted."

I knew the princess's reputation: an idle, pleasure-loving woman who seduced and kept young men. But my uncle insisted that this woman was responsible and trustworthy, not to mention enormously influential. She had never betrayed her word. Katarin and Marianne would be much safer on this yacht than in our regimental quarters. I could not deny this. Despite our best efforts at security, some of our junior officers have been killed under what could only be categorized as unusual circumstances.

Katarin and Marianne had been silent during this conversation, but now Katarin spoke up.

"I am willing to trust the princess," she said. Marianne agreed, although I could see the fear behind their confident-sounding words.

Yuri started, as if surprised they could speak, and frowned. In his world, women, especially noble ones, are not supposed to have their own opinions—they are expected to follow their fathers or husbands.

My uncle Yuri's proposition, like the map, needed careful investigation. Yet what were the alternatives? Indeed, Yuri thought our situation was urgent. He said we should not even return to our billet—the ladies should go straight to the harbor.

"What about our belongings?" Katarin asked.

"The princess will give you a generous allowance to buy what you need in Constantinople."

"But we cannot leave everything—we brought family treasures on that wretched retreat from Kiev," Katarin said, clearly distressed.

"I shall go back to our quarters and get our luggage. There are things I must retrieve as well," I said, brushing aside Uncle Yuri's alarms about my own danger. "This is my price for allowing my family to depart with the princess. I should return within the hour. I shall meet the ladies at the quay and accompany them out to the yacht. I want to meet this princess and see her boat and crew before letting them go."

Yuri swore upon the soul of his grandfather that in my absence he would protect the ladies to the end. I caught his meaning that he would be joining the passengers on the yacht. I understood his wish to leave—obviously, he would be in danger should the Reds take over Odessa, but I thought of all the civilians who would also want to leave but not have the means. The thought caused me to dislike this man of religion even more. But he was vowing to keep my family safe, and so I could only smile and thank him.

At 1630 hrs. [4:30 pm], I ventured forth from our billets with Vlad, Shav and with everything of importance to us. We arrived at the quay before the others, and I breathed in deeply of the fresh air. We waited near the foot of the Boulevard Steps, their great breadth and height [longer than a soccer field], crowded with people entering and leaving the city. Out in the harbor, a dozen French warships were moored. They were a formidable line of defense against the Reds, perhaps the last. But did the French have the will to employ such power? Their military was shattered by the Great War and only now, with Germany bound to pay, do they plan to rebuild. I fear they might just leave Odessa and abandon us to the Reds. Until recently, the harbor has been frozen solid, and the water is still clogged with ice floes. Rumors are circulating that the French will withdraw as soon as the ice clears, probably in less than a week. If so, many of the people here would rise up against us and go over to the Reds. We know these bolshevik elements exist in Odessa, but we lack the manpower to ferret them out. We live atop a powder keg. A spark could come anytime, from anywhere.

It was nerve-wracking waiting for the ladies to arrive on the quay. I noticed a knot of men—eight or ten—among the crowd coming down the steps. They were a group, judging by their ragged, filthy uniforms, and the way they bawled and jostled each other suggested that they were drunk. But that could be just a ruse, I thought, as they came straight toward us.

"Those men are a disgrace," I shouted to Shav, who took my cue and raised his pistol. The villains scattered in all directions.

Then there were the beggars. A young girl approached me, almost skeletal in her rags, holding out her hand for money. She seemed to be without fear. I bent down and looked into light-less eyes. She was just the advance guard of a horde of such creatures. I hesitate to refer to them as children as there appeared to be nothing left of their innocence. I gave the girl a few coins and threw some more at the other ragamuffins to create a small riot as they dove for the coins. They formed a temporary cordon against possible assailants.

The arrival of the princess's large Hispano Suiza automobile broke up the melee, and I was relieved to see my ladies and Uncle Yuri. Their chauffeur was a tall blonde woman, a modern-day Amazon. I could not help staring as she effortlessly lifted the trunks and carried them to the motor launch that would take us out to the yacht.

The yacht was really a small ship and, like the Hispano Suiza, bore the hallmarks of great wealth and luxury—usually attained by massive corruption. Once on board, a woman in work clothes escorted the four of us to the princess in her quarters. Yuri introduced her as the Princess Alexandra Mytrovna. She was tall with regal bearing. Her wavy blonde hair was piled atop her head, and she wore a high-necked wine-colored dress adorned only by a jewel-encrusted Orthodox cross on a gold chain. Her visage was surprisingly pleasant.

I kissed her hand, then, looking around at the others, asked if I might have a word alone with her. They withdrew—although I did not miss Katarin's mischievous smile as she left.

"You look surprised to get a look at me, Colonel Markov," the princess said. "Perhaps you've heard about me as a wicked woman. Greatly exaggerated, I assure you, and quite deliberate on my part. I've spent a lot of money to cultivate my bad reputation. It's vital to my operations.

"Besides, I'd never try to seduce you. It's obvious how much you and your lovely wife love each other."

I began to relax a little. The princess was a serious woman.

"Let's get down to business," she said. "Passengers on this journey will be females only. Thus Father Yuri is the odd-man-out. I really despise him."

"Why is your crew all female, then?" I said.

"Why not?" she said with a grin.

"The Black Sea is dangerous," I said. "Hostile ships, even a few pirates. An all-female crew . . ."

"They are trained fighters, Colonel. You must not underestimate them. You can inspect our guns on the foredeck. My crew is more than capable of using them."

"You must understand that our ladies are not trained fighters. My wife is expecting a child. She needs special care. We have also taken on a young girl, Alexandra, seriously damaged by drugs and other abuse."

"Yes, I know her and her predicament and shall be happy to provide whatever she requires. And thank you for rescuing her from that vile Zhidy, Sandikoff, as well as killing him. Further, all your ladies shall receive much better care here than with an all-male crew, would you not agree?"

That seemed inarguable.

"I wish to do something special for you," the princess said. "Your removal of that villain Sandikoff was a great blessing for me. Come to Constantinople after your mission, Colonel. I shall see that you are generously compensated."

"No need," I said, but she pressed my hands and repeated, "Come to Constantinople."

I trust this woman, rightly or wrongly. Katarin is pleased that plans are settled. She and Marianne remained on board, and my wife shall arrange for the other ladies to join them early tomorrow morning. I had but a brief time to make my farewells to Katarin and Marianne as the trunks were secured on board. But then Katarin and I had already said our farewells last night. With blessings and wishes for good fortune all around, I took my leave. A warning to be careful seemed unnecessary.

Vlad expressed a strong wish that I stay on board and depart with the ladies. He reminded me of the network of limestone caves under the city of Odessa that criminals—literally the "underworld"—used to make their way through the city rapidly and undetected. Assassins could enter houses from the basement. "I remember," I said, then reminded him that, even though I appreciated his concern, we still had much to accomplish before leaving. On our way back to the regiment, I told Vlad and Shav we would be departing at 2000 hrs. [8:00

pm] for our secret mission. Vlad said the men were ready as we spoke. Their efficiency is a good omen.

I feel horribly empty with the departure of Katarin and Marianne, but I must focus on the charts Uncle Yuri gave me before meeting with my staff. If they aren't accurate, this could be the last entry in this journal. May God watch over us.

As I was returning to quarters from my staff meeting, I heard a shot, then a second. Before I could draw my pistol, Grigori had shot and killed another assailant after my bounties. How had the intruder maneuvered past our sentries? Who was he? He wore the loose-fitting sharovari pants and a high-necked blouse of a Cossack officer, but his pockets had no identification. Those pants were not his own— they had bloodstains in places he had no wounds. His hands were scarred and calloused, not the hands of an aristocrat. He likely stole the garments from a Cossack he either killed or found dead. A clumsy attempt at misdirection, probably by Makhno's anarchists. How depressing that he is another Muzhik. We shall soon be facing hordes of them. Ever since the uprising in Petrograd, as they now call it, these people have been filled with resentment and revenge. I used to hold these Muzhiks in high regard because they produced our food, but now, many are the landlords slaughtered by their own tenants. And the travelers slaughtered, robbed or worse. But the prospect of remaining in the city is equally frightful. These are indeed perilous times—condemned if we do, damned if we don't.

Calling the man who saved my life "Grigori" seemed inadequate, and so I asked him if I might address him by the more familiar "Grisha." He agreed, saying perhaps we were even now—he was in my debt for all the medical supplies I secured for him. He did ask to call me "Misha." Thus some good has come from the whole business with Sandikoff and his confederates.

I conclude with one more positive note. One of General Deniken's aides, an observer at the meeting, told us of a confirmed report that the Emperor and the Royal Family were not, in fact, killed by the bolshevikii. Elite troops from the Czech Legion freed them all. The Emperor is now in Vladivostok, preparing to lead all loyal Russians against the Godless usurpers in Moscow and Petrograd. This news gave us the lift we needed after our recent reverses. I am now eager to lead my men after the devil Sabantsevski.

PART THREE

Saturday, 5 April 1919, On Campaign / 1820 hrs. [6:20 pm]

Captain Anatoli Sergeyovich Dubowski arrived last evening, and I brought him up to date on our mission plan.

Before leaving Odessa at 2045 hrs. [8:45 pm], I divided my forces in two to increase our chances of success. Captain Dubowski, assisted by Vlad, departed from headquarters while I left with my contingent from Sandikoff's warehouse. Grisha is with my troops, driving the metal supply/medical wagon with his horse in tow. Shav commanding the rear guard. The weather was quite cold.

I had been tempted to go through the more familiar route in Bessarabia to the west. However, the Romanians and Reds are fighting constantly for supremacy there, and we do not know who is in control. Thus we went east through Ukraine, passing single file through Red lines. We know how to pass quietly—being experienced raiders, having often passed through German, Austrian and Ottoman lines. The Reds were dismantling their tents and loading up gear, and their noise muffled our progress. But we could ill afford a single mistake. I focused on my breathing and the aroma of smoky wood, remaining on high alert. Jesus rode with us, granting us success. In truth, the Reds' lines were some of the easiest we have penetrated.

Once at the rendezvous point, I led a prayer for our safe transit and our continuing good fortune. Yet too many people know at least the outlines of our mission. I wonder if the Reds let us pass through because we are riding into a trap. This would not be the first trap we have faced. Being back on campaign has cleared my head and brought back memories of past traps we have evaded.

We have made camp on a hill that affords us a view in all directions. I just posted pickets to warn us of anyone approaching, and I am now sitting at one of our campfires to get warm and take advantage of the light to write. It is a cold, dark night. There are only a few other campfires in the area, and perhaps our intelligence from Uncle Yuri was right—that Red forces in Ukraine are mainly to the west of Odessa, with only skeleton forces elsewhere.

I have enjoyed being back in the saddle with my black charger, Élan. "Élan" is the same name I gave my two previous black chargers. But this one is the finest, I believe, and best exemplifies the meaning of his name, "vigorous spirit." The word also refers to French military philosophy in that innocent time before and during the Great War and means constantly on attack, never static, never retreating. After the catastrophe of Verdun and the mutinies, that changed, of course, and the French army fell back to being a purely defensive force. I am no longer a Francophile. Nonetheless, the idea behind the name continues to appeal to me as a cavalryman, especially as a Guardsman. It still expresses our spirit.

What memories attach to my valiant chargers, as well as my saddle that rests on a branch nearby! The pliant, down-filled curves of my beloved saddle remind of our Cossack tradition. It originally belonged to my great uncle Iaroslav, a Hetman [Cossack chieftain] who fought against the infidel before his death on the battlefield in Crimea. My uncle passed it to his son, my cousin Ivan Sergeyovich, who gave it to me when I joined the Imperial Light Hussars. It makes me both happy and sad to look upon it. It has been with me in my success, yet what chaos and death have come upon the world during that time.

All this chaos and death sprang from the clumsy assassination in Sarajevo of the Austrian Archduke Ferdinand and Duchess Sophie by a nineteen-year-old Serbian fanatic. The Austrians, demanding punishment of our little Serb brothers, provoked the cursed war to preserve their thousand-year Reich. It is now broken into many states, fighting and bickering over the spoils, like vultures with a corpse. Moreover, the Serbian Black Hand secret police, which financed the assassination, is trying to draw all of the South Slavs into their new Kingdom of Serbs, Croats and Slovenes under the Serbian king Alexandar. Truly, God does work in mysterious ways that are beyond my limited comprehension. And the assassin, Gavrillo Pincep, reportedly died of tuberculosis in an Austrian prison in 1918. Or so they claim. I learned a long time ago that the Austro-Hungarian officers should not be trusted, in part because they knew their decadent Reich would lose the war and lied to keep the soldiers fighting—though they defected en masse anyway.

It is hard to believe now, after nearly five years of fighting, how enthusiastically we greeted the news of war in 1914. On to Vienna! On to Berlin! This modern war would be glorious, and brief! As if to punish our hubris, God made us blind to the obvious. Our tactics had not significantly evolved since the Napoleonic Wars, but the technology of war certainly had. The machine gun, above all else, became the master of the battlefield as countless men fell before its power.

During the summer of 1915, Emperor Nicholas II had decided to replace his uncle, Grand Duke Nicholai Nikolayevich, as supreme warlord. The Grand Duke was reassigned to the Caucasus Mountain Front as viceroy and commander-in-chief of the Russian Caucasus Army fighting the Ottomans [Turks]. Most of our regiments went as well. Our squadron had done such valuable service, however, that it was decided we should remain at the Austro-German Front for a while. We became lost in paperwork in Petrograd's headquarters and were not reassigned for over a year.

In truth, I did not push the issue. I had heard tales of the blood-soaked Caucasus Front and was in no hurry to rejoin my brother officers there to fight the heathen Mohammedans. I have since learned that Rasputin, the damnable monk, wanted the Grand Duke exiled, far away from the Court. And with the Emperor at the Front, he could wield his power over the Empress and her children in Petrograd. However, I do not believe the malicious rumors from irresponsible bureaucrats about his sexual liaisons at the Court with the Empress and Grand Duchesses. Nor do I believe the rumors that the Grand Duke was relieved of command because he had moved all non-Russians—Germans, Poles, Mohammedans and Zhidy—away from the Front. That was just common sense during wartime.

The Grand Duke established his headquarters in Tiflis, Georgia, and we joined him there in the summer of 1916 to continue with our centuries-long war against the Turk and other Mohammedans. One of our goals was to push the infidels far back past Constantinople in order to restore the Hagia Sophia to its rightful place as the foremost cathedral of the true faith—Pravoslavni [Russian Orthodox]. Politically, we wished to make the Black Sea a Russian lake to gain access to the Mediterranean for our ships. Our original deployment, I learned later, was to coordinate with the British colonial forces that had established beachheads in the Dardanelles at Gallipoli in 1915. Ah, what might have been.

We had great faith in the Grand Duke. He was a commanding presence, with great height and piercing eyes. Had he been a Muzhik, he would have commanded respect. The mission of the Imperial Horse Guards Regiment, including my squadron, was to reconnoiter the land and probe the Turkish lines. There could be no question of the loyalty of the vast majority of Georgians, as they are true Christians. When we rode east into Azerbaijan, however, we encountered numerous Mohammedan Azeeris around the oil center of Baku on the shores of the Caspian Sea. They were ostensibly the Emperor's loyal subjects, but one always had to be prudent, as their loyalties could lie with the Turks, their co-religionists. The Azeeris are barely civilized. They veil their women; they engage in endless blood feuds.

They are cunning and devious, yet I learned to tell the difference between allies and spies. Our most reliable allies proved to be the Christian Armenians, whom the Turks persecute.

We raided the Turk lines for captives to interrogate. Sometimes we interrogated them immediately; other times, if their information seemed particularly valuable, we took them back to Baku and the island prison of Nargin for further sessions—after which they would be left to perish of the diseases rampant in the prison. I justified this based on their beastly treatment of British and French prisoners. The few German officers we captured were taken to Tiflis for interrogation, where the surroundings were much better. We fought the Turk demonically, knowing that capture by those heathens meant we would never see our homes again. The mercy of God saw us safely through trials that might have destroyed lesser men. A fuller account of my campaigns is contained in volumes V through VII of my war journals, now in the safe hands of my dear wife Katarin. I miss her terribly and dream of her most wonderful farewell.

Saturday, 5 April 1919, On Campaign / 1000 hrs. [10:00 am]

Vlad arrived with his forces an hour after sunrise to report dreadful news. Their leader, Captain Dubowski, was assassinated last night as they were leaving Odessa. It was about an hour after curfew and the streets were dark. Suddenly a man in a long black coat ran out from the shadows, firing a pistol repeatedly. The captain fell. Vlad returned fire, wounding and capturing the attacker.

The captain had died instantly. The column returned to headquarters, where the captain was taken to the mortuary. Vlad interrogated the assassin and learned two crucial facts. First, the man belonged to the Zhidy Association of Armed Combatants. Second, his intended target was me—in revenge for the death of Boris Sandikoff. Now we know which side the Zhidy are on. The damned assassin was executed forthwith, with no delay. The column then left Odessa. Led by Vlad, they passed without incident through the Red lines.

May God have mercy upon Captain Dubowski's soul.

Sunday, 6 April 1919, On Campaign / 1800 hrs. [6:00 pm]

Today we followed the Dniester River north towards Kiev, making our way far enough inland to avoid patrol boats. I wonder if the cupolas of St. Vladimir Cathedral still shine from atop the high city as a beacon to navigation on the river. I have always considered Kiev my second home, and my mind wandered to all the wonderful times I have enjoyed there. Many of my troopers were born in Kiev and its environs. It is galling that we are not leading an expedition to liberate the city. God willing; however, we shall be doing precisely that in the future.

We are now on the vast steppe stretching all the way to China. This is truly the country of God, for the distances are so vast that man's measurements, such as versts and kilometers, are meaningless. Only God can truly comprehend it. Such a place makes a man feel insignificant, even lost—not only in place but also in time. My view is the same enjoyed by Scythian and Cimmerian warriors, as well as the Amazons (those female warriors of the Sarmatians), in the time before history. The same seen by my Cossack ancestors fighting the Roman Catholic Lithuanians and Poles for mastery of the land. I am following in that great Cossack tradition as I stalk the Pole Sabantsevski.

In late afternoon we came upon a beautiful valley and pitched camp atop the south rim. I reconnoitered the valley, walking Élan, encountering nothing of tactical value but breathing in the vernal smells of the trees and grasses now coming back to life after the long winter of hibernation. There was a time—it seems a thousand years ago—that Corporal Stantuski, my batman [servant], would have performed this duty for me. But he defected to the Reds. Why? I do not understand. He was well-treated in the regiment. Officers and troops—shall the relationship ever be what it was? Even if we defeat the bolshevikii, we can never return to the Old Order. I can see that the Old Order was imperfect, even if I think of it through a haze of nostalgia. How it could be made better is a conversation for another time, after we defeat the Reds and march in parades of victory through St. Petersburg, as it must again be called. Besides, should it be the will of God that I ride in such a parade, He shall surely grant our leaders the wisdom to rule. However, should I not live to see such a parade, I shall know that I have remained faithful and true to my beliefs, even in the face of eternity. For when Sabantsevski and I meet again, only one of us shall remain. That is my duty not only to my country, but to my sacred honor as well. A warrior cannot ask anything more than to satisfy the two demands of duty and honor. Even though the Imperial Horse Guards no longer exist, I shall always be, in spirit, a Guardsman.

Sabantsevski expects Whites to be conventional thinkers. He is probably right more often than not. Yet, as any cadet would tell you, it is a mistake to underestimate your enemy, and I do not. We are relatively relaxed at present but remain vigilant. I have sent out scouts and doubled the guard around our encampment. As always, we have a few surprises for anyone who might wish us harm.

I love this place. Patches of snow remain in the shade, and there is a slight chill lingering in the air, but spring is clearly on the rise. I love the fresh, clean aromas carried by the breeze. After the stench of Odessa, it is paradise. We have finally stowed our face masks.

This place reminds me of my childhood on my father's estate. One's childhood always seems idyllic in retrospect, but in truth, mine was. The bolshevikii propose such a utopia. I know that the world could never be that secure and carefree for everyone, but the man with little or nothing must find the bolshevik promises irresistible. And that, in miniature, is the nature of the war we are now fighting. The Reds kill to spread fear and panic amongst the populace, but our side cannot do that if we are to prevail. While we must always be on guard against the stranger, we must balance prudence with friendliness.

I must not lose my faith in my troops. We must be vigilant against spies, saboteurs and traitors amongst our ranks, like Stantuski—for a man can change sides almost as easily as he changes his shirt. But I have known my troops for many years, and we have mutual trust. If I allow prudence to degenerate into paranoia, then I have lost much more than just victory in the field.

Monday, 7 April 1919 / 1630 hrs. [4:30 pm]

I shall not soon forget that lovely valley where we camped last night—but not for the reasons I thought. Several of our scouts had not returned by dawn this morning. That is not unusual, given the way they operate, but they should have returned by 0800 hrs [8:00 am].

I mounted a search party with Sergeant Kapolski and a few volunteers. Not far from camp we found a man hanging from a tree. It was Corporal Barinski. He was naked and had been savagely beaten, abused and burned. I have known him for many years, and his fate was a blow to my heart. I sent for Shav and the rest of the squadron, save a few men to guard the camp, and volunteers dug a grave for the corporal. Meanwhile I scanned the valley, focusing my field glasses on the opposite ridge of the valley. There I saw a band of black-leather-jacketed chekists—Dzerzhinski's devils.

The best plan was to attack them from both front and rear, and I sent Shav and his men around the position. Further examination as I waited determined that most of the enemy wore the broad-brimmed black hats of Zhidy—so here were more Zhidy looking for revenge. They had a truck—probably an Austin three-ton, with a Vickers machine gun mounted in the bed. Since the truck was covered with a canvas roof, I could not know their exact numbers, but experience told me there were about sixteen.

As I watched, a dozen or so chekists hauled a barrel into place and rolled it down the hill. I heard muffled screams. A few men chased down after it. When it stopped, they pried it open and withdrew a bloody body, which they added to a pile of some ten or so other bodies, most surely dead. I restrained myself from ordering an immediate attack, knowing I must wait for more men. Two more such spectacles followed.

The moment Shav and his men arrived, we charged up the hill. So intent were the chekists on their gruesome task that we caught them off guard. We soon routed them, killing nine, capturing the others. Unfortunately, their commander was killed in the process and would not be able to provide us with any serious intelligence. While the surviving chekists dug graves for their tortured enemies—at gunpoint—Vlad and I investigated the barrels.

Faint moans issued from one, and Vlad pried off the top. Inside was the horrible sight of Corporal Schroeder, another of our scouts, lacerated by multiple spikes. Blood gushed out of his wounds. He was barely alive.

"Lieutenant Colonel Markov," he said. "I did not tell them anything. Nor did Corporal Barinski. Nothing at all."

"You did well, Corporal Schroeder. You are a hero. I am very proud of you. You will have your reward."

I held the corporal's hand as Grisha bent down to examine him. Grisha shook his head to indicate no hope.

"Please end this for me," Corporal Barinski murmured, and I gestured to Vlad, who gave him the blessing of a bullet to the head to end his agony. The other victims of the barrels were all dead. What cruel barbarians these chekists are. I have heard rumors about the chekists using smaller spikes in their prisons as an interrogation technique. These larger spikes—about thirty centimeters [six inches]—were not just to torture but to kill in an agonizing horror. Those appalling deaths would be used to spread fear, for had we not intervened, the mutilated bodies would soon be displayed in nearby villages and towns.

Once the poor victims had been buried, we executed the chekists with bullets to the head. Honor required that we show them more consideration than they had shown my troops. Seeking revenge for the death of Corporal Schroeder, Corporal Mansur drove his trench knife deep into a chekist's stomach so he would die slowly and painfully. I stepped in to finish the job with a bullet. I then assembled the men and reprimanded Corporal Mansur. While I understood their anger and desire for revenge, I said I would not tolerate such unprofessional behavior. The chekists may be barbarians, but we are professional soldiers. We did, however, leave the chekist bodies for the scavengers, taking their stores and Vickers before burning their truck. I had considered taking it with us, but it cannot go where our wagon goes, nor as quietly.

When we first fought against the Germans and the Austrians, there was a certain amount of chivalry for captives, at least amongst the officer corps. As the war intensified, however, such courtesies became increasingly rare. Today, such notions seem quaint. Truly we have entered a new dark age of barbarism. I felt nothing as we executed the chekists.

But I am clear in my purpose. One of the chekist victims was a girl of perhaps fifteen with the sweet face of a child in the process of becoming a woman. She was badly bruised, and her ragged Muzhik clothes were torn. The chekists had clearly violated her before shooting her through the base of her skull. I would wager she had no political beliefs, so why was this dear young girl killed? Do they fear the people in whose name they rule so much that even such a girl is a threat to their power?

I have no illusions about the dangers women and girls face in a war. But usually, they are not killed, even after violation. My heart grows heavy with the thought of my wife and daughter on the sea and pray that God protect and shelter them in this time of trial. Some might think I should not have abandoned my family to the mercy of strangers, but my mission is crucial: Sabantsevski must be destroyed at the earliest date. No one has a better chance of success than I. Not one of the surviving officers of the Regiment knows his devious mind better than I. Because I declined the chance to destroy him before the Great War, I must do it now. I must accept the responsibility for all the misery he has authored since that time.

I am really undertaking this mission for Katarin, our children, and for our children and great-grandchildren, for our descendants to come, you for whom I write this account. If one does not fight to preserve the present and future for those one holds dearest, then what is there to fight for in the end? If I do not fight, then who will? Some of my men fight because that is all they know. They might have been, let us say, shoemakers and been perfectly happy, not suspecting what they were missing. But many of them fight for the same reasons I do—to protect those they hold dear and for their comrades who fight alongside them. I believe there is no higher calling for a man. A just cause brings out a man's élan. Any trooper forced to go back to some mundane craft like shoemaking after we win this war would be a miserable wretch.

Monday, 7 April 1919, Encamped / 2200 hrs. [10:00 pm]

Shav brought me a chekist volume he found at the site—the unit commander's record since leaving Moscow. I read of their activities in Ukraine with particular interest. It is a bare account, with no names in the volume, only designations such as landlord, class (former class, rather), and the ubiquitous "enemy of the people," modified by gender, each followed by a number. It confirms what I already knew— that they attacked our estate and killed all of my family and our retainers—whose only crime, as far as I know, was not being members of the proletariat. I cannot bear to write more about this catastrophe. What has become of the world when a person can be tortured and killed for the class to which he was born, over which they have no control? I understand the desire of the oppressed for revenge, but revenge should be limited to a quick execution.

At the end of the chekist volume was an explanation of the numbers next to the person's description: the method of torture and death. Decorum prevents me from describing any of the ghastly tortures in this journal. I shall only say that it is as though the gates of Hell were flung open, and the very devils and demons themselves sprang forth upon our land to inflict their torments upon the living. I cannot comprehend a human mind that would permit—no, encourage such horror and degradation. Here is proof of the degraded condition of mankind in this chaotic world. And it scares me. No, I am terrified. I shall mourn my family and all the denizens of our estate as long as I live.

PART FOUR

Monday, 7 April 1919 / 2400 hrs. [Midnight]

Earlier tonight, I drank far more vodka than I should have to dull my pain over the deaths of my parents and siblings and those of our friends on adjacent estates. I wasn't expecting visitors, but at about 2300 [11:00 pm], I heard a knock on the door to my tent. It was Corporal Mansur, who had also been imbibing freely from his vodka ration. As he entered, we rather drunkenly saluted each other. He looked distraught, and I told him to stand easy and speak freely.

"I cannot rest, Lieutenant Colonel Markov. I need to explain," he said. "I know I behaved dishonorably when I stabbed that chekist vermin, but he killed Corporal Schroeder in that horrible way, and Schroeder was... he was my special comrade." Mansur began to sway. I told him to sit.

"I see," I said, nodding gravely, trying not to look surprised. "Special comrade" has a distinct meaning. Homosexuality has long been a fact of life in the Russian military although seldom acknowledged until recently. Before the bolshevik coup, I would have escorted him personally to a military prison after such a revelation, but now we are more tolerant. Today, "special comrades," usually young and unmarried, are openly acknowledged. I had observed that Schroeder and Mansur were close friends but had not thought further about it. In my squadron, everyone's private life is his own affair.

"Corporal, I cannot excuse your lack of military discipline but what you have told me shall mitigate your punishment," I said, thinking that it would probably suffice to deny Mansur the promotion to sergeant I had been planning. "We shall deal with this tomorrow. Now return to your tent and sleep off the vodka. We have a long ride before us."

I cannot condone the poor corporal's actions, but neither, in good faith, can I punish him. The killing of one's special comrade has its own traditional set of rules that fall outside the standard military code. This young man's lover had died an unspeakable death. His murderer deserved no more consideration than a mad dog—something to be put down immediately.

On second thought, I shall promote Mansur tomorrow.

After this interview, I did my usual check of the perimeter, speaking briefly to some of my pickets. The cold and fragrant air acted as a tonic for my spirits, and I began to shake off the effects of the vodka. The camp is orderly and quiet—no noticeable drunkenness or raised voices, although I have no doubt the men are deeply affected by the events of the day. Today we lost two of our brothers—two comrades, each a warrior, a cavalryman, one of us. While I grieve every time one of them is killed, I do not display my grief before the men. A public display of emotion would be unspeakably vulgar. My troops feel the same way and behave accordingly. The adversity we have faced over the past five years has made us a unit. That is our bond.

Something else has been troubling me. Captain Dubowski knew the details of the mission as far as Kiev, but now that he is dead, I am the only one who knows them. If I am killed, the mission would have to be abandoned. I cannot give Sabantsevski such an easy escape. I do not think my shavetail Ensign Karneski would be able to lead such a complicated mission and, in any case, he would surely be no match for Sabantsevski. The only other man I consider capable of leading the mission is not an officer. It is Grisha. My decision is probably unprecedented—guardsmen led by a civilian—but this is an extraordinary situation. I shall brief Grisha at the first opportunity tomorrow.

I should be explicit about the nature of the enemy we pursue. Sabantsevski is evil, but at least he is a Roman [Catholic] Pole. He purports to believe in Christianity, albeit of an alien dogma. But the ranks of the bolshevikii harbor persons of such cunning and cruelty that their ilk has not been seen since the age of barbarism. Particularly among the Asian peoples of the south, where Tartar blood still flows strongly in their veins, the capacity for cruelty knows no equal. Horrors I witnessed amongst the Mohammedan Turk in the Great War still haunt my dreams. The Battle of Sarikamish, for instance, in the winter of 1915. It was during January and February in the mountains between the Ottoman Empire and Armenia. The battle was a stunning victory for the Russian Caucasus Army over the Turkish Third Army—23,000 Turks captured. But what I remember best— what haunts me—is the 32,000 or so Turkish soldiers frozen to death in the mountains. Their leader, Enver Pasha, was dressed in leather and furs, but the troops' uniforms were in tatters. Many had no boots. Some had lost feet and ears to frostbite. The corpses looked as though they had been starved to death. If Turk officers treat their own troops so badly, you can guess how they treat their enemies. I fear the horrors ahead of us will pale my present nightmares into insignificance.

The only thing unifying Ukraine now is the true faith of Pravoslavni. Once that is removed, barbarism will return, with chaos, anarchy and death on a scale unknown in modern times. We cannot let that happen.

Tuesday, 8 April 1919, Evening

Spring rains are upon us, and we have been riding through mud. We would prefer not to dissipate our energy on skirmishes with hostile forces, but the flatness of the steppe sometimes makes it unavoidable. This morning we encountered a squad of irregulars from some faction or other and suffered some minor casualties before driving them away.

Yesterday we passed through a desolate zone with many a burned and deserted village. In one barren place where there had been fierce fighting, we saw no sign of any living man, woman, child or horse among the burned huts and rusted detritus of war, save a pile of rotting corpses. There were no supplies to be salvaged there. I am well pleased that our supplies and foodstuffs from Sandikoff and the chekists we just defeated appear sufficient to get us through. May we traverse this war-torn region and complete our mission before we run out.

Even when we reached country less devastated, we did not see Muzhiks out doing their usual spring planting. Only a few women and old men were in the fields. More often people were breaking the sod and sowing seeds around their own huts, presumably to grow food for themselves. But still no young, vigorous men. They must be away fighting for one of the factions.

There were exceptions. In one village, we were met by about forty armed Muzhiks who were guarding the main communal hall. Presumably the village valuables were stored there, and I assumed the "valuables" were wheat and other grains, Muzhiks being unlikely to have gold or jewels.

"Death to anyone who enters this building," the Hetman said. There was no bowing and scraping when he said this, just defiance. His men mumbled and grunted, and a few waved their rifles about.

"And good wishes and good fortune for your village," I said with a brief salute as we rode on. They certainly showed us no respect, I thought, irritated for a moment. But then, did we really deserve any? My father always taught that it was our responsibility to protect our tenants. And he always did, to the best of his ability. But what protection had the Whites provided to that village lo these past five years? Precious little, I fear.

In some villages the elder was respectful, doffing his hat as he spoke with me. In others, it was clear that the elder would as soon shoot me as talk. Everywhere we sought intelligence on the whereabouts of the Reds but learned precious little. The Germans had come and stolen their grain, or the Reds had come and stolen their grain, or the Whites, or the Nationalists, or the Greens. They only knew that someone in uniform had taken their precious grain stores. And they wished a curse on anyone in uniform—and all foreigners. Everywhere we went, we saw signs of malnutrition, if not outright starvation. Since little planting is going on, I foresee a calamity of Biblical proportions here in my Ukraine. At present, everyone is powerless to prevent it.

By the grace of God, at the end of the day we came to a village where we were welcomed. Like a thousand other villages, its name is of no import. We were allowed into the main building and now have been fed. The officers are housed in a vacant hut. It is very pleasant to have shelter in an actual dwelling with a fireplace. Nothing has been said so far, but I suspect the villagers want us to stay and protect them from the brigands who roam this area. I asked about Sabantsevski, but no one seemed to know anything about him or the whereabouts of Red forces. Can that be true? I have posted pickets in and around the village in case of bolshevikii perfidy.

I have a few minutes of leisure to write here before I sleep. It is a luxury to light my pipe without considering the wind. My beloved Katarin is never far from my mind, but she sweeps to the fore at moments of quiet. How I miss her now, thinking of her long blonde hair, spun from pure sunlight. Her face would shame the immortal Helen; her figure surpasses that of Aphrodite. Perhaps I exaggerate, but may not a husband indulge in such minor vices?

Besides, I have seen Katarin under circumstances very unusual for those of our rank—childbirth. Noble ladies give birth with a doctor or, more commonly, a midwife who drugs her during labor and delivery; then the baby is handed over to a wet nurse. When Katarin was expecting our second child, we were traveling back to our estates near Kiev for the birth. Although she was only in her eighth month, we were dismayed that she went into labor. The baby was coming quickly, and we took shelter in yet another nameless village. Since the only midwife available was young and inexperienced, Katarin begged me to assist her as she removed her clothing. The midwife had no drugs, and my wife endured the pain as bravely as any soldier.

It was a hot summer day, and when even Katarin's undergarments became sodden with perspiration, she asked me to help her remove them. Before the midwife could cover her with a clean sheet, she lay naked, a modern-day Eve. The heat had disarranged her hair and makeup—all social artifice was gone, but I have never seen her more beautiful. Once the baby arrived—our Marianne—she chattered on excitedly, without concern for her own appearance. As she took the baby to her breast, I saw the true Katarin. I felt I had been admitted to a secret society ordinarily denied to men. This is our bond and shall be forever. Although I should add that my eternal adoration of her had already been established. She is the perfect soldier's wife, always cheerful and bright when I am in her presence. She excels in all the wifely arts and is a fine mother to our children, whom I also miss greatly.

Perhaps I indulge her more than I should, but I am grateful for her charming and diplomatic ways, which have been an asset to my career. Ever since getting settled in the regiment in 1899, she has fit in beautifully, well-liked, even loved by all.

This fact—Katarin's magnetism—is actually at the core of my mission, although few people know this. But I must write the truth here. It began in 1909 when Katarin and I returned to the regiment in St. Petersburg after a posting at our embassy in Paris. A young officer had recently joined the regiment, Lieutenant Nicholai Janovich Sabantsevski. I was then a captain, proud of my regiment and my country. Sabantsevski claimed to be Polish, the second son of a count from north of Krakow, near the Austro-Russian border. He had not matriculated at the Pages School, as had most of us, but was educated mainly in Warsaw. He had learned fencing at an early age from a Viennese master in Krakow, and excelled in the art. He quickly built a reputation as the finest swordsman in the Imperial Horse Guards.

From the first, I knew he was not cut from the proper cloth of a Guardsman. He had no respect for anyone or anything. He scoffed at tradition and ceremony, telling us we were dupes for allowing ourselves to be seduced by "the ancient dead hand of the past." God had granted this man a handsome visage, a quick mind and abundant charm and grace, but he did not have the wisdom to use these gifts properly. He regarded most of the regiment as his intellectual inferiors and the ladies of the regiment as mere diversions to satisfy his lust. His effrontery was astounding. At a regimental ball, within my earshot, he attempted such liberties with my own beloved. She dismissed him easily, as she might a naughty child, and I said and did nothing. But later he tried to seduce her again. This time she was clearly irritated, and she publicly humiliated him. He laughed it all off, but clearly, she had wounded his vanity.

Now this is the import of the matter. I am ashamed to write it, but I must, as it helps explain my position now. As a regimental officer of the nobility, I should have called him out upon the field of honor at that very moment to defend my wife. But he, as the accused, would have the choice of weapons, and his choice would be sabers. Katarin forbade me to challenge this expert swordsman. She feared that he would certainly kill me, and she said she could not bear to be the cause of my death. Her argument made perfect sense—but it ran contrary to the code of the regiment. No one ever mentioned the incident again, but I knew there was a cloud over my reputation, even though I was known as an expert shot and my bravery on the field was beyond question. After that, my relations with Sabantsevski were tense but amicable enough on the surface. He seemed amused by me, as by all Ukrainians, and we would debate for hours and, in the end, settle nothing.

In 1911 he was denounced for an affair with a major's wife and another indiscretion. This time his actions had gone far beyond attempted seduction. Other officers hated him as much as I, and there was a general cry for the colonel to exile him to Siberia. During his time in that hellhole, he became infected with the bolshevik virus. Yet the Russian Army had not yet finished with this man. By 1916 our situation had become so desperate that he was recalled from Siberia to serve as a field commander in a different regiment. I have to admit that the scoundrel has charisma, and he soon gained the support and loyalty of his troops, enjoying enormous success in campaigns against both the Austrians and the Germans, even against the German army's elite—their stormtroopers.

But his real loyalty lay with the bolshevikii, not the Emperor. After the Emperor was forced to abdicate in 1917, Sabantsevski led his troops back to Petrograd [St. Petersburg during and after WWI] and played a major role in the October coup d'état. He came to the attention of Lenin, who, after personally probing his politics and his loyalty, became his patron, giving him a secure post in Petrograd. But the canny Sabantsevski saw that Petrograd was by no means secure. He requested a Red Army command. And so, outfitted with the best equipment and horses to be had, he set out with his most loyal and dedicated men to make over the world.

It should also be noted that he always left himself an escape route should the fortunes of war turn against him. He pursued his goals with great vigor and enthusiasm—and what a trail of woe, tears and destruction he has left! His world is that of the narcissist—a place of black and white, with no shades of gray. You are either his follower or his enemy, to be eradicated. He is like a plague to be eliminated from this earth. Only then will our border regions know a measure of peace. Only with his defeat and death can reconstruction begin.

And only with his defeat and death shall I be able to settle my score with him. I no longer worry about my own reputation. That "cloud" has dissipated, thanks to my valor in battle—both in Manchuria, against the Japanese in 1904, and in the Great War.

There is yet one more reason I have to eliminate this villain. I have recently learned from reliable sources that Sabantsevski is not the son of a Polish count, as he claimed, but the son of a prosperous merchant. Thus he gained admission into the finest regiment in all the Russias by falsifying his credentials. He played his role so convincingly that he fooled even his most ardent critics, including myself. There can be only one punishment for such dishonorable behavior—a punishment I shall administer or be killed in the attempt. Such concepts as duty, honor and truth may have no place in our modern secular world, but this squadron still holds them dear. They remain the cornerstone of a just and honorable world and the heart of the Old Order for which we fight. That is the order I strive to create out of the chaos of the present.

Wednesday, 9 April 1919/ Midday

This morning we departed from the village. As we learned last night, indeed the villagers did want us to stay and protect them from Red partisans operating in the area, and to say that they were displeased to see us go would be an understatement. Some gathered and brandished their rifles as if prepared to restrain us by force, but they thought better of it as we mounted up, flourishing our superior firepower and perhaps reminding them, with our fine uniforms, of our superior power.

I confess I sympathize with their predicament and even briefly considered staying a while to help these people in this no man's land where we are almost cut off from orders from the High Command as surely as if we were at the bottom of the Black Sea. Have I mentioned that I "forgot" to bring our radio equipment? We are our own command for good or ill. But before I could make such an offer, Private Agnikov and Private Valski volunteered to stay behind and instruct the villagers on the proper use of their rifles, which they recently bought from Germans. The two privates seem to have a powerful desire to help these people, and I suspect women are involved in their decisions. Although to be fair, they are both from small villages in

Siberia, and I believe they feel kinship with the villagers. Since their offer averted what might have been a bloody riot, I had no objection to their plan. Agnikov and Valski say they will rejoin us in several days at our next point of rendezvous. Privately I do not think we shall ever see them again. I hope to be proven wrong.

Wednesday, 9 April 1919 / 1900 hrs. [7:00 pm]

I had no idea today should take such a horrific turn. After our midday meal, we rode about an hour before coming to another village. It had been attacked only a few hours earlier by Sabantsevski and his band of brigands, as we were informed by a few terrified survivors. These wretches had been spared by Sabantsevski so that they could report his atrocities to me. He and his men had looted the village of everything they wanted and molested the women and girls. Such acts are despicable but not unexpected for revolutionary forces. But these men did things that were not only beyond the rules of civilized warfare but also beyond my imagination. I cannot bring myself to describe what I witnessed. Perhaps after some time has elapsed, but not today.

I desperately want to keep going after Sabantsevski now, but if we press on, we may grow careless and blunder into an ambush. He is not going to leave Ukraine because his mission is to defeat us, and we shall pursue him until he is ours. The outrage he committed today only heightens my desire for revenge. We will camp under the stars tonight. May my mind not remember what my eyes have seen so that I can have the mercy of sleep.

PART FIVE

Kapolski's scouts have been shadowing Sabantsevski's forces and reported this morning that they are traveling about eighty kilometers [50 miles] ahead of us. Unfortunately, they are a considerably larger force than our intelligence reported. I would risk an attack on this larger force, hoping to catch them by surprise, but only if I knew for sure that Sabantsevski was actually present. Kapolski did not see Sabantsevski at the head of the force. Is that significant? Perhaps, since the Reds know he is our target, he is safe in Moscow, with these forces bearing his name as a trap. Perhaps he is within their ranks dressed as a common soldier. But I will assume that Sabantsevski is with these Red forces that bear his name until I am proven wrong. Kapolski has been trying to capture a Red to interrogate without betraying his scouts' position but hasn't yet succeeded. No doubt he will. Kapolski is ever resourceful.

So far we have had only three casualties, but this far away from headquarters and the remote possibility of reinforcements, we can ill afford even those. Nearly everywhere we go, we meet hostile forces. Some are organized, but most are motley crews of Muzhiks or God only knows what else. We have passed countless deserted villages, and once-fertile fields are now fallow and choked with weeds. Everywhere we see the detritus of war—bodies, spent munitions, broken weapons, artillery shell craters. In some places, smoke is so thick it blots out the sun and gives a reddish hue to the moon.

We may be in the End Times. The antichrist has risen, and the final battles will be engaged. As the Prophet Joel says in the Acts of the Apostles:

And I will show portents in the heavens above
And signs on the earth below,
Blood and fire, and smoky mist.
The sun shall turn to darkness
And the moon to blood,
Before the coming of the Lord's great and glorious day.
Then everyone who calls on the name of the Lord shall
be saved.

Our pickets have reported seeing many strange and horrible sights at night—armies of the dead marching past our encampments, crosses burning in the sky and similar unexplained phenomena. I do not know if these are hallucinations, superstitions or bizarre realities. I am awakened during the night by strange noises, but when I rise to investigate, I see nothing more than smoke and mist. Many of my men believe that we are in the Final Days and that they will soon be in paradise with the Lord. I believe in my heart that this attitude is what keeps the men going.

Last night I could not bring myself to write of one incident that shook me to my core. Now I feel better and able to face it. By putting it on paper, I hope to exorcize its power over me.

It was yesterday afternoon in the nameless village that Sabant-sevski and his troops attacked so brutally. We began to realize what had happened when we reached the village church and saw that a priest had been burned at the stake as though he were a heretic. The charred corpse was still chained there. The church was burned, and within the ruins was a pile of burned corpses. They were heaped toward the west end, near what had been the front door.

A faint moan led us to another priest lying nearby. He was pinned to the ground by a large spike through his abdomen and barely alive. Grisha and I bent down to speak with him. He could hardly speak. We had to strain to hear his words, which I will never forget.

"They came, those soldiers—the same ones who had attacked my village a few days ago. That monster who commands them ordered the men to get everyone in the church—everyone in the village. They made Father Nikita and me help, and we did, thinking it would help keep our people safe. Then they took us outside and tied us up, did this to me, set my old friend Father Nikita on fire. They locked the doors of the church and set it on fire. While we could still see. While we could still hear the screams. May God have mercy on their souls and welcome them into Paradise."

Grisha examined him and shook his head at me. He offered the dying man a shot of morphine, but we heard him say, "No. This is the Will of God. I am being tested." Although the priest's body trembled and tears soaked his long black beard, his face radiated peace, as if he were already in another world.

"Leave us where we are. We will bear witness for the next passers-by."

I do not know how long the priest survived, but I am in awe of his faith and his courage.

The Muzhiks oppose the Reds, and Sabantsevski's goal is to terrorize the populace rather than convert them. His fertile mind devises ever more hideous ways to subdue the Muzhik. It might be supposed that Muzhiks would be easily swayed by promises of a glorious and liberated future under the Red banner. But the Muzhik has the soul of an anarchist: he wants nothing more than to be left alone to cultivate his land and enjoy his simple pleasures. Thus the anarchist Nestor Makhno is an effective leader of the Muzhik Greens. But the Reds do not tolerate any resistance, and Makhno's forces are currently no match for either the Reds or our Whites. But things are changing rapidly, and I cannot rule out any possibility. Makhno can draw from millions of Muzhiks, and—given the atrocities Sabantsevski and the Reds are committing—they might grow strong enough to wreak a terrible revenge.

Sunday, 13 April 1919/ 1800 hrs. [6:00 pm]

It has now been three days since I have made entries and a truly hellacious time it has been. It has rained relentlessly, turning the steppe into a sea of mud and rushing water. Yet the rains have also extinguished the fires and the smoke, which might have been the cause of the strange phenomena that have troubled us. Such wet conditions make for a most difficult transit, slowing our progress. We saw very few people still alive, nor did we at first find any shelter where we could light a fire or sleep. We camped in the driest places possible and ate our rations raw and cold.

I have endured such conditions before, and knowing that they are temporary gives me the courage to carry on. Nevertheless, the flooding has its special horrors, especially the sight of bloated corpses in fields where battles were recently fought or in the swollen streams. My only consolation is my oilskin, which I purchased in the Baku bazaar during the Caucuses campaign. This garment has proven its worth on numerous occasions, and it again kept me relatively dry, although the rain was so heavy yesterday that I was soaked.

I must record, with great sadness, that Ensign Karneski was caught in a flash flood while fording a stream. He was proving to be a fast learner and, given time, might have become a good officer. I shall write his family upon my return, as I shall do for all my fallen comrades. We have thus far lost four, which is not yet critical. Although if we continue to lose men at this rate before we even engage our main enemy, I will have to make serious adjustments to our plans.

We finally found shelter in yet another nameless abandoned village, where we were able to make a fire to dry us out. We slaughtered Corporal Barinski's horse, which fed our party to the satisfaction of all. I am comfortable now, sitting here with my pipe, and will not write of my ailments from long days of riding. Nor of the difficulties in keeping my charger in fighting condition and ensuring that my men do the same for their horses. The pleasures of a good pipe, a ration of vodka, a dry house and a warm fire are almost everything I need on campaign.

The only element missing is my dear wife. What has become of her and the other ladies? I do trust the Princess, but the danger of crossing the Black Sea with only a deck gun for protection is considerable. Would they have been safer if they had waited for the evacuation and departed on a French Corvette? I go over and over this in my mind, but always conclude that I had no choice. The Colonel of the Regiment has always seen to it that the regiment's ladies were promptly evacuated from danger, but that dog Kamaranski did not. He cares not a whit for such concepts as honor and chivalry, which is to say, the protection and well-being of our ladies. Had I not made the arrangement I did, I know that my ladies and precious daughter would surely have been subjected to even greater dangers. The common run of soldiers can devolve into animals in the face of defeat, especially with cheap vodka and other intoxicants. Too often I have seen their handiwork during these two long wars. Therefore, I pray that the Princess proves to be an adequate protector. It should be me, but I must be here, doing what I am doing.

These are also perilous times for both girls and boys growing into adulthood. I have heard tales of decadence and debauchery in parts of Europe as young people, even those of old and honorable families, have discarded pre-war morality and now lead lives dedicated only to physical pleasure. They seem to believe that their world might well not survive, so why not snatch forbidden fruit in the little time remaining to them? Such thoughts are seductive, and I confess that sometimes I long to emulate them. Then my sanity is restored, and I know that such behavior will earn the Wrath of God. I also know that

I am part of the force that stands opposed to those bolshevikii who would destroy the world with their godless ideology.

Should we fail, then who will be left to stand against such a tide? A bolshevik victory would make us nostalgic for the worst excesses of the vilest emperors of all the Russias, which would seem moderate by comparison. I have seen what modern technology, in the wrong hands, has accomplished. Tsar Ivan Grosni—the Dread [translated as "Terrible" in the West]—killed many of his subjects to maintain order, but his methods of torturing and killing were nothing compared to those of the antichrist Lenin and his lackeys Trotski and Dzerzinski. The spiked barrel used to torture Corporal Schroeder was mild in these devils' arsenal. They use any means to crush dissent. In the Lubyanka Prison in Moscow, where chekist brutality runs rampant, men and women prisoners have set themselves alight on their cots rather than endure another day at the hands of these devils.

Such brutality is beyond even Hobbes's imagination, and even if we ultimately triumph, I fear we will inherit a shattered world with little left worth preserving. Such thoughts chill me a thousand times worse than the cold and damp of recent days. Perhaps a new world will arise out of those ashes, perhaps not.

I have to believe there is a purpose to all this. Thus do I pray for the coming of the Kingdom of the Lord, as has been foretold, with a peace which passes all understanding. That can be the only positive outcome to this satanic situation.

My other consolation is Katarin. It drives horrible thoughts of the world, present and future, to think of my wife's lovely form, her lovely visage and golden hair, her long graceful neck, her succulent breasts, her long legs and her most feminine place, which she calls her love canal because she adores what goes in and, even more, the children who come out. It is Madame Daria's instruction that allows us to acknowledge such natural truths.

It has been nine days since we last joined and yet it seems an eternity. I so long to be reunited with her. Together we shall face the future and make it a better one on our small piece of Earth.

I have decided that this shall be my last mission. The Guard no longer deserves my undying loyalty. Kamaranski is a disgrace who failed to protect my own and the other ladies of the regiment. I have tolerated a great deal during my career, but this is the final straw. I may yet shoot him dead.

Monday, 14 April 1919/ 2230 hrs. [10:30 pm]

A warm sun greeted us when we set off this morning, and our spirits were lifted. Shortly before noon, we arrived at a small lake shaded by trees, which are now rare in this part of Ukraine, where most of them have apparently been cut down for firewood. It was pleasurable to splash about the lake, washing off the grime of days past. We also bathed the horses. Washing Élan brought happy memories of washing our horses long ago when I was a youth on my father's estate. Putting on clean uniforms afterwards buoyed the men's morale even more.

Thus restored, our thoughts turned to our rations and how they would soon need to be replenished. There is little opportunity to forage on the steppes, as most of the villages we have passed have already been plundered. However, the other villages are well fortified, their supplies in closely guarded buildings.

We are not the only ones looking for food. We have passed several expensive automobiles by the side of the road—Daimlers, Hispano Suizas, Rolls-Royces, not to mention the fine carriages. Inside are corpses that were stripped of possessions and left to rot. They were city people seeking food from the Muzhiks. City dwellers are slowly starving since so little food is being produced. Do they not realize that the Muzhiks, too, are short of food? How could they flaunt their wealth in such a vulgar manner? The bolshevikii have incited class resentment everywhere. These city people made themselves obvious targets for robbers or resentful Muzhiks.

We stopped in one village, and I sought out the elder. He bowed, hat in hand, seemingly reluctant to look me in the eye.

"What about these automobiles?" I asked him. "Who killed these people?"

"I know nothing about that, your honor," he said, turning his hat around, shifting his feet. He gave me a toothless smile, affecting great innocence of any rich people looking for food. "The only people who have come here are robbers—foreigners. They rode in a few days ago and took almost everything we have."

"Where can we buy some food?" I asked.

"Nothing around here."

"Where can we find those robbers, then?"

The old man crossed himself several times and looked at me as if I were insane to ask such a question. Finally, he gave me a probable location but suggested we give it a wide berth. I told him I had no doubt the brigands were dangerous, but they appeared to be the only source for food. Would his men like to join us? I asked, having noticed some well-dressed villagers with expensive-looking hunting rifles, late of the city people, no doubt.

"Oh, no, your honor," he said, resuming his bowing and scraping. "We have what we need."

That is the typical Muzhik attitude: no concern for the future when immediate wants are satisfied. After thanking the elder and wishing him good fortune, we searched out the brigands' lair. I was not interested in attacking them, lest we lose more men. Nor did I want to punish them for theft. Perhaps they had lost their homes. No doubt they were as desperate and without resources as we were.

To our surprise, what we found was a log compound boasting an Imperial German flag fluttering in the breeze. This was no temporary encampment but rather a well-constructed defensive position. A quick reconnoiter of the site showed that it was surrounded by a ditch of about 3.5 meters [12 ft.], with breastworks into which spiked logs were sunk at a menacing 45-degree angle. It was high enough that, even on horseback, I could not see inside. A drawbridge led to the entrance gate.

I decided to take Vlad with me—should they allow us in—leaving Grisha and Shav in charge of the men. I gave Shav strict orders that should we not return, he should continue on the mission rather than attempt to rescue us. He protested strenuously, but I reminded him that Sabantsevski was our target, not the Germans. After a proper display of loyalty and concern, he finally agreed, as I knew he would. Then Vlad and I set out under a white flag of truce.

Sentries challenged us at the gate. Since my German is rudimentary and French might provoke an unpleasant response, I told the guards, in English, that we wished to see the commanding officer. "You English?" one said, raising his rifle. "We are Russians," I said, although he seemed not to understand until I said, "Nyet, Russki." With that, he called to the sergeant of the guard, who opened the door.

Inside were two, maybe three, log buildings surrounding a parade ground. A young, robust man escorted us to the far building and an office where we were presented to a slightly older officer behind a desk. He studied us closely before rising to greet us, introducing himself in English as Captain Schell. I asked him if I might speak with his superior officer.

"I am in charge," he said, standing straight and clicking his heels. "I am the last officer remaining. And who are you?"

I thought I might be able to relate to the captain as a fellow cavalry officer, but efforts at collegiality quickly failed. After all, his army had suffered a humiliating defeat, and he was quick to take offense. I ventured to ask why he remained in Ukraine so long after the war ended. He replied that since reports of the fatherland were not encouraging, he and his men had no desire to return. They were the last outpost of a regiment based in Kiev. Last fall, their major was assassinated by the Zhidy Association of Armed Combatants, and it was his own squadron that had finally found and killed the assassin. As far as he knew, their regiment no longer existed. And our intelligence confirms this.

I expressed my sympathy by saying that, in the end, no one had truly won the war. Could we purchase provisions from him? He inquired curtly what we had to offer in exchange. "What do you want?" I asked. He said he would be interested in military materiel or gold.

"I can probably send for adequate payment," I said, not wishing to imply we had money or other valuables on our persons. He again appraised us, finally noting that Russians were always looking for food.

"What faction do you fight for?" he asked.

Somewhat insulted that he did not recognize my light green tunic. I replied that I was a cavalry White Guardsman fighting for the White cause. This brought the first smile to his face.

"You fight against the Bolsheviks?" he said. When I replied that I most certainly did, he extended his hand and said we could parlay.

"But I do not have much time," I said as Vlad and I took seats. "I have ordered my second-in-command to take action should we not return in good time." Of course, I did not specify how much time that would be.

"Do you not trust me?" the prickly young captain asked.

"I trust no one outside of God and my own men," I replied.

Herr Schell called in an orderly to record our needs, and we spent some time negotiating a fair value. At one point, when we came to an impasse, the captain offered us a mysterious liqueur he referred to as "kummel." He told me it was extremely popular where he came from. The liqueur was clear as vodka but with a thicker viscosity; it tasted like rye bread. Things relaxed a bit, and I asked Herr Schell where he was from. Leipzig. When I said I was from north Kiev, near Chernobyl, he said he had been there and seen great mansions in ruins, a statement which sent a chill through my heart.

His men would probably have to decamp before the end of the

summer, he said, since there was little food in the region beyond their own supplies. He and many of his men would probably join the Freikorps, a paramilitary army fighting the Reds. Former German soldiers were being paid well to join. The Freikorps were having success in Estonia and other Baltic states, in Germany too, where in January, they had quelled an attempted revolt by the Spartacists, a bolshevik group. Many of the Spartacists had been rounded up and their two leaders—Karl Liebknecht and Rosa Luxemburg—executed. Herr Schell said he hated all communists and used several epithets I will not repeat to describe them.

Our fellowship of feeling over hatred of the bolshevikii broke our deadlock and our negotiations proceeded quickly. I dispatched Vlad to fetch the gold, along with a strong escort for our provisions, and I waited with Herr Schell as a guarantor of our good faith. As we sat over another glass of kummel, a Turkish captain entered the office. He was stocky and formidable looking, with a long, nasty scar on his bearded face. Saluting formally, speaking Turkish, he asked my name. It was an unusual request, I thought, but I had little choice but to comply. I stood, and he moved so close to me I could smell his sweat. He then informed me, in broken English, that he was a veteran of the prison on Nargin Island in Baku harbor, and I had put him there.

"I led the troops you ambushed in the Southern Caucuses mountains," he said. "You interrogated me, do you not remember? I swore a sacred oath that I would have revenge for my imprisonment on Nargin, and for all my men who died there," he said, or words to that effect, grasping the hilt of his sword as if to kill me on the spot. Simultaneously I drew my sidearm, cocked it and aimed it between his eyes, hoping it would not jam. I would shoot if he made another move.

We faced each other across the abyss in a moment that seemed to last forever. To my relief Captain Schell shouted something at this mad Turk in German. The Turk barked back in German. He dropped his hand to his side and, as he turned away, ran a finger across his throat.

"He said he shall kill you later," Captain Schell said, though I did not need a translation. The Turks always seemed to have noses out of joint about something, he went on, apologizing profusely for the man's unseemly behavior.

"He is not a proper officer," Captain Schell said.

"What is his name?" I asked.

"Tariq Aziz," he answered.

I thanked the captain for his intervention but did not relax my guard. I believe he had simply been protecting his buyer rather than exercising military courtesy. I would remember this Tariq Aziz—one more villain trying to kill me.

How did this Turk come to be in Herr Schell's command? I asked. When the German army moved into Ukraine and other parts of the former Russian Empire in 1917, they released all the prisoners of war—German, Austro-Hungarian, Bulgar and Turk. Tariq was merely one of the prisoners who offered his services to the German army. Being skilled at barter and theft, he quickly became invaluable. This was the first time he had ever acted so reprehensibly, Herr Schell said. Schell assured me that Tariq Aziz would make no further trouble for me.

When Vlad returned with payment, we loaded our supplies and went on our way without further incident. After wishing Herr Schell good fortune against our common enemy, we left the German camp on good terms.

For the rest of the day, I thought about the Turk. Yes, I had treated him and his men harshly, but they were hardly innocent victims. Shortly before the battle in which he was captured, he had led a raid on a Christian village, where his forces carried out a barbarous slaughter of civilians, although the village had no strategic value. During the interrogation, I asked why he had engaged in such heinous slaughter.

His reply: he was simply doing as his religion had taught him. The village of unbelievers stood as an affront to his beliefs, and he had killed, or ordered killed, a nest of men who were doomed to eternal damnation because they drank alcohol and gambled. The women were also damned because they were shameless, naked harlots. They were clothed when I found them, I countered, not naked, but he looked at me as though I were mentally defective. Without the veil, they were "naked," not proper women of virtue. They were all infidels.

"And they were killed for their 'sins'"? I asked again. He nodded proudly, adding that they were also "Armenian scum, not worthy of further thought."

At this, I left the room and told my men to throw him in the worst section of the prison. Ordinarily, an officer would have been spared this fate, but I was so enraged by him that I broke with protocol. For I knew by then that he had been responsible for similar raids on Georgia and Armenia for at least nine years from his base in Azerbaijan. Now, I thought, this bastard would learn about damnation firsthand.

I was amazed that he had survived, but now I realized that it was probably his beliefs, misguided as they were, that had kept him alive from day to day. I also now recognized the depth of my own contempt for the captured Turks, which allowed me to deliberately throw them into a prison where typhus and diphtheria were widespread, giving no thought to their fate. To me, they were just infidel scum. At that moment, I realized that Tariq Aziz and I were more alike than not.

Doubts and questions I have been trying to suppress rose to torment me. My faith has been shaken by the events of the last five years of war, especially now. Have I been following the wrong God? Could a just God allow all this misery? Or am I and all the others merely latter-day Jobs? Are we being tested in preparation for the Final Days? How can one mortal man even begin to know the answers to such weighty and ultimately unanswerable questions? Did God give us reason merely so He could torment us with such questions?

On the other hand, is it best to be like a simple Muzhik woman and merely believe without questioning?

A new fear arose as we rode along. Tariq has vowed to kill me. What can Captain Schell do to stop him? His assurance was meaningless. Tariq has probably already stolen away from the German compound with his followers. He will simply have to join the long queue of those who wish me dead.

Our dinner tonight restored my spirits—canned Polish ham along with a nice bottle of Riesling wine, a feast. The wine brought up a happy memory of Kiev, summer of 1918, with Katarin. We were in a bistro one evening in a quarter where all the cafes and bistros were filled with people and song. Despite the bolshevik coup in Petrograd the previous October, the Ukrainian Nationalists, under the German Army, had restored sanity to this small corner of the Russias. That night it seemed that civilization would return, that even a great cataclysm could prove to be temporary. A memory for which to fight. Perhaps, if God so wills, for which to die.

Yet I think now of the brutality we saw today as we approach Kiev. We entered a burned and devastated village. Thirty or forty bodies hung from wooden gallows, including White troops, now rotting. Tortured before being hung. This will be our fate if we are captured, I reminded the men. Together we silently dug a pit to bury the bodies. The sour stench of death and decay, which I know so well, has returned to stay in my nostrils. Not even the wine or vodka could dislodge it. Several of the bodies wore the light green tunics of Guardsmen. How discouraging that the enemy took my brothers alive and dealt them such a horrific end. How can it be that they surrendered rather than fight to the last man? They were probably ordered to lay down their arms by an inexperienced commander who thought that his troops would be well treated. I know such men exist in positions of leadership, but I cannot fathom how they have remained so naïve in the face of the Reds' barbarity. Surely they will soon lose their illusions.

It cannot be like the Great War when some officers continued to believe in the essential goodness of the enemy. These were officers who had served only on the Austrian Front, where whole regiments of Slavs gladly surrendered, regarding the Russians as liberators from their Hapsburg oppressors. My service in the Caucuses Front dispelled any illusions I might have had about the nature of war. There we faced a clash of civilizations, the age-old struggle against the forces of the Orient, be they Hun, Mongol, Mohammedan, Arab, Persian or Turk.

Today we face another clash of civilizations, between Christian and heathen—the godless bolshevikii. In that struggle to the death, we need the cooperation of the Germans, such as Herr Schell and his troops, to defend the very center of Europe. How rapidly events are changing in this new world. Perhaps in the distant future, we shall fight the Mohammedan Turks or Arabs once more.

I am still haunted by the tortured and burned priests as I sit writing this. Sabantsevski no doubt knows we are tracking him and his horde, and I believe he committed this latest outrage as a taunt to me. "Look what I do with impunity," I almost hear him say. When we finally engage him, we shall mete out the punishment he so richly deserves. He will find that honor, duty and justice still exist. Just as Tariq's hatred kept him alive in the hellish prison, so my hatred of Sabantsevski warms me even in the coldest moments. He is the personification of the Red Ukrainian Army. Even worse, he brought shame on the finest regiment in the Russian Imperial Army, and for that, there can be no pardon nor forgiveness. I shall, with God's help, see to that.

PART SIX

Sunday, 20 April 1919, Outside Kiev/ 0600 hrs. [6:00 am]
Easter. Christ is Risen.

I am remembering another Easter morning in the last spring before the Great War. I was in Kiev with my family after the Vigil at Santa Sophia Cathedral. As the sun rose, we walked in the procession, following the crucifer with his gold cross and the priests in their scarlet vestments through the streets, bells ringing, everyone chanting the wonderful news of rebirth and redemption. Then Mass, followed by the family feast of lamb roasted on the spit. And, of course, the exchange and admiration of Pysanky, our unique, intricately patterned Easter eggs.

I wonder if the Bolsheviks are allowing a procession in Kiev today?

The commissars want to suppress religion completely and would no doubt want to prevent such a public display of devotion to God, but do they really have the power? Would their rank and file really have the will to overcome the people in a matter so important to the Ukrainian spirit?

It has been six days since we left the German Army compound. We aimed to arrive a day early for our rendezvous with the agent Aishna, and we have been riding hard to make up for our slow transit during the days of torrential rain. But we must rest and regroup now, and so I have time for a summary of the recent events.

We rode in such a fashion as not to engage with Red units and have not seen many. We were compelled to engage with one rather rag-tag and poorly armed Red unit and killed all. May God help me, but I confess I have never enjoyed simply running men through with my saber as much as this. We captured documents from their leader, a rough brute of perhaps thirty-five years. They confirmed my suspicions that while the Reds hold Kiev, they do not control much else and should be ripe for an early counterattack.

About sixty kilometers [37 miles] out from Kiev, I noticed villages where all the few survivors wore masks, presumably against typhus and Spanish influenza. Thus Grisha has again issued face masks. In other places seemingly untouched by those diseases, we have seen the unmistakable handwork of something even more deadly, the cheka. Everywhere are more weed-choked fields with the dry, white skulls and bones of past massacres.

Sergeant Kapolski has reported that Sabantsevski's troops avoided Kiev, likely out of fear of disease, and their rampage across the countryside continues. Sabantsevki attacks wherever he thinks he can find the Muzhiks' food supplies. Battles are being waged over granaries. Men, women, even children are tortured to reveal their whereabouts, and bodies continue to mount. Wild dogs and other scavengers are growing fat, presumably on human flesh. Worse still, where dogs have yet to feed, naked bodies lie by the roadside, the marks of torture readily visible. People of God deserve a better fate than this; they should be buried in holy ground. If we were to start performing even the most rudimentary of burials for these poor wretches, however, we would not be able to advance. It would take us a year to reach Kiev. It is a pity that their corpses play into bolshevik hands by serving as a grisly reminder of what happens when one does not cooperate with the bolshevikii and their Red Army.

I confess that the carnage we have ridden through has left me numb, but I force myself to pay attention enough to register the extent of Red crimes. I am used to seeing dead soldiers. Such is the nature of war. Even dead civilians, as civilian deaths do occur as unfortunate by-products of war. Here, however, the enemy has waged war on the populace as well as our forces. Why? Are the bolshevikii so devoid of reason, or blinded by their ideology, that they fail to see if they kill all the Muzhiks, there will be no one left to plant and harvest the crops Russia has always counted on from Ukraine? No matter who you are—Christian, Zhidy, Mohammedan, Turk, German, bolshevik or Eskimo—you still must eat. And how can that happen when there are no crops to harvest because they were never planted? Actually, it seems as though bolshevik ideology—everyone equal in a classless society—would unite them with the Muzhiks. Muzhiks, like those at the bottom of any society, would like to be the equals of everyone else—and who can fault them for that?

Perhaps the bolshevikii will not succeed in conquering Ukraine. Muzhik support for Makhno's Green forces appears widespread. If the Greens prevail, how could the bolshevikii hope to control them? Even though the bolshevikii are ruthless, they are small in number. How could they compel so many millions of persons to toil in the fields against their will? The Muzhiks might simply hoard their grain and let bolshevik city-dwellers starve. This is what encourages me. While the bolshevikii might well triumph in the short run, they cannot rule in the long.

No one with eyes and reason can doubt that the world has gone insane. The Great War produced many smaller conflicts all over the globe as age-old tribal animosities, no longer contained by civilization, erupted from long slumber. Plagues have been unleashed upon the world in the wake of that war. I have heard that the Spanish influenza has already killed more than the Great War. Many regions still suffer from typhus and dysentery. Classified reports reveal that farther to the east, the Afghani are blighted by the bubonic plague, the same disease that swept through our land in the seventh and fourteenth centuries. If history is a reliable guide, it will soon be upon us. Indeed, if such plagues recur with any regularity, we are overdue.

Perhaps, as I write these words, some Asiatic chieftain and his forces are preparing to escape the plague by sweeping down on a weakened and divided Europe, as did Attila, the Scourge of God, and Jengis Khan, and bring the plague with them.

Lenin presides over all this strife and chaos, preaching the gospel of universal revolution. But what he seeks is not a society of equals but power for himself and his commissars. He has declared aristocrats and Muzhiks enemies of the state. And when whole categories of people are declared to be enemies of the state, where does it end? There is always someone else who becomes suspect and is designated an enemy—a counter-revolutionary—despite any evidence to the contrary. In Lenin's revolutionary state, the survivors, as they face disease, starvation, or execution, will envy the dead.

Loyal White Russian agents plead our case in the major capitals, but so far, to deaf and war-weary ears. The bolshevikii have agents who tell the most outrageous lies about our Whites and their cause, and gullible writers repeat their slanders in the newspapers. Their dupes believe that the bolshevikii want nothing but peace and justice—the peace and justice of the mass grave, that is. That "peace and justice" lie has become an article of faith with them. So many believe it because they yearn for a new world to replace the old world they lost in the war. Bolshevism has the allure of something new. That makes the task for those of us who know the truth a thousand times more difficult.

I cannot allow anything to distract me from the mission to find the arch-bolshevik Sabantsevski. Even my personal safety. Kapolski also reports that Tariq and his band are following us at a distance, waiting for an opportunity to strike. I have no doubt we could slaughter every one of these damnable Turks if we engage. But they are such tough, persistent soldiers that we would surely lose men in such a struggle, to say nothing of the time we would lose. And I might lose my life, which would sabotage the mission. It is Sabantsevski that General Deniken has sent us to defeat, not Tariq Aziz. While I would love nothing more than to lop off Tariq's infidel head and put it on a pike for all to see, that pleasure must be postponed until our mission is done.

In the meantime, I am a target for Tariq and God only knows how many others, and that is the reason I have remained somewhat aloof from my staff and the men. I do not sleep among the men, as is my custom, and I often ride a short distance away with only one other rider with me. Such aloofness is not my custom, but I think they understand the reason. And I will tell them everything when the time is right. I am sure they know how deeply I am concerned for their well-being and morale. The food supplies we purchased from the Germans have helped restore both.

Tomorrow I go to Kiev for final intelligence and full information about my mission. I have not yet decided who will accompany me, but I shall sleep on it tonight and pray God to grant me the wisdom to make the correct choice. The wrong choice could mean disaster for our mission.

Markovs have seen war, pestilence, famine, invasion and natural catastrophe beyond measure. I have no doubt that many of my forbears who faced such challenges felt the end of civilization was nigh. Yet I shall state it again: because of the progress we have made in the technology of death and devastation, the fate of a nation has never hung by such a slender thread. For the sake of future generations, I must steel my will for the coming struggle. To that end, I once more pledge my life and sacred honor to the survival of Ukraine. Nothing matters beyond that.

Monday, 21 April 1919, Kiev / 2400 hrs. [midnight]
Easter Monday

We are camped a safe distance out of Kiev. At dawn, I received a very young courier from Mayr: Arbaha, a girl who could not be older than eight. She said our contact, blue-eyed Aishna, would be at a specific café today at noon, wearing a red cloak. I asked Arbaha if she knew Aishna, and she replied, "Of course, she is my aunt."

Getting me to that meeting required careful planning. I chose First Sergeant Shav as my companion rather than Vlad or Grisha. If I am walking into a trap, Shav will make a formidable bodyguard. Frankly, I cannot afford to lose either Vlad or Grisha. I put Vlad in charge of the men. We planned to rendezvous at 2200 hours [10:00 pm] this evening at the gap in the old city wall. (It is an unmistakable landmark, created when the Mongols breached the city in 1240.) The plan for the squadron was full of risks: since they could hardly announce their presence by crossing a bridge directly into the city, they would have to cross the Dnieper elsewhere. We deemed the best option to be a ferry raft some ten kilometers [6.2 miles] north of the city. Men are vulnerable on a raft in the best of circumstances, and it would take multiple trips to get all the men across. We knew circumstances were not ideal, as the river is swollen from the spring melt and rain. Loss from drowning was a real threat. And pray God the Reds didn't know about the ferry and have guards posted there. Once across, they would approach the city a few at a time and gather at the rendezvous point. They needed all their skill, and luck, to pull all this off.

Shav and I rode toward the city until we were about a mile away. Our plan was to pose as White deserters looking for opportunity in the Red cause. Such men are found in all large towns and cities. Since deserters do not usually have horses, we simply walked in. For that same reason, we did not wear face masks. We have enough stubble to look as though we've been on the road a few days. The dirty tunics we wore had belonged to common soldiers from some non-elite regiment—I had bought them for my senior men last year in Kiev to use as when they needed to disguise themselves. Shav and I had carefully rid our persons of any evidence that we were Guards, since deserters from the Guards would be met with high suspicion and shot on sight.

Nor would I want to be recognized as an officer since an officer would have useful information.

The weather was perfect for our purposes, cloudy with some light river fog and a chill to keep us alert. In the distance, I could see the statue of St. Vladimir, the founder of Kiev. My heart soared that this symbol of the city had so far survived the iconoclastic bolshevikii. Then I saw the blue-green and gold dome of the Church of St. Andrew. No doubt the monks and priests are no longer there. Then the buildings of Podol, our artisan's quarter.

We approached the Chain Bridge over the Dnieper. Not surprisingly, at the entrance, Red militia were manning a blockade to check the identity card of every person attempting to cross. (Curious, I thought, that a main entry into Kiev should be protected by regular troops, not militia. Is there a manpower shortage?) I had tried to get Red identification cards, but that proved to be far too risky. It was Shav's idea that we pretend to be drunken deserters. The trick to appearing drunk is to have enough alcohol on our breaths to be credible but not drink so much as to impair our reason, and we found that balance.

When we were stopped by two militia men, I said, in heavily-accented Ukrainian, "We've come to Kiev to join the forces of liberation. We've had enough of being on the losing side."

The guard looked suspicious, and I feared the worst. Then Shav looped his big arm around the smaller guard and, slurring his words, said, "Any problem with us proceeding, friend?"

"Why don't you have any identification? Everyone has identification, you fool."

"The officers took our papers. Everybody wants to desert. They thought that would stop us," Shav said—though he said it much more plainly and blasphemously.

That seemed to make sense to the men, and the taller one wrote out day passes for us. But before handing them over, he said that if we wanted to extend them beyond today, we must report to the nearest cheka office early tomorrow morning. There would be grave consequences for not doing so.

"Certainly, sir, certainly," Shav said, saluting and grinning. "And have a drink, with our blessing." He pressed the half-empty bottle on the man. "We stole this from our captain, so enjoy. And you too," he said to the shorter man. The other guards at the blockade were all laughing, at which point I retrieved the bottle and pretended to shove Shav along.

Armed with our passes, we crossed the bridge into the city. I have such happy memories of walks across this graceful structure in better times. On the other side, we were stopped again by Red Army troops. They looked more professional than the militia and asked us several questions in a hostile manner. Not so easily charmed by Shav, they rebuked us for our drunkenness.

"Find some place to sleep it off. Report first thing tomorrow to the Cheka or else."

I decided on a dangerous gambit. I said I wished to see the chekists today. The soldier shook his head and said that no one wants to see the cheka before they are called. Besides, the cheka would not tolerate our inebriation. We each took a swig of vodka before heading on our way.

As soon as we were out of sight of the troops, we took stock. A clock on a nearby church seemed to be functioning, although the church itself was clearly abandoned, and we saw that we had an hour or so before our appointment. I wanted to look around the city. Much to my surprise, the trams were running, although no schedules were posted. Before long, one came along. It was so crowded we had to stand. People stared at our disheveled uniforms, our unshaven faces. Differences were to be feared here now. I realized that the bolshevikii had brought a form of mental illness with them—no one trusts anyone else.

Kiev was no longer the city I knew and loved. By the time we reached the Kreschatik, the main artery, I was weeping. In the summer of 1918 when I was last here, the Kreschatik was a bustling promenade of shops and cafés. Now most of the businesses were either boarded up or burnt out.

The people on the tram and in the streets appeared to be better fed than the Muzhiks we had been seeing, but only slightly. But, just as in Odessa, corpses hung from lampposts—some hanged just recently, others in a state of decay. In lots left vacant by the total destruction of buildings, we saw stacks of dead bodies, and rifle fire suggested that more death was taking place. Not far from the Opera, we saw a heap of men and women recently executed by firing squad, their bodies still writhing and spasming in the final stages of life. Troops marched throughout the city in disorderly fashion. Frequently the tram was stopped at a roadblock, and a soldier would board to examine identity cards. Thankfully, these brutes seemed satisfied by our day passes and our claims to be on our way to enlist in the bolshevikii cause.

The stench of the city—a combination of death, decay and human waste—is still in my nostrils. Yet, in the midst of all this ruin, people were engaged in the normal wartime pursuits of bartering, drinking and fighting.

The tram was moving so slowly we got out to walk. A block or two along we joined a raucous crowd at a vacant lot. Curious about what they were straining to see, we pushed to the front. Militiamen and soldiers were bent over a dozen or so women lying on tables, hands bound above their head. The women's clothing was torn to below the waist, or torn away completely, and the men were ravaging them, as their companions cheered them on. Other men stepped forward to take their turns. The women lay still and quiet—were they that afraid? Or already dead? The women were all types—young, old, pretty, ugly, healthy, even deformed. These Red savages were brutalizing women, any women they could get their hands on.

"We need to stop this," I whispered to Shav, "but it would be suicide to try. Too many drunk Reds here."

"It would doom the mission," he whispered back.

"Who are you?" someone snarled at us. Others started grunting and pointing at us, presumably because we weren't laughing and shouting with the crowd. Thus, we joined in the noise, raising our fists, trying to look excited and gratified like the others, meanwhile shuffling back through the curious, the depraved, the sadistic voyeurs of this dreadful spectacle. We had already seen far too much. We knew now what happened to the women when the Reds were finished with them: they were stabbed. The Reds did not consider them important enough to merit a bullet to the head.

My heart was like lead as we plodded on. I had seen so many horrors on this journey that I had no real emotion left. It seemed appropriate that so many of the cafés I used to frequent were now either closed or reduced to rude drinking establishments. Curiously, voices emanated from some of these places, even though they were shuttered. Sounds of a party came from my old favorite, the Bilbocquet, now shuttered. I assume it is now a bordello or gaming establishment for the bolshevikii elite. Of course, *they* still party, although they banned vodka in 1917 as the curse of the working class.

So many of the houses and buildings we saw were only half-finished or partly painted. So much for the "Ukrainian revitalization." In 1918 the Nationalist Symon Petliura and his Directory announced an ambitious program of architectural restoration to help rebuild our Ukrainian cultural traditions. Even in those early days, some skeptics said the project was nothing more than an elaborate theatrical backdrop with actors running about in traditional Ukrainian costume.

Petliura's intent was to give Ukraine a distinct cultural identity after the long Russian occupation, but the result is, in fact, more like a comic opera. The current bolshevikii regime seems to be concerned only with punishing their class enemies. The cheka's main task now is to eliminate war profiteers and kulaks, or so I conclude from posters lining the streets. I was not familiar with the word "kulak," but found out that it means "rich Muzhik," surely an oxymoron. But now that the bolshevikii have killed the landowners, anyone owning any property is a kulak. The meaning of "war profiteer" has been expanded downward as well. Anyone who has a great deal of money is called a war profiteer. The bolshevikii don't seem to care what you do as long as you don't have a significant amount of property or money. Unless you are opposed to the regime, of course—then you are also a target.

When it was almost time for our rendezvous, we headed back toward the Opera and Theater Street (where all the theaters were closed) to find the designated café. We seated ourselves at a small outdoor table to wait, pistols at the ready. A waiter wearing a dirty white apron finally came around to our table. He was wheeling a wooden cart with bottles of Red Star Vodka and earthen mugs. As we had come to expect, he asked for our identification. Our day passes had a number, which he wrote on his pad.

"What are you doing in Kiev?" he asked as he scrutinized our dirty uniforms.

"Just trying to build up our courage to meet with the cheka. We want to stay here in this beautiful city," I said.

He laughed as if understanding something unspoken and leaned down to say, "Many of our customers here are doing the same." And he set a bottle and two mugs on our table. When I asked him how much, he said it was free and moved on.

The vodka was coarse and fiery, like something the Muzhik drink, but the price was right. I recalled this café when it had been a fashionable destination with a different name. Then it had crystal goblets for premium liquors, not earthen mugs and Red Star. But all signs of its former elegance had been stripped away, and being here was like sitting amongst the ruins of a once-great building. We attracted little attention from the other patrons, who were a mixed group—some soldiers, some civilians, probably a mix of Reds and deserters. I suspect most were deserters. Our presence added to the strength of their numbers. They must have identification, though—perhaps some were informants. All I wanted was to meet our contact and get out of Kiev. Whoever chose this place for our rendezvous must have considered it the best of a number of worse options.

Our contact, Aishna, was supposed to be alone and wearing a long red cloak. After what we had seen of Kiev, it would be remarkable, I thought, to see a woman on the street alone. The women we had seen were either riding in carriages or open automobiles, accompanied by important-looking men, or they walked the streets under the dubious protection of a soldier. Women were vulnerable to attack or abduction—even under the protection of men. I overheard some of our café companions loudly boasting about their exploits with women—one rogue even claiming that he was wont to enter a house and take the wife, then kill the husband if he happened to be about. "Sounds boring," said another. "Not enough of a challenge."

We were astonished to see a veiled woman in a long red cloak walking briskly through the tables toward us. I wasn't expecting a veil. Would not Mayr have sent a Christian woman as our contact? Very few Christian women wear veils, especially not red ones that cover everything but their eyes. Her eyes met mine—yes, the blue, blue eyes. Before she could reach our table, though, she was grasped by a big rough fellow.

"Give us a kiss, girlie," he said. Suddenly she reached into her cloak and withdrew a fearsome dagger. And what a dagger! It flashed in the sun, and the ruffian backed away. I recognized the dagger immediately as the kind popular with assassins in this region—Damascus steel. It can kill quickly in the right hands, and this woman's stance and the way she handled it left no doubt of her proficiency. For the record, this knife is a twenty-centimeter [10 in.], double-edged, curved spider dagger with a five-centimeter [2 in.] blade. It was horrible to be the target of such a weapon, as I knew. Tariq Aziz had a dagger like this.

The crowd seemed to take in a collective breath as this woman approached our table. A murmur arose as she sat on Shav's lap rather than take a chair. I was flabbergasted as she dropped her veil below her chin and grabbed our vodka bottle and took a gulp. Her hair was black as a raven's feathers and just as shiny. Then she kissed Shav passionately, at the same time deftly sticking a small envelope into his tunic. When she came around the table to me, I had my first good look at her face: blue almond-shaped eyes, short turned-up nose—a nose wide enough to keep her from being beautiful. But she was erotic—there was no doubt about her erotic power. Her eyes, lined with kohl to make them larger, could easily hypnotize a man. In the next moment, she was on my lap, kissing me, then pressing her full, soft lips to my ear to whisper that she would meet us again in about an hour at a certain corner in the Upper City. Meanwhile she inserted another envelope into my tunic. Then another kiss, longer this time, which aroused me beyond all reason.

Someone jarred me with a thump on my shoulder—the brute who had been bragging about taking women in their own houses. "It's my turn now," he said, calling Aishna a vile word. She sprang to her feet, grabbed his belt, and whipped out that dagger again, thrusting it just under his manhood.

"I could cut through your trousers and move this dagger right up your foul body," she said loudly in Russian, though using more colorful words. The ruffian laughed scornfully until he looked down at his situation. Like the first man, he mumbled something and retreated to his comrades, trying to sound tough by berating her in vulgar, scatological terms. She strode after him, grabbed his throat and held up her dagger.

"See my spider," she said. "The ancient penalty for your filthy words is to cut out your tongue. For your unwanted advances, I should geld you. I know about your crimes against women and their husbands. The penalty for that is death. How do you plead?"

"A thousand pardons, Madame, I had no idea who you are. I meant no harm," he said in a wheedling voice.

"Stop your blather. It is too late for pardon. But you are fortunate. I am in a good mood. I will not torture you."

A deep thrust of her dagger ripped open his throat, which gurgled and began to spurt blood. He tried to stanch the blood with his fingers but fell to his knees. Holding his head by the hair, Aishna bent over and ran her dagger into his heart, twisting it around before pulling it out. She jammed her boot on his chest to knock him down and hold him until he stopped writhing. Then she wiped her blade on her cloak and lit a cigarette. I recognized its pungent aroma as a Balkan Sobranie. There was a moment of silence before cheers rang out. She smiled, turned and disappeared in the direction of the Upper City.

"My God," Shav said to me. "What a show. Not what I expected from a courier."

"Nor I," I said. "I would have thought she would be as inconspicuous as possible. Someone will surely report this. We have to make it look like she chose us at random.

"These Kiev girls are certainly friendly," I said loudly, looking around the café, trying to catch the eye of our neighbors. "And lethal!"

"Never seen anything like it," Shav chimed in with a laugh. "Who on earth could she be?"

We remained seated at the table for a while, drinking vodka. A few men tried to engage us in conversation about the incident, but we just shrugged and said we were as mystified as they were. The body of Aishna's "admirer" remained where it had fallen and was largely ignored.

When the fuss died down, I rose and said, "Time to see the cheka." Still holding on to the vodka bottle we had brought into the city, we left the café, walking in the direction opposite to the one Aishna had taken. Once off Theater Street, we stopped to see if we were being followed. No one who could be a chekist or a soldier was behind us, and so we turned toward the address Aishna had given us via the Andreivskii Spust. I was churning with questions about Aishna but tried to put them aside as we made our way through the streets. Everything in Kiev seemed to bring back memories. A little church where I had gone to a funeral was now tightly boarded up, as was the store where I had sometimes bought shoes.

The Andreivskii Spust reminded me sharply of Constanza. I have a particular reason for writing here about how I got to know that worthy girl. It was in 1896, when I was eighteen. I was in Kiev for my Bohemian summer, as my father liked to call it. He had sent me here to live on my own in a small hotel and, with his blessing, sow my wild oats—to learn about real life before joining my first regiment as an ensign [second lieutenant]. On my first morning in Kiev, I was sitting at an outdoor café on this very street, having a light breakfast, watching the locals, all of whom looked artistic and glamorous to me, as they strolled by. But mainly, I was waiting for ten am, opening time at the La Maison Blanche, a genteel house of relaxation and recreation for gentlemen so exclusive that it was known to only the most select. In my pocket was a letter of introduction from my father to the madam. To say I was excited to begin my initiation into the world of men does not begin to convey the way I felt.

A young woman walked toward my table. She was unusually tall and slender, wearing a light blue caftan that swung freely about her ankles. She looked familiar—I vaguely remembered her remarkable red hair and black eyes—but I could not place her. To my astonishment, she sat down at my table and asked me to buy her a Russian tea.

"I am Constanza," she said. "Madame Daria's daughter."

Madame Daria—my mother's spiritual advisor. For the past three summers, I had studied with Madame Daria, at my mother's insistence. I had seldom seen her daughter because she had been away at school. Constanza now told me that she had recently graduated from a girl's boarding school on a large estate outside Tsaritsyn. She was nineteen.

"My mother has asked me to teach you the ways of women and men this summer."

Thus Mme Daria had a different idea for my initiation than my father. I did not find it difficult to agree that summer morning. I could go to his old haunt, the Maison, any time. Constanza was an enchanting sight. Her adornments were exotic—bangles or bracelets stacked in a row on each arm up to the elbow, a brown leather choker with a stone in the center (probably her birthstone). An unforgettable scent—light but musky—wafted from her. Her face was young and unfinished, yet somehow opaque, mysterious.

Constanza asked me a series of questions about my experience, especially with sex. That was very little. My heart belonged to someone—Evgania, a pure angel, who gave herself to God—but she was only a dream. Constanza was very much flesh and blood, however, and even though she was only a year older than I, much more worldly and confident. I was increasingly drawn to her, especially when she began to describe what we would do in bed. How could I resist being taken to her house around the corner from the café?

We went upstairs to her bedroom, where she disrobed and stood naked and at ease before me. This was the first time I had ever seen an adult female undressed. She was small-breasted with erect nipples and a neatly trimmed pubic triangle. An intricate tattoo on her left breast caught my eye, but she declined to explain it. She might tell me one day, she said. In any case, it was hard to contain myself, much less think, as she undressed me. I was hopelessly aroused. We coupled and explored each other's bodies the whole day and, after a quick dinner, the rest of the night.

I learned right away that what Constanza wanted from this connection was a child. She did not want a husband or conventional family like other girls I had known. She wanted to become pregnant. She and her mother, Daria, would raise the child, she said, along with other children she planned to have in the future. No one would ever know I was the father, just as Daria had never told her who her father was. I just accepted this extraordinary situation, not, as I say, being in a condition to think things through.

"Stay here with me," Constanza said to me the next morning. "I have much to teach you that Mother wants you to know."

My education was to extend to history and politics as well as sex. Like her mother, Constanza was an Armenian nationalist. She was in Ukraine to raise money to fight the Ottomans, who had committed such atrocities against the Armenians in the Great War. I learned the Armenian language and also the tragic history of that country. The more I learned, the more I was determined to help. Constanza began to introduce me to her friends and allies in Kiev. Several times we spent evenings with Mikhail Bulgakov, said to be an up-and-coming writer. By the time I was to leave in the fall, she was pregnant. I asked her to marry me, but she declined, saying she still had much to do.

After I joined my new regiment, I never saw or heard from Constanza again. I wrote her two or three letters, but she never answered. I let it drop, which proves, I suppose, that although I was drawn to her, I never really loved her. My heart, at that point in my life, still belonged to my boyhood love, Evgania, who still haunts my thoughts from time to time to this day, despite my deep love for my wife Katarin. I will likely think of Evgania for as long as I draw breath.

But today, the sight of Aishna, still in her red cloak and awaiting us on the cobblestones, brought my mind back to the present. We were in a residential area of housing blocks of no special character. Like most of Kiev, it looked shabby. She led us to her house on St. Alexei's Street, which was very familiar to me.

"Do you know who lived here before the war?" I asked as we entered her building.

"Most families who lived here were killed, or they emigrated," she answered noncommittally.

The reception room of her house was well kept, though not richly appointed. We could finally relax after a long morning of being on high alert, and I suddenly felt very tired.

"Would you like to rest?" Aishna asked me, and I could not resist the appeal of napping in an actual bed. As she led me upstairs, I had a sense of déjà vu. I fell on the bed, and the last thing I remember is hearing the voices of Aishna and Shav, speaking in rapid-fire Georgian.

Several hours later, I awoke. A smiling woman stood at the foot of the bed.

"Hello, Mikhail Antonovich."

"Of course," I said, smiling too. "I should have known. Constanza."

Her abundant red hair and black eyes were unchanged, but she had filled out, her face now more defined by her intelligence, her breasts and hips more fully rounded under her simple dress. As she kissed me warmly, I decided she was even more striking than when I first knew her.

Over the course of the day, I learned that Constanza was now the famous Mayr, leader of La Revanche, and this was one of her safehouses. And she had married, after all. Her husband was Captain Jacques Baron Charbonnet, leader of La Mort. Her formal name, seldom used now, was Baroness Lucine Sarkissan. Both she and her husband were skilled at intelligence operations, he having been with the Deuxieme Bureau, the intelligence service of the French Army. I should have been surprised but was not. It all made sense now.

Mayr briefed me thoroughly on the situation in Ukraine. Sabantsevski's last known location was east of here, some fifty kilometers [31 mi.], but his troops are always on the move. She proposed that Aishna join our mission as a guide because of her matchless knowledge of the land and its resources. Aishna was her star pupil, and I could trust her completely, Mayr said. I have reservations about this. Mainly I fear that a woman's presence in the squadron will be disruptive. Nevertheless, I did accept Mayr's offer. Aishna is no ordinary woman—she is clearly canny and knowledgeable. Perhaps a bit wild, but I believe I can keep her in line.

I also learned that Mayr has three children. Two are daughters. One, named Daria, is a teacher and mentor in Beirut, like Daria, her grandmother and namesake. The other, Kalama, worked with Mayr during the war but was killed in June 1917.

"Is either Daria or Kalama my child?" I asked.

"No," she said. "They have different fathers. My child by you is a son. His name is Tomaz. He is in Paris raising money for La Revanche and La Mort. Rem—we just call it La ReM. That is all you need to know about Tomaz for now."

It was clear that Mayr would tell me no more, and I determined to put this unknown son out of my mind. What she wanted to talk about in the short time she spent with me was her special organization, the Legion of the Black Widow Spider's Revenge on the Turk. I had heard of the Legion—a band of women warriors—but had thought it just a myth. Yet the Legion was very real, she said. Its present aim was to fight the Red Army and harass the bolshevikii, which I thought a wild ambition for a women's organization. Mayr asked if I would agree to train them further in tactics, scouting and raiding once my mission was complete. I said yes, I would be honored. And if the way Aishna handled that brute in the café that morning was any indication, Mayr's Legion had real potential. All too soon, she left me, citing another appointment, saying she hoped we would meet again in better times.

The aroma of supper sent me downstairs, where Aishna sat with Shav at a small wooden table by the stove. Now she was dressed like a man in a black high-necked blouse, pantaloons and knee-high boots. Seeing her without her cloak, I was struck by how young she was, surely no more than twenty. Earlier she had seemed much older, judging by her confident bearing and bold sexuality. But then, innocents do not survive for long in such a situation as we find ourselves.

Again, her eyes captivated me. Katarin or Marianne would never wear such dramatic eye makeup, but it looked perfect on Aishna. I wondered if the beauty mark by her right eye was natural or applied. And what hair she had! Black and glossy, it was now loose, falling to her waist. It was hard for me to take my eyes off Aishna as we ate our simple meal of chicken and rice and drank a fine Armenian wine.

Shav was preoccupied with her as well, and I had the impression Aishna had seduced him in the course of the afternoon. We talked desultorily. Aishna praised Mayr as her "mother, her teacher." Among other things, she revealed that "Lucine" means "mysterious like the moon," and she certainly is.

When it was time to meet Vlad and the men, Aishna put on a hiker's pack and scabbards with her spider scimitar and curved dagger, saying she would follow Shav and me shortly. We had her assurances that the point where Shav and I were to meet the squadron was beyond the perimeter patrolled by the Reds, and we headed that way. Unfortunately, her information was incorrect, or out of date, and just before we reached our destination, we were stopped by a militia patrol of six men on horseback. The sergeant told us they were looking for Heghine Khachaturian and the Baroness Lucine, who were reported to be in this part of the city. All they knew was that these women are Armenians. Baroness Lucine—my Mayr! In my best semi-drunken tone, I replied we knew nothing about either one. And truly, I did not know who "Heghine Khachaturian" was.

Next, the sergeant asked for our identification and checked our numbers against his list.

"You met with Heghine Khachaturian at a café earlier today."

"Oh, you mean the woman in the red cloak?" I asked, although I used a ruder word than "woman." "We don't know who the hell she was. What a wonder____. And the way she killed that man! We had to go along with her. Didn't want her to cut our throats!"

Shav joined in with noises of agreement. I went on to suggest that she was one of the many women driven insane by the death of a beloved husband during the Great War.

"Yes, she is a madwoman, all right. All of our information suggests she is crazy. But anyway, what are you doing out so late? It's past curfew."

"Curfew? We didn't know there was a curfew," I said, repeating the story about being White Army deserters waiting to see the cheka about joining the Red Army. "Just looking for a place to sleep under the stars before we report tomorrow morning."

By this time, the other guards were shifting around on their horses, apparently eager to get on with something more interesting than a couple of drunks. But this sergeant was cleverer than the usual Red guard.

"We'd better take you in now," he said, drawing his pistol. "Your meeting with the Khachaturian woman this morning is just too suspicious."

Going to the cheka was out of the question, and the decision to fight and, if necessary, die fighting here was an easy one. I nodded to Shav, and simultaneously we reached into our tunics for our pistols. Without hesitation, I shot the militia sergeant in the head while Shav killed another.

Suddenly a third man lost his head. Aishna was behind him on her palomino gelding, scimitar flying through the air. A volley from the dark caught the three other militia men by surprise as they raised their guns to shoot, knocking them to the ground. Our men had come up quietly, having dismounted a short distance away. Shav and I mounted two of the militia horses, swiftly making our escape before more militia arrived. Vlad, brilliant soldier that he was, had not only managed to get all the men across the river but had established a defensive position much closer to the wall than I expected. He had been shadowing the patrol we had just wiped out, foreseeing they would be a threat to Shav and me.

Not until we returned to our camp did Shav reveal he had been wounded in the shoulder. I too realized that I had some superficial wounds. Grisha is now operating on Shav.

Aishna/Heghine (what shall I call her?) came with us, as planned, and I have put her in her own tent, guarded by two reliable men. I know so little about her, but Mayr Lucine has heartily endorsed her, which carries great weight. "La ReM," Mayr's organization with her husband, Baron Charbonnet, is first-rate. This Legion Mayr talks about must have some importance. But tomorrow morning, I will summon Aishna to my tent and discover more about her. Can I really keep her under control? I am growing more in awe of her seductive powers—it is clear that she has conquered Shav. Besides, every time I see her, I find her more attractive, even with that short, flat nose. I must keep my distance. I must not betray Katarin.

This long, long day was a success. I now possess the latest intelligence on Sabantsevski as well as the coordinates for rendezvous with the rest of another squadron. We shall proceed to act upon that tomorrow.

As I prepare for sleep, I have the pleasant mental image of St. Vladimir, lit against the night sky—as always, a beacon to ships on the river—as we rode away from Kiev tonight.

PART SEVEN

Tuesday, 22 April 1919, outside Kiev / 0900 hrs. [9:00 am]

I have met with Aishna, and I believe she has already made an important contribution to our mission. At about 0600 hrs. [6:00 am] Corporals Malinski and Betenov, her guards for the night, brought her to my tent, where Grisha was also present. Like most men, apparently, he seemed taken with her appearance. Once again, she was dressed in black, her stunning eye makeup in place even at that early hour. We ate a hearty breakfast of ham, croissants and tea.

When I asked her to tell us about herself, she replied that she was not yet ready to share her personal story beyond stating her age as twenty-three. Her role, she said, was to ask questions about our tactical situation and what we need.

"At least tell us your political persuasion," I said.

"I am an anarchist," she said, lifting her chin, looking proud.

"Really?" I said, motioning toward a small gold Orthodox cross she wore around her neck. I had just noticed this cross, which surprised me, as she had in no way behaved like a religious person. Nor are the true faith and anarchy usually found in the same person. But I am learning that she seems to delight in defying preconceived notions about herself. Despite her adult age, she clearly still has some of the wild child about her. Consistency does not seem to concern her.

"The Bolsheviks and their Red Army are the mortal enemies of anarchism," was all she had to say on that subject.

"What we need most is weapons," I told Aishna. "And a headquarters."

"I can give you both, not far from here," she said. She never lacks confidence, I am learning. She described a shtetl the Germans had used as their local base of operations in 1917–18, now abandoned. It not only has huts but also two larger buildings for shelter from pogroms, which the Germans had further fortified. We will need all the defenses we can get, for Aishna revealed something disturbing. The cheka have armored cars, and we have no defense against them. "The advantage," she said, "is that it appears to be just another abandoned Zhidy village. But it certainly is not."

Tuesday, 22 April 1919 / 1400 hrs. [2:00 pm]

Our squadron arrived at the shtetl yesterday at 1025 hrs. [10:25 am], and I immediately set up pickets to watch for the cheka.

By 1200 hrs. [12:00 pm], we had moved into the huts while Shav and Vlad explored the fortified buildings. Aishna took me to look for a cache of weapons that she and Mayr Lucine believed to be here. Mayr had learned about it from a German soldier she had seduced, then shared with Aishna. (I am trying not to be shocked by the tactics of these women.) When his troops left this place last year, they buried a number of weapons crates. Mayr said we could take what we need, but we have to leave enough for her own operations.

"What percentage would that be?" I asked Aishna.

She thought that forty percent would be more than adequate.

"Why did the Germans leave so many valuable weapons behind?"

"Is it not obvious?" she said. "They planned to come back as conquerors."

I cannot say I was surprised. Of course Germany wanted Ukraine as one of their spoils of war. Ukraine is always a tempting target because of its agricultural abundance (at least in normal times). But it is also a gateway to Russia, and, as I read in a classified report before leaving on this mission, the German Kaiser's primary goal in the Great War was to destroy Russia before she could fully industrialize in the next ten years. Thus his gambit of sending bolshevikii in a sealed train from Switzerland to Petrograd so as to destroy us from within. The German Freicorps forces fighting the Reds in the Baltic States are just the vanguard of a larger force that will eventually invade. The Poles wanted Ukraine too. They got western Galicia from Austria at Versailles, then fought the Reds to get east Galicia. Their next goal would be the annexation of western Ukraine.

I set two men to digging for the weapons. The German soldier's directions were accurate, and we discovered several crates. First, we found two boxes of Mauser Gewehr 98 rifles. This is an exceptionally fine rifle for an infantryman but too long—1250 mm [4.9 ft.]—to be practical for cavalry. Nonetheless, we loaded them in the wagon to use during unmounted defense. Next, six boxes of Mauser C-96 Broom Handles, a semi-automatic pistol with wooden rifle stock that can easily be fired with one hand from a saddle. Then some semi-automatic Mauser M-1912 pistols with a twenty-round magazine and abundant ammunition.

By late afternoon, we had twenty boxes, enough for the entire squadron. I was concerned that none of these weapons could pierce armor, though, and we needed defense against chekist armored cars. But perhaps the Broom Handles would do. During the war, I had heard rumors that a Broom Handle would pierce armor plate if you reversed the bullet—that is, inserted it backwards so that the flat end of the shell comes out first. That could save us, if it worked. I instructed Shav to find an iron plate 2.5 cm [1 in.] thick and set it up as a target. When Shav and Aishna realized what I proposed to do, both demurred. It was too risky. They were certain the pistol would explode, killing not only me but anyone else nearby.

"If you must test this theory, I should be the one to fire the pistol," Shav said. "I'm expendable."

"No. It's my idea. I must be the one to take the risk," I said. "Call everyone to observe, Sergeant. They won't believe it will work unless they see it."

I aimed the pistol at the plate and, after a quick prayer, squeezed the trigger. When I opened my eyes, the plate had a good-sized hole in it. Shav and Aishna cheered, as did the others. Now we have an anti-armor weapon, and thank God I am alive.

And now we have even more.

"Surely there are other rifles equipped with Mauser K armor-piercing bullets," Aishna said, leading me back to the holes we had dug, which will make good traps for the armored cars, by the way. From a particular point, she instructed me to walk twenty-five paces. I summoned two fresh troopers to dig there, and we soon found crates with more weapons like we already had. With more digging, though, we did finally find four boxes with abundant K ammunitions. We now have more than enough to meet our needs. Perhaps we are taking more than our share? I assure Aishna that we will return here after our mission and re-bury everything Mayr could need, although I do not think she believes me.

Meanwhile, the men had been preparing the shtetl for attack, and, accompanied by Aishna, I inspected their work. The space between the two fortified buildings is now blocked by a large log almost 5 meters [16 feet] long. Infantry and cavalry could jump over it but not an armored car, at least not quickly. Fired at the cars from the rear, the Ks could do real damage. Satisfied, I returned to my tent to complete this journal entry.

Tuesday 22 April 1919/ 2330 hrs. [11:30 pm]

After my final check of preparations for defense of our cantonment, Aishna asked if I would accompany her on a reconnaissance ride around the area. I gladly accepted. I needed to refresh my knowledge should we be forced to fight the cheka and their auxiliaries away from the shtetl. Besides, we are near the great forests west of Kiev, which have remained largely uncut because of the myriad possible threats there—brigands, Reds, Green Muzhiks, mobs of White or Red deserters, Ukrainian Nationalist forces. It is almost impossible to predict whether Nationalists will be hostile, neutral or supportive. Obviously, Aishna needed an escort in such territory. Vlad was left in charge of military matters, Grisha in charge of general deportment.

Armed with our Mauser Broom Handles and 1912 pistols, Aishna and I set out on horseback for a very interesting foray over the steppe and into the forest. After the pressure of the Mauser test shot, I relaxed a bit, grateful to breathe in the clean, fresh air. It also felt good to get away from camp, where, sadly, there is always the threat of being killed by one of my own troops, no matter how remote. This is a war of ideas, and you can never know, until too late, who has become infected with the bolshevik virus. Even my "anarchist" riding companion, Aishna, could be so infected. I still knew very little about her except that Mayr Lucine endorsed her. Up went my guard again.

We had been riding in silence, but suddenly, as we came to a clearing in the forest, Aishna began to speak.

"Let's stop here, Lieutenant Colonel. I want to tell you a story. Do you know what happened at the shtetl during the German occupation last year?"

I did not. As she recounted, when the Germans first came in the fall of 1917, the harvest was in the final stages. They confiscated food from all the villages in the area but treated Zhidy villages differently from Christian ones. Whereas Christian Muzhiks were allowed to keep ten percent of their produce, the Germans took all the Zhidy had. At the shtetl where we were camped, Germans forced the Zhidy to load all the grains onto trucks that drove it to a central railhead for transport back to Germany. The Zhidy were left with virtually nothing, and wherever they went to buy, beg or borrow food, they were refused. Muzhiks rebuffed the Zhidy's pleas to purchase even a portion of what they had. The Christians went further: they attacked and looted the shtetl. The Zhidy were made to clean up the mess and make everything appear as before. Then the Christians ravaged the Zhidy girls and women.

"The men were brought to this clearing. There were fifty-three of them. They were shot or, in some cases, knifed, beaten or tortured to death. The Christians laughed as they did all this, saying they were simply preventing the Zhidy from starving to death and should be thanked for their humanitarianism."

I had seen enough mass graves to recognize the one in that clearing.

"What happened to the women and girls?" I asked. "Were they buried? We found no bodies in the shtetl."

"The prettiest were sold to brothels in the area. Those not so pretty were sold to brokers who sent them to Australia or America."

I recall my first visit to Kiev's famous White House. It was the first year after my summer with Constanza when I was a lieutenant and still single. The letter of introduction from my father gained me instant entrance into the elegant salon. Lovely girls in provocative attire walked back and forth before me until I made my selection. Where they might have come from or why they were there never entered my mind. They were simply there, as they were supposed to be, existing only in the moment.

Same with the Zhidy. Last year in Kiev, Katarina and I heard talk in the cafés and clubs that the surly Muzhiks were not relinquishing their grain, but that seemed to be happening in another world. Pogroms, the eternal pogroms, were as much a part of the landscape as the fields of wheat. The Zhidy were victims—the weak and oppressed—the role their God had chosen for them. Perhaps they received some great reward in the afterlife, although I was not certain they believed in such a concept.

Here in Ukraine, the pogroms have been more frequent and violent than elsewhere in the Russias, I believe. That is at least partly because it was part of the Pale of Settlement, that area where, from 1825 to 1917, Zhidy were allowed to settle, albeit with many restrictions. Christian Muzhiks regard the Zhidy with deep suspicion, linking them to some degree with the Turks. In the south, Zhidy live in proximity to the Turks in the Balkans. When Turks conquered Constantinople, they allowed the Zhidy to remain there and practice their strange rituals. Ukrainian Muzhiks suspect that the Zhidy feel loyal to the Turks—their Mohammedan masters—and would collaborate with them at a moment's notice to conquer Ukraine.

I also understand that our Christian Muzhiks hate the Zhidy as "Christ killers" and allies of the hated Mohammedan infidels, but in no way can I condone such slaughter. Some Muzhik believe that even Lenin is Zhidy. Certainly, Trotski is, and several of the most prominent of their leaders.

This whole business is surely a great conundrum.

"Why are you fighting for the Whites?" I asked Aishna.

"I fight against the Bolsheviks," she said again. "I am an anarchist."

"Are you associated with Nestor Makhno and his Green Forces?"

"No, such ragtag forces have no chance of victory. I simply wish to be left alone by the government to live as I see fit."

Such an idea was very un-Russian, I told her. In Russia, order is prized above all else.

"I am not a Slav, obviously," she said. "For all I care, Russia can go straight to hell."

"It certainly is well on its way," I said.

She shrugged, saying that the devil you know is always better than the one you do not. I thought it imprudent to tell her that even as we spoke, General Deniken was fighting for a unitary Russia and would never allow the sort of individualism she espoused.

I am still astonished at her claim to be an anarchist. Is not our present situation anarchy? What sane person would want to continue living in such Hobbesian brutality? Anarchy has always been the greatest fear of Russians, especially in Ukraine, given our history of invasion and bondage. Ultimately a nightmare of chaos and crime, with separate tribes ruled by local warlords in our failed state, ripe for invasion. I believe this will be the reality of bolshevik rule. But a strong, independent person such as Aishna might be able to live the life she wants, at least for a while. I looked at her anew, astride her Palomino gelding. She certainly has the bearing of one of those legendary Amazon warriors who roamed these lands in the time before history.

Actually, at first glance, Aishna might be mistaken for any other member of my squadron. Her black garments—blouse, pantaloons, boots—are virtually indistinguishable from a man's. Her long hair is tied back, like many of my men's, though with a narrow red ribbon with a black widow insignia rather than a leather thong. What is hers alone is the earring in her left ear—with another black widow spider insignia, identifiable by its tiny red bow tie. As I rode at her side, only a glimpse of the swell of her breasts would indicate her gender.

Again I asked Aishna to tell me more about her background.

"You know all you need to know," she said, looking away. "My name. My age. My politics."

"You are not a Slav, you said. What is your nationality?" I asked.

"I was born in the Republic of Armenia," she said. "But my parents were Persian. Therefore I have no 'nationality.'"

"Then why are you associated with Mayr, who is Armenian to her core?"

Aishna looked at me as though I were brainless. "Mayr Lucine's intelligence network is the finest of several in the Caucasus, the best in Ukraine."

As we rode through the forest, we avoided trails, fearing that we might encounter a hostile party. These woods bordered my mother's estate, might even have been part of her estate, and the smells and sounds reminded me of my youthful explorations on horseback. When we came to a ridge I recognized, we descended its slope and came to a tributary of the Dnieper and a private spot where Constanza and I often had picnics. The river was no more than seven to ten meters across [23 to 32 ft.] and not deep enough for large boat traffic. It seemed like a safe place to stop and water the horses.

Thinking of the carnal pleasures of picnics with Constanza, I decided to have a wash in the river. Dismounting, I removed my blouse and hung my Broom Handle and pistol belt on my saddle. As I waded into the river—which was icy cold—I was surprised to be joined by Aishna, who had also removed her blouse. She was splashing her breasts and under her arms—shaved, I saw with even more surprise. At first, I was astonished by her brazenness, but then I realized that she was not trying to be seductive. In fact, she seemed unaware of my presence.

"Do not stare!" she said.

I quickly replied that I was simply admiring her, not staring.

Hands on hips, she turned to face me, laughing, "All right, but you must think of me first as a warrior, not as a woman. I expect no special consideration because of my gender."

"Yes, of course," I said, but that was hardly possible for a gentleman. By revealing her femininity, Aishna had revived my chivalrous concerns about having her in my squadron. Nor could I ignore her firm round breasts, which only one so young could still have, or her wine-dark nipples, erect in the cold. Nor could I avoid seeing the panoply of tattoos above her breasts and along her lithely muscled arms.

"There must be many stories behind those tattoos," I said, for lack of anything better to say. Some were large, others small, but all intricately patterned and obviously symbolic. "And that one, on your left breast. Mayr Lucine has that one. She had it even when I knew her as a young woman."

And neither Constanza nor Mayr had ever told me what it meant. "I assume that is your Amazon one."

"Perhaps, but sadly I can't tell you more. All the others are from my campaigns with Mayr's Legion of the Black Widow Spider's Revenge on the Turk."

"Oh, that is no more than a myth," I said, trying this gambit to entice her to reveal more of her history. "I heard rumors about this Legion during the war but never saw any mention in army dispatches or documents we captured from the Ottomans."

"The Ottomans would not mention the Legion," she said. "They were humiliated to be defeated by women. Therefore they suppressed reports of our victories. Since the legion was not part of the Russian Caucasus Army, again, no mentions."

"That is absence of evidence, still not proof of existence. Besides, Mayr Lucine told me to be careful. Many women claim membership in the Legion who never really fought for them."

I knew I was going too far. While I was unarmed, Aishna was wearing her Damascus steel dagger, which she now withdrew.

"Remember how the criminal I killed yesterday reacted when he saw this?" she said, pointing to the black widow spider emblazoned on the dagger. "He was terrified, especially because he knew he had violated our ancient tribal rules."

"Still not proof."

"Bon Dieu, you are impossible. All right. Tell me what you know of the Legion."

I recounted how I had first heard of them while serving on the Caucasus Front during the Great War. They were supposedly a modern-day Amazon cavalry who raided the Turk and Azeeri, armed with scimitars, lances, and bows and arrows, as well as conventional weapons. Stories were told about how they would attack a Turk camp just before dawn, fire a volley of pitch fire arrows into the tents, then kill or capture all the men and take their supplies. Then they would return to their headquarters—no one knew where—in Georgia or the northern Armenian mountains."

"We were free, brave women, not affiliated with any army, and we knew what our fate would be if we were captured. Hence this curved dagger. Good for self-defense, but also good for cutting our own throats or stabbing our hearts to avoid capture. But not just any woman can claim to be a Legionnaire. There is one sure way to identify one of us. Do you know what it is?"

"Yes, I think I do. Mayr told me her members have a large spider tattoo over their canals of love."

Aishna laughed at my primness about what she called "ma vagin." Then she dropped her pantaloons to reveal her pubic region. It was completely shaved, something I have never seen before, but the astounding thing—and I blush even to write it here—was a terrifying tattoo. It is large—about twenty-five-centimeters long [9.8 in.] and represents a black widow spider. It is similar to the image on her dagger but with a mouthful of razor-sharp pointed teeth. Its head is just above her canal of love, with legs going down around it. The pain of getting that tattoo must have been horrendous. Also, as I now recall the sight of her, I realize she has no body hair whatsoever, which is quite unusual for a noirette. Having her body hair removed must also have been terribly painful.

"That is proof, alright," I said.

"I joined the Legion in 1915, when I was nineteen. I learned how to use a lance, bow, pistol, scimitar and knife. I was awarded my spider after my tenth kill in battle. That is also when I got my Legion nom-de-guerre—Aishna, to replace my old civilian name, Heghine Khachaturian. Getting the spider was very painful, but it was such a great honor I endured it gladly."

Realizing that Aishna was not in a hurry to cover her most intimate parts and determined to deflect any thoughts of seduction, I continued talking.

"There are rumors that you go into battle bare-breasted, like the Amazons thousands of years ago. And that you torture your captives in unspeakable ways. And that Mohammedans kill themselves rather than be captured by the Legion."

"Yes, almost everything you have heard about the Legion is true, except going into battle with bared teats. Early on, some of us did want to show the Turk that we held Turkish military skills in contempt, but they soon realized their teats were too exposed. Therefore we began wearing a thick leather band around our chests for protection. As for the torture, that is true. You know the female black widow is twice the size of the male, and she eats her little mate after copulating with him. Think about that."

To change the subject, I asked her about her rank.

"Ithnayn Thalatha, or two three."

Aishna explained she was in the Second Company and leader of platoon three of five. A company in the Legion is fifty women. By the end of the war, Mayr had twenty companies made up of Christian, Jewish and even some non-religious women who had come from all over to fight the Turk. She had no trouble replacing dead and wounded with new recruits. French was their common language, at Mayr's insistence, and learning French became part of the training. Aishna is quite fluent in French, and she is also one of Mayr's French teachers.

She noticed me looking at a long scar on her left side.

"From a scimitar," she said. "It happened in 1917 when seven hundred legionnaires attacked and largely destroyed the Ottoman garrison at Kharput. Kharput is one of the sites of the Armenian genocide in 1915."

While Aishna was igniting one of the barracks at Kharput, a Turk had snuck up behind her and slashed her side. She retaliated by slashing his belly with her curved knife, leaving him to die slowly and painfully. This was just one of countless raids they had made on the Turks and Azeeris.

Aishna untied her hair and dunked her head beneath the icy river, then retied it. She must be impervious to pain and discomfort.

"No more questions," she said as we dressed.

If she wishes to be mysterious, I see no harm in that—unless it interferes with our mission. And my reservations about having her in my command remain: simply by existing, such a free and stimulating woman may cause havoc in my command. But the positives outweigh the negatives. I shall have to monitor this situation most carefully. My thoughts return to her naked body—I confess it—but it helps to remember that a woman such as I would marry—a lady—would never dress as a man or be so immodest in the casual, public way this woman warrior can be. I cannot imagine my Katarin being so immodest, although she is distinctly not priggish in private.

"Before we go, let me do a little scouting," Aishna said, and she walked away, leaving me with the horses.

Soon she returned, saying she had found some women around a bend in the river, washing clothes, and they had given her some valuable information. They were expecting a visit by chekists and perhaps even a Red Army unit tomorrow, perhaps as early as tonight, and taking advantage of this relative peace to get their washing done. If they were arrested, they would at least have clean garments to begin a prolonged detainment—or meet death. I acknowledged this womanly logic with a smile.

We rode on toward Kiev without seeing anything of interest. From a ridge overlooking the city, I glimpsed the familiar cupolas of Santa Olga of Kiev. I rejoiced that this great church still stood and said a silent prayer for the holy fathers and mothers, especially my Aunt Katiya in her nunnery. She is probably under the rule of the godless bolshevikii now.

Farther down the ridge was a Red encampment. From the safety of a thick stand of trees, I tried to assess how great a threat it posed. I passed my field glasses to Aishna. Neither of us could observe any unusual activity. Judging by the size of the camp, it could accommodate about 250 men. I estimated their able-bodied complement to be about two hundred, assuming about a twenty-five percent reduction from disease or wounds. The men I saw looked malnourished, and their uniforms were ragged and mismatched. I reduced my estimate of their combat-ready troops to about one hundred. Some were barefoot Muzhik conscripts—typical Red cannon fodder troops in Ukraine. If this was the Red Army unit the washerwomen were expecting, it was not so fearsome—it could be worse. Vehicles entered and left the compound as we watched, but no armored cars. Everything appeared to be normal. Nevertheless, we shall avoid this camp when we move on from the shtetl.

"It would be great fun to attack that camp when the Legion is reunited," Aishna said.

"When might that be?" I asked, still trying to get more information from her.

She merely shrugged.

It was time to turn back to our base. We returned via a different route to complete a circle of reconnaissance. In about forty minutes, we came upon a trail that I recognized, and I recalled that there had been a military encampment about two kilometers [1.2 miles] along this trail to the north. This could very well be a base now for either the Red Army or the chekists. It was late—the sun was low in the sky—so in the interest of time, we risked riding on the road, as there was no other traffic in sight. When we were within a few hundred meters of the camp, we returned to the trees and proceeded with our weapons at the ready. The forest seemed tranquil, with nothing save the sounds of the wind, the birds and the animals. We tied up the horses, moving on foot for the final approach. We saw no pickets; the barracks were quiet. Not a soul in sight anywhere. Wary of a trap, we pressed on.

Broom Handles drawn, we dared to approach the first barrack. A horrendous smell met us as I opened the door. Covering our faces with our kerchiefs, we entered—eyes watering from the foul, noxious odors. Stacks, piles, rows of blackened, decomposing bodies, like so much cordwood. We backed away, gagging, and closed the door on this hellish scene.

"Victims of the Spanish flu," I said, and Aishna nodded, eyes wide and filled with tears.

"We had better inspect the other buildings, get a sense of the extent of this," I said. "Please go back to the horses. No point in both of us doing this."

Although she was clearly terrified of the plague, Aishna, to her credit, insisted on coming with me in case I encountered guards. Thus did she display her courage and earn more of my trust.

As we left the compound, I asked what she knew about the Spanish influenza in Kiev. There had been rumors of an outbreak last fall, another over the winter, but neither of us had definite information. But here were bodies, hundreds, if not thousands of them. It was clear to me that Skoropadski's Nationalist Directory had brought the victims here and left them to freeze over the winter. There was some justification for such action: to prevent further infection and panic. But I had no doubt there were more cynical motives at play. To keep the inhabitants of Kiev from realizing the severity of the outbreak. To refute rumors about the outbreak in the wider world, maybe to refute news of the very existence of infection in Kiev. There is now no doubt that all the Four Horsemen are assembled here—war, famine, pestilence and death.

I said as much to Aishna as we rode away.

"Yes, Commander," she replied. "Russia has always been a violent culture. Muzhiks, in particular, always seem to be fighting, killing their enemies in gruesome ways, especially here in the border regions. The Great War just ripped the veneer of civility off the truth."

I was struck by how acute her analysis was, also by how she called me "Commander." While she had insisted that I call her by her nom-de-guerre, she had never called me by my name.

"Shav is an exceptionally good man," she said out of the blue. "Do you know him well?"

I told her I had first met Shav on the retreat from Kiev. We had fought many battles against the Reds, and he could always be depended upon. He was a natural warrior and a superior addition to my squadron. She commented that he was extraordinarily strong, and from her expression, I had no doubt of her meaning.

In time she spoke, at first, so softly I had to strain to hear. She said that after dismounting last night, Shav had saved her life by taking the bullet from militia fire meant for her. Since Shav served under me, she would now be responsible for my life. While I recognized her Armenian reasoning and sense of honor, I felt uncomfortable having Aishna as my protector. But then I realized that, even though she was not a "lady" as defined by my code of chivalry, she was a very capable warrior who must follow her own code. Thus I thanked her and told her I had many enemies who would like to kill me. She asked me about them and listened most attentively as I told her of Sabantsevski. She said that such a man should be buried up to his neck, then ridden over by our entire squadron. While that was an interesting idea, I had other plans for him.

I told her about Tariq Aziz the Turk. She spat at the very mention of "Turk." She said she would love to disembowel him with her dagger, cutting ever so slowly. As I mentioned other enemies, she appeared to have some manner of slow horrible death planned for each one of them. In truth, she seemed to relish the idea of disposing of all my enemies as gruesomely as possible. I recalled what I had heard in the Caucasus: "An Armenian woman is passionate in love and even more passionate in revenge."

Tariq and his men must be the ones following us, she said, telling me some of what she knew. When I asked her to elaborate, she said that was all I needed to know at this point.

"My trade is information. One of my official titles by 1917 was

Legionnaire Mistress of Interrogation, an expert. But I would never betray any of your information for any price or circumstance since you have defended my homeland against the Turk." But she used a rather colorful scatological metaphor to describe the Turk, one that would surprise me even coming from a trooper. With that, she spurred her horse and said she was going hunting for Tariq. She refused to let me go with her on the grounds that I had to prepare the troops for tomorrow. She was correct, and so I reluctantly watched her ride off amongst the trees. She obviously felt this was a duty she had to perform in order to cement my trust. She also appeared to think that killing this Turk would be great fun.

I now think her the same as one of my troopers. However, while we may hide what God has made us for a time, the ruse cannot endure for long. Although she acts very much as a man, there can be no mistaking her femininity, especially in her incredibly expressive eyes.

Shortly after Aishna left, I heard a loud and terrible noise. I rode toward it as rapidly as a grasshopper to water and, from a safe distance, used my field glasses to see an armored train bristling with canons and machine guns, belching smoke and fire from the top and steam from the bottom, covered in a streamlined red skin of armor and looking for all the world like a demon from Hell. It boasted many Red flags and clearly transported someone of importance toward Kiev. Owing to their limited finances, the bolshevikii cannot be promiscuous with the use of such a monster. I could not read the banners identifying the person being transported. I have heard that Sabantsevski travels on such a train, as do Kamenev, Zinoviev, Dzerzhinski and even Lenin. It is not Trotski, as this is much too proletarian a train for the high-living commissar.

Whoever it brings, this cannot be judged as anything less than an event of the utmost importance. Troops traveling on such a train must be of a much higher caliber than the rag-tags we have faced thus far. The war in Ukraine has just now taken a turn for the worse. My troopers and I will bear the first brunt of this development. It is a challenge we shall meet with firm resolution and, if need be, fight to the death. May God help us in our hour of trial.

PART EIGHT

Sergeant Kapolski and his men are out on patrol this morning. I have just reviewed our plans for defense with the remaining men and am satisfied that their morale is high. I have also made a final inspection of the buildings.

I assume the chekists will come in armored cars, supported by Red cavalry from a local garrison. I do not anticipate any difficulty from cavalry. Our Vickers machine gun, along with four well-placed snipers, should suffice to destroy them.

Most likely chekists will arrive in Austin-Putilovs, and our goal is to immobilize them forthwith. A word about these vehicles. Our English allies supplied Russia with these cars in the Great War. Rather, they supplied Austin motors, transmissions and chassis that we then armored. Each Putilov car has a crew of five. It is a formidable machine, 4.9 meters long [16 ft.] and 2.84 meters high [9.4 ft.], with aft mounts of two side-by-side Maxim machine guns. It weighs 5.2 tonnes [5.7 tons]. Yet it has only fifty horsepower and is thus fairly slow. (The Austin-Kegresse, which has been fitted with a tracked drive on the aft section for improved traction, is even slower, but they are rare, and I do not expect any today.)

The first order of business is to destroy the Austin-Putilov's tires or tracks with grenades—not easy because the wheels are protected almost to the ground by armored plates. The next objective will be to penetrate the car's armor, which is 7.6 cm thick [3 in.]. I did not know whether our K bullets would suffice. Again I had Vlad make a metal sheet target, this time 15.2 cm [6 in.] thick, about twice the thickness of the car. When I fired a clip of five K bullets from a distance of one hundred meters [328 ft.], two penetrated and three bounced off. But from twenty meters, all five pierced. Good to know—we must move in toward our targets.

But, as I told the men, there are many unknowns. Perhaps improvements have been made on the Austin-Putilov. Or the cheka could attack with another kind of car, even a tank. We must expect surprises, but if we remain disciplined and lay down a crossfire with all the new weaponry in our arsenal, we will carry the day. We shall also use petrol bombs, which have been effective against armor. I ordered the troops to make more petrol bombs. We have a fifty-liter [13.2 gal.] drum of petrol on the wagon for that purpose, along with some empty vodka bottles. The men have been instructed to scour the grounds for more bottles. This will keep them occupied until the battle, for waiting is always the hardest part.

I reminded the men that no Reds should be allowed to escape the scene of battle lest they reveal our position and bring on another attack before we can depart on our mission. There were no questions following my review of the plan, but I could read the men's faces— sheer pleasure that they were about to engage with the enemy. Indeed, a spontaneous cheer arose from the men. I vowed to them that we will enjoy the sweet taste of revenge against the cheka before the day comes to an end. We will remove the mark of dishonor placed upon us by the cheka, with every man acquitting himself as a member of an elite cavalry squadron should.

If morale were a physical weapon, we would be indestructible. However, the stress on us all still manifests itself in ways we cannot control, such as the inability to sleep. Or, as in my case, in extraordinary dreams. I have read Freud, whose ideas, in my view, are little more than fodder for salon chatter. But thanks to my mother, I know that dreams do have special significance. What some educated persons may dismiss as simply unrelated images are as real to me as the paper of this journal.

Madame Daria taught me about dreams. She—an Armenian and the mother of Constanza/Mayr Lucine—truly had the power to see. She and Constanza lived in a beautiful cottage on our estate, on 1.2 hectares [3 acres] given by my parents as a thank-you gift and as compensation for her ongoing counsel. She is reputedly a descendent of the Maga—that priestess and Zodiacalist of the ancient Amazon female tribes. Some might dismiss a Maga as Muzhik superstition, with no place in our modern scientific age. Some might condemn her as a witch, but that is too facile. Mme Daria is not a hag but a handsome, mature lady. She is learned in areas that can only be described as the supernatural, that is, beyond science. My mother consulted with her on a regular basis, as did my father on occasion.

I first got to know Mme Daria when I was an adolescent, a fourth-year student at the Page Academy. During a holiday, my mother sent me to study with her to "broaden my view of the world." I considered myself possessed of the best modern ideas, and at first, I treated Mme Daria with condescension, as only an arrogant schoolboy would do. She took no offense at my ignorance and proceeded to teach me of her world. Much of her instruction had to do with dreams, which she called the door to the soul. All one needed, she taught, was the courage to turn the lock and enter. I left her instruction, which seemed all too brief, with the highest respect for her and her ways.

Whenever I returned home, I always spent some time with her and perhaps gained another grain of her wisdom. On my last visit home before my summer with Constanza, I asked Mme Daria if she could tell what my fate would be. Yes, she said with a smile, but she would not share such information, as it would be too great a burden on me. However, she did make a few general statements about events that would change my life. She said I would be given a great task.

Another prophecy, which I have been thinking about lately, is that late in my life, a woman would appear—Aishna? Mayr Lucine?—to render assistance in a demanding situation. Such prophecies were broad enough to apply to anyone, like fortune-telling by a huckster, but they are coming true. Her parting advice was simply to live each day as though it were my last. I have done so since that day.

There is something else. I have felt the hand of God grasp me to His bosom as if protecting me for some purpose of His own. Once on the Galician Front, for instance, we were under heavy bombardment by the Austrians. We were exposed on a salient without proper shelter. I vividly recall how the bursting shells from their huge Krupps artillery drew nearer to our position with each salvo. I thought it merely a question of time before the shells ripped our position apart and sent us all to our final reward. Then, miraculously, the shelling ceased, and we were spared. And, so, armed with my armor of faith, I have become relentless in the pursuit of my foes.

Last night I had a horrible nightmare. For several nights, I have dreamt of the two priests who were so gruesomely murdered in that nameless village. It began last night as it has in the past, but the body of the priest burned at the stake morphed into a naked Aishna. She was hung by her wrists from a large hook on the wooden scaffold. But the setting now was the vacant lot in Kiev where we saw the women being raped and the rabid crowd gathered around them. Aishna looked older in the dream, perhaps thirty, but her beautiful body was now scrawny and emaciated, and discolored by bruises. Her head was shaved, and her spider tattoo virtually burned away. Only her deep blue eyes were the same; otherwise, she was scarcely recognizable.

Before her stood a tall, muscular man wearing a black hood and a long white butcher's apron. As the crowd roared, he raised a long knife and cut a horizontal gash across her belly, then pulled out her female organs and flung them away. I could see the agony on her face but could not tell whether she was screaming. I prayed for her to die, for her agony to end. Over her was a large sign, "By Order of Stalin, Revolutionary Justice for our Martyred Comrade."

I awoke, aching, my nightshirt drenched with perspiration. I have no idea who "Stalin" is. That word means "made of steel" or "man of steel." This must refer to someone who has seized power in this nightmare world, but over all the Russias, or just Ukraine? He could be Sabantsevski—but he was the kind of devil who would have seduced Aishna, not butchered her. Should I tell Aishna? As Mayr's star pupil, she no doubt believes in dreams—but what good can knowing of this nightmare do her?

I rose and summoned Vlad. "Has Madame Aishna returned?" I asked him.

"No, not yet, sir," he said, adding, "You do not look well, sir." He insisted on escorting me back to my cot.

I lay there a while, unable to sleep. I had the keenest sense that I am no more than a wraith visiting amongst the living. It was as though Mme Daria was telling me that I shall not survive this mission. No matter—death has been my boon companion for these many years of service to my Emperor, regiment and country. Nothing I do will change my fate. This conviction gives me a new sense of courage. It frees me from my fears.

Wednesday, 23 April 1919 / 1000 hrs. [10:00 am]

We remain in that excruciating waiting mode. Sergeant Kapolski should be back by now. I still wonder about the identity of the dignitary or dignitaries on board the armored train. We need to get a chekist prisoner for interrogation, then move on toward our objective.

Where is Sabantsevski? If neither Aishna nor Sergeant Kapolski can get definite information, I am determined to visit my Aunt Katiya at her nunnery in Kiev, as she is likely to have the latest on the military and political situation in this area. That would be exceedingly dangerous, of course: the cheka would expect me to go there.

On the other hand, they know who they are dealing with and might well think I would not make such a cadet move. If they post pickets in the area, my troops can deal with them, having outwitted pickets now for many years.

In truth, however, my primary reason for going there would be to have the privacy and space for some prayer and silence before my confrontation with Sabantsevski. I pray the nunnery remains unscathed. Surely not even the Reds would consider harming the Holy Ladies of God, a move that would alienate the people they seek to control. But at this point, no barbarism by the Reds would greatly surprise me.

I've been weighing all the options, even leaving before chekists can arrive, thus not further depleting our ranks. After all, our target is Sabantsevski, not the cheka. Engagement has other terrible risks. Any chekist survivors who escape could reveal our position to the garrison at Kiev and bring down a brutal new attack in force upon this shtetl. We can defend this position against a rapid ambush but not against a concerted attack. Yet the men clamor for engagement with the cheka. They long to avenge the deaths of their two gallant comrades—Corporal Schroeder, tortured and hung, and Corporal Barinski, stuffed into the spike-embedded barrel. What manner of deranged minds can conceive of such debasement? I have heard that bolshevikii scour prisons and insane asylums for chekist recruits.

Wednesday, 23 April 1919 / 1600 hrs. [4:00 pm]

I must try to record the events of this momentous day before they begin to fade. At 1130 hrs. [11:30 am] Sergeant Kapolski reported that he and his scouts had spotted a column of two armored cars, type undetermined, with a Red cavalry escort heading towards us. At noon we were attacked. The cavalry led the charge. As expected, they jumped over the log barrier easily but were caught in our trap, mown down from behind by the Vickers and four snipers. Next came two Austin-Putilov armored cars, which were stopped by the log. They did not seem to grasp that they were now boxed in on all sides from our protected positions. Grenades destroyed their wheels as they were attacked on their flanks by the armor-piercing Mauser Ks. The bullets made a terrible racket as they ricocheted around inside the cars, despite the felt lining of the interior. Our snipers shot from roofs at the cars' gunners and commanders. Once the cars were incapacitated, they were set aflame with petrol bombs. The crew of the second car tried to escape the flames but were easily mown down by our rifles.

It was all over very quickly. The Reds lost over twenty-five men, not to mention the destruction of two armored cars. But I felt sad rather than triumphant. Sergeant Kapolof and Corporal Ingen from Sergeant Kapolski's squad were killed on the way back to the shtetl. And the whole engagement seemed to have been too easy. When this patrol fails to return to camp, a larger force will doubtless come in search of them. It would not surprise me if an artillery barrage were to commence at any moment, but the only sound in the air has been the birds returning after the noise and smoke of battle. Could the Reds have such inferior leadership that they fail to follow up on the loss of such a squad?

We need to close down our operations here, but I want to wait for Aishna. I cannot sacrifice the welfare of my troops for her, but I do want to permit her some additional time to report. In truth, and despite my nightmare, I am still unsure of where her loyalties lie. With us? With the Reds? Or simply with herself, to the exclusion of all others? I still struggle with the idea that she is an anarchist, someone who does not believe in rules or laws. She cannot have been captured and forced to reveal our position. There has not been enough time for the Reds break her. Her spider tattoo and the scars on her body testify to her ability to withstand pain.

One interesting outcome of the attack today: we have a prisoner to interrogate. Shortly after the attack, Vlad brought him to me. He had identified himself as a commissar, but he looked like a scrawny weakling next to Vlad, more like a raw recruit than a Party official. But he wore the cheka's characteristic black leather jacket, and I knew by his hard expression that I was faced with a vicious killer.

Standing straight, the prisoner said, "I am an officer of the All-Russian Extraordinary Commission for Combating Counter-Revolution, Profiteering and Official Corruption."

"My, that's impressive," I said, noting that such bravado must mean that the situation in areas controlled by the bolshevikii must be deteriorating. Vlad and I shared a good laugh.

Vlad noted that Sergeant Kapolski and his squad had found the prisoner following at a safe distance behind his column.

The implication that the "commissar" was a coward was so clear that the prisoner took a swing at Vlad, who flung him easily against the wall as though flicking a bug from his uniform. No doubt Vlad could have broken him easily, but I wanted to interrogate him in my own way.

"Vlad, thank you, I shall continue from here," I said before he could deliver another blow. "You are dismissed, with my thanks."

"Take a seat," I told the prisoner, who slowly picked himself up and took a chair. With my Mauser machine-pistol at hand on my makeshift desk, I finished some paperwork and let the prisoner regain some composure.

"What is your name?" I asked at length.

"I cannot reveal any information to you, Lieutenant Colonel Mikhail Antonovich Markov," he said to my surprise.

"I see. But you have me at a disadvantage. You know my name, but I do not know yours. So, I repeat, what is your name?"

"I shall tell you only my *nom de guerre*. It is Fyodor. I am a commissar. My business is information."

"And what further information do you have on me?" I said. He spoke with such authority that I was beginning to realize that, despite his youth, he was actually a person of some import, not a hooligan, as I had initially thought.

He said he knew about my key personnel as well. As he spoke, he moved his lips slightly upward in what might be construed as a smile. He knew my mission as well—to kill Comrade Commander Sabantsevski—and I would never succeed, he said. The Commander was far too clever to be killed by such an operation as mine. The cheka had thoroughly infiltrated the White Command structure up to the highest levels, he said.

"I do not believe you," I said.

He shrugged indifferently.

"I want the names of those traitors," I said.

He laughed—at least that was how I interpreted the peculiar noise coming from his throat. "The persons who betrayed you are most likely already dead. They were White officers who learned secrets and passed them on to us because their families were being held hostage."

He described what amounted to a perfect operation. When disloyal White officers are discovered, they are accused of treason and executed. Until their inevitable discovery, however, the Reds have excellent sources of information.

"Are families ever released in exchange for the information?"

He shrugged. "Some White officers have betrayed both the Cheka and their families. But by then, they are compromised, and your people deal with them harshly. Just as you did with Lieutenant Vladimir Antonovich Tomsk for his 'dereliction of duty' during your retreat from Kiev. He was actually a saboteur."

"I do not believe you," I said again, although what he said revived my paranoia about Red traitors in our ranks.

"Have you heard from Katarin and Marianne recently?" he said nonchalantly.

I rose, walked around my desk, and punched him with enough force to knock him to the floor. I was outraged that he even knew their names, much less dared to speak them.

"No one is safe from us," he said, wiping blood from his mouth and trying to rise to his feet. "You have no idea how many of your troops, including officers, are perfectly willing to betray you because they believe in the rightness of the Bolshevik cause."

"Who are you?" I said in disgust as he re-seated himself. He seemed vaguely familiar. His accent was upper-class. I placed him in Moscow or thereabouts, and his resemblance to a fellow officer had become increasingly obvious.

"I knew your father, Captain Vasili Alexievich Antonov," I said. "He was in my regiment, killed on the Galician Front in the summer of 1915. He had a son named Vasili. That must be you. How old were you when he died? Eighteen? Nineteen? How tragic it must be to lose one's father at such an impressionable age. Why have you betrayed your father, your family, your class, your country by joining the cheka?"

"No, no, that is not me," Fyodor muttered as I spoke to him. "You are mistaken. My father was a worker in the Tula Ammunition Works. I was a farm worker."

"Show me your hands," I said. Even from some distance, I could see they were well-tended, even manicured. They were the hands of the scion of a well-to-do family, not a farm worker. No doubt Vasili Vasilievich Antonov had gone to the St. Petersburg University, where he had his empty head filled with socialist nonsense. I was disgusted with this student revolutionary and his romantic notion of a *nom de guerre*.

"So, Vasili Vasilievich, tell me now what you know about my wife and daughter," I said, rising from my chair, putting my hand on my Mauser.

I had his attention. "All right," he said. "They are prisoners of the Cheka, but so far they have been spared any duress."

"That cannot be. They are no longer in Odessa. They are out of the chekists' reach."

"So you think," the prisoner said. "We know they were evacuated, but when they landed in Sevastopol, they were betrayed. We also have the families of several other officers."

"Do you have proof?" I said, shaken more than I wanted to admit.

The prisoner pulled a small notebook from an inner pocket of his jacket, which I seized and examined. It had a list of names, many of which I recognized. Katarin and Marianne were on it. The notebook looked official, with its various stamps and seals.

"Anyone could affix seals and stamps to a cheka notebook with a fake list," I said firmly. My hope was based on the absence of two particular names, the Princess Alexandra and the other Alexandra, the poor abused child we had rescued from Sandikoff. If the cheka really had Katarin and Marianne, they would have the two Alexandras as well.

"What would you require as proof?" he said.

"Nothing. Nothing short of seeing my family in chekist hands would persuade me you have them." As I made this declaration, I forced myself to appear calm and confident—the hardest thing I have ever done.

Meanwhile, this scoundrel ran his mouth, saying I would probably never see my family alive again, even if I cooperated with them in some way. But at least their deaths would be quick. If I did not cooperate, their deaths would be unimaginably slow and painful.

"Do you think I would try to bargain with you monsters?" I said. "One can only negotiate with honorable men."

I said no more on this score. I would never tell him that both Katarin and Marianne knew what capture by such an unscrupulous enemy meant. We had a deadly protocol. If confronted with death or torture they believed they could not endure, they would take poison. Ever since this terrible civil war had begun, both Katarin and Marianne carried a small, jeweled vial of a quick, painless poison on their persons.

I have often bluffed about my hand in cards, but never have I played for such high stakes. But what else could I do if "Fyodor" was telling the truth? There was no way to verify his claim that my darling ones had been captured. I could not even request a meeting to see them lest that be the occasion for a deadly ambush.

Fyodor now became quite angry. Standing and flailing his arms in the air, he asked me what manner of monster I was to so thoroughly disregard the welfare of my family. Did I not know my so-called mission was hopeless? Did I not know that the White cause was hopeless? For what was I fighting? A regime that was doomed and had already been cast upon the ash heap of history.

"Join me in the creation of a new and better world. You're a great tactician. Look how you demolished my patrol! The Bolsheviks could use a man of your abilities. Your men would be welcomed by my comrades. They have seen the future. They are working toward it, as Commander Sabantsevski and his troops are doing."

I must admit I was impressed with this young man, if for nothing else than his gall. Here he was, certain of execution, yet he was trying to get me and my troops to defect. I could only laugh. He sat back down.

"Just tell me," he said. "Why are you fighting for the *iberat régime*?"

I could easily have ignored his question but decided to try to answer it, perhaps thinking that even now he could be reconnected with his Russian heritage.

I spoke of duty, honor, country. I spoke too of Pravoslavni, the faith that holds the Russias together. Then I proceeded to give him my objections to his bolshevism, which are fundamental. I am not now, nor have I ever been, impressed by men who preached a secular religion, for that is what bolshevism truly is— the belief that it is possible to achieve perfection in this world. First, because it requires the emergence of a new type of man—a more perfect being. Man is inherently flawed and can never be perfect. The perfect is the enemy of the good or the workable, as is so often the case.

Fyodor, of course, claimed to be that new man, *Homo Sovietica*, Soviet Man. "Are you merely content with the workable?" he said. "Do you not aspire to anything better than that?"

"I aspire just up to the border of where the 'new man' is required. You should know the border, as you are in the business of removing imperfect persons from this world. But once the slaughter begins, where does it end? Or does it turn into terror, as the French Revolution did? Where can it end? Will Lenin or Trotski or Dzerzinski be the bolshevik Robespierre? And what about their valuable officer on the front, Commander Sabantsevski? Is it not likely that he will be the Red Napoleon who will seize their power and usurp the revolution? Consider this, Vasili Vasilievich. By killing Sabantsevski, I shall actually save the bolshevikii."

"Why would you do that?" he asked, looking confused.

"I have known Sabantsevski for a very long time," I told him. "His regime would be much worse than yours."

"Bolshevik leaders have also read their history," he said. "They have learned from the mistakes of the Jacobins. There will be no Thermidor military takeover by a new Napoleon. There simply will not. Politics—I mean the will of the Party, the proletariat—will remain supreme. No single officer can gain enough power to rule the Party."

"Really," I said with a smile. "You obviously have no idea how a real military unit operates. Should a commander wish to oppose the party, he merely needs to kill the commissar and march on the capital."

"That won't happen," he said. "All the commanders have been vetted for their political beliefs. None of the commanders is so fanatical."

"I suppose I should just abandon my mission. The Party will certainly take care of such an ambitious and resourceful officer as Sabantsevski, who will never bow to the will of the Party or anyone. So much for their vetting."

I thought he would try to refute my comments about Sabantsevski. Instead, he said the new order would fight as long as it took.

If the Capitalists destroyed the new order in Russia, the proletariat, now empowered, would simply emerge elsewhere. After all, the people have no estates to which to return, nothing of value awaiting them in the old order. They have every reason to continue the struggle until ultimate victory.

Fyodor paused and looked around the hovel. "I will never leave this room alive, but someone is already waiting to take my place at the Cheka. That is why you will never succeed. We are willing to die and take many of you with us for our cause while deep in your hearts, you know that if you fail here, there is still the rest of the Capitalist world for you to retreat to. Your life is too good to die for. You wish others to die to preserve your rank and privileges. Your mission is doomed, and so are you and your world."

I was intrigued by this young firebrand and wished to continue our conversation. But time had become the enemy. Perhaps that was his intent—to hold us here just long enough for an attack to be mounted.

I summoned Vlad to take charge of the prisoner, making him personally responsible for Fyodor's safety. Looking back at the young man, I told him not to get any ideas of leniency. If he did anything to endanger the mission, Vlad would deal with him severely. "Bind, blindfold and gag the prisoner. We are decamping in thirty minutes. I shall announce our destination later."

As Vlad removed the prisoner, I asked if Aishna had returned. Vlad said no.

"I understand now," the prisoner said over his shoulder. "You're willing to sacrifice your family for your mistress. You are a degenerate."

Vlad punched him in the stomach and slung him over his shoulder. As they left, the prisoner was yammering about the bolshevik cause to Vlad. A waste of breath, of course.

Yet I must admit Fyodor had stung me. Even though Aishna was not my mistress, nor likely to be, he was correct. I am a degenerate. I should at least attempt to rescue my family. May God forgive me for what I have done or not done.

I am filled with dread. The specter of Reds in my command revives my paranoia.

Addendum, Thursday, 24 April 1919 / 0400 hrs. [4:00 am]

We departed from the shtetl and rode the last part in the darkness to our new position. We have now made camp by a stream in the forest northeast of Kiev. Sleep has proven as elusive as ever. I remain troubled by Fyodor's comments about Sabantsevski. If the Party would, in fact, execute him if he becomes too powerful, is this mission merely a waste of time?

No. I know Sabantsevski. That is why I am uniquely suited to head this mission. I shall not be dissuaded from carrying it out. Sabantsevski will never submit to any political authority, of that I am sure. Nor will the bolshevikii eliminate someone as valuable as he. I am eager to discuss these matters further with young "Fyodor." He might have some potential for us.

I must try to sleep for a few hours. Then we must continue to move.

PART NINE

We are camped atop a hill on the steppe about seventy kilometers [43 miles] east of Kiev, waiting for reinforcements from the Kharkov garrison. We are expecting at least a hundred cavalry, a detachment from the force that defended the city against the Reds. That force has now evacuated westwards. With these reinforcements, we shall go to the nunnery for the latest information, then continue on to Sabantsevski himself. After his death, which will deprive the Reds of their most able commander in Ukraine and thus further weaken their cavalry, we will raid the Red lines of supply. All this in support of our goal of liberating Kiev in the not-too-distant future, God willing.

Meanwhile, Tariq is on our heels. That damnable Turk and his followers are harassing us. His forces have grown—I do not know by how many. However, his tactics show his band is not yet prepared to kill me but is merely toying with us to increase tension. Last night they woke us with rifle fire. Sometimes they fire random rounds into our camp during the day, then disappear. I grant that they are particularly good at disappearing. Several patrols have gone after them without success. But we shall not spend further time or resources on them until they perpetrate some actual harm.

Aishna has not returned. Does the presence of Tariq mean that he has killed her? Surely not. Were she dead, they would likely toss her severed head into our camp. My hope is that she never found him and that she will rejoin us soon.

Earlier I asked Vlad to bring the prisoner to me for further questioning. But as soon as his gag was removed, he started berating me for sleeping apart from my men and my horse. He claims Commander Sabantsevski stays close to his men at all times, although I doubt it. Sabantsevski is too much the "aristocrat" and snob for such fraternization. Simply wearing Muzhik attire, as Sabantsevski likely does, does not a proletarian make. And, as I have already noted, my troops are safer if I do not sleep near them. Tariq shall likely steal into my quarters one night and try to slit my throat as I sleep. If so, it shall not be as easy as he might think. He is only the latest enemy who has sworn to kill me. Others have tried such melodramatic exploits without success.

I now believe, after listening to Fyodor, that the bolshevikii shall kill Sabantsevski when the war is over, as he would no longer be of value to them. But I do not intend to wait for that—our combat is personal. It is maddening to live in a vacuum, knowing nothing of the progress of the war outside of my immediate area of operations. I long for news of the war and especially of my family. Not knowing about my darling wife and daughter is the worst torment of them all. There may be some truth in what Fyodor has told me about them.

I have made little progress questioning Fyodor. He just regurgitated his drivel from Thursday. I had Vlad re-gag him and take him away.

Saturday, 26 April 1919 / 1210 hrs. [12:10 pm]

I cannot decide whether to be discouraged or jubilant. About 1000 hrs. [10:00 am] a courier brought news that is both alarming for our mission and joyful for me personally. To my surprise, he was Baron Jacques Charbonnet—leader of La Mort and husband of Mayr Lucine. He came from near Tsaritsyn [Stalingrad/Volgograd], making his way through the lines with a small patrol to bring us a sealed dispatch from General Deniken. His primary news is this: we shall not be gaining any reinforcements for our mission. General Deniken has diverted the Kharkov troops, including the cavalry, to the Don River Basin to support his counter-offensive against the bolshevikii holding Moscow and Tsaritsyn.

"What about Kiev?" I asked.

"That will have to wait," Charbonnet replied. "But the general is confident you can complete your mission without reinforcements. He is relying on your resourcefulness. He says you know the area well. You know Sabantsevski better than anyone. That's why you're leading this mission."

That was gratifying, but what he said next is troubling. La Mort is also after Sabantsevski, and not only him but also his commissar Koba.

"We believe Koba is as dangerous as Sabantsevki, perhaps even more so."

"Shall we join forces, then?" I asked.

"That's not necessary. My men are shadowing you now, and among them are six highly trained assassins. They're your backup. They have orders to engage only if you fail."

Then Charbonnet handed me his courier bag, saying he would leave it with me a few hours while he briefs his men.

I am ambivalent about this development. It is always good to have a backup, but I was not expecting the task to be carried out by assassins rather than regular soldiers. At best, assassins could kill only the two leaders, after which their command would be taken over by the ranking officers. Better than nothing, but not by much.

A word about Charbonnet. This is my first look at him. I do not know quite what to make of him. For one thing, he is amazingly frank. He declared our personal connection right away, although it could be the cause for a duel. He knows that his wife and I had a youthful affair and that his stepson, Tomaz, is mine. He said this without apparent emotion. He also told me that he had met Constanza/Lucine at the

Deuxième Bureau [French Military Intelligence], to which she had come for help in establishing her new agency. Since he had recently ascended to a baronetcy with the death of his father, he was in a position to resign his post and join her cause. Together they formed La Mort and La Revanche (La ReM). So this is Mayr's husband.

He still wears a French officer's uniform, has red hair and beard, and is slightly shorter than I. He is a bit of a dandy with a fashionably pointed and waxed moustache. There is something of the rogue about him, a quality that is attractive to the ladies. But intense black eyes belie his seriousness. And he is obviously a valiant and experienced soldier to have passed through hostile territory to reach us.

I searched the dispatch pouch to see if Deniken had given me any magic seeds to allow me to quickly grow horses and troopers. Where can we find allies? I know there are Nationalist partisans operating in the area, but I have not seen them. I have no way of contacting them, if they even have a unified command structure. Even if they would be amenable to helping us. Deniken has now publicly declared that Ukrainian nationalists cannot also be Russian patriots. Even though the general is a brilliant and respected commander, I must disagree. We need all the allies we can find. I wish he would refrain from speaking on political matters. The French will not help us. A dispatch describes the French Navy's shameful withdrawal before the battle for Odessa. They seem to be allies of the bolshevikii, not ours. The Americans and British will not help us because their war is over. They did send small expeditionary forces to northern Russia, but most have now been evacuated after a chaotic and useless effort. To whom can we turn for help?

Is our mission even possible now? if so, what changes need to be made? If the mission is no longer feasible, what are my options? I have no desire to lose my troops in a suicide mission. If I abort, however, General Deniken would likely have us all shot. Either way, we are dead.

Yesterday I could have accepted death with equanimity, but today I have reason to live. Charbonnet also brought a letter from my own beloved Katarin. She writes that Princess Alexandra Mytrovna evacuated her, Marianne, Alexandra and all the ladies from Odessa with great generosity and hospitality. They are now safely in Constantinople, where they are staying in the Stanbul section of the city with other prominent White Russian exiles. Their quarters are guarded to protect them against Reds and other killers. My heart rejoices as I read these words. If only I could leave this wretched hell and rejoin my family there.

The general was kind enough to include the news that my son Vasili, who is still serving with light cavalry in the Don River basin, has again been mentioned in several dispatches for his courage and gallantry. I beam with pride at these words. While I should like to have him here, I also realize he is likely safer on the Don Front. My hopes for the continuation of the military tradition in the Markov family rest upon him. Perhaps, after the war, he could seek a position at the university in Kiev. He is highly intelligent and would make an excellent professor.

We may have to wait for the next generation after him for that to occur, however. The struggle against bolshevism will continue on and on, even when we win this military struggle. Bolshevik-inspired revolutions have burst forth and so far been suppressed. Where will the next major uprising occur, and will it be suppressed as well? In the wake of the Great War, there are countless places in turmoil, countless people with grievances, real or imagined. Red agents merely provide the match for the explosion.

Bolshevikii and their kindred Marxian spirits hold sway with the intelligentsia and liberals in many countries. They do not realize how vulnerable they are. Before the 1917 coup d'état, the Kadet [Constitutional Democratic] Party in the Duma [parliament] strongly supported the revolutionaries, even their terror tactics, with money, propaganda and safe houses. After the first revolution, they held five portfolios in the new socialist government. But after Lenin seized power, he killed the Kadets *en masse.* They were the first of the liberal supporters to suffer this fate but hardly the last. I have seen first-hand how the bolshevikii and cheka wiped out the intelligentsia after taking over Kiev.

After mulling over the implications of the general's dispatch, I assembled the men to inform them of our new situation. As is now required, I outlined our options and left the decision up to them. I would rather face Sabantsevski alone than with men who are not committed to the mission.

Corporal Stephanowski was the first to say that the lack of reinforcements made no difference to him. We had proven we could defeat superior enemy forces. I thanked him for his vote of confidence in the mission but also noted that Sabantsevski's forces will be of a higher caliber than those we have fought so far. The corporal acknowledged that but said it still made no difference because we have prevailed in the past. Also, we have a mission to complete. There was a general buzzing of conversation in the ranks for some minutes before a cheer went up, attesting to the continued commitment of the troops.

I thanked them, then said I would now return to my tent. Any man with doubts about the mission should then step forward. That person would be doing both himself and his comrades a favor by honestly stating his doubts now. He could leave with Baron Charbonnet within the hour. I would not think less of him, nor, in my view, would his comrades.

It is strange sometimes, this new republic democracy we have in our army, but it also makes sense from a practical standpoint. It is the result of a great tactical failure that must not be forgotten. In June 1917, the Russian army stood to capture Tsargrad [Constantinople]. This capture had been a dream of the Russians for five hundred years. Admiral Alexander Kolchak and General Deniken jointly formed a flotilla for this purpose. Yet when the fleet landed, the troops rebelled and refused to invade the city. Their reason? They had fought long enough. General Deniken learned a great deal from this episode. Now that we have these new procedures in place, I see the fervor in the eyes of my troops.

Grisha reported that no one stepped forward. The men were somewhat insulted that I should even suggest that anyone might abandon his comrades-in-arms. I am filled with pride that my men have such an intense sense of loyalty to each other and to me. My fears about traitors among them have also been allayed.

I summoned Fyodor for no other reason than to torment him with my new information that he had lied about my family being caught in Sevastopol. He scoffed at the news.

"No one is beyond the reach of the Cheka," he said belligerently. "It makes no difference whether the person is at large in Russia, Europe, Asia or the Americas. They cannot escape the revolutionary justice of the commission. If one agent fails to capture your family, another will take his place until they are captured. We can always kill our targets in an explosion if all else fails. How old is that letter, anyway? Your women are probably in prison now," he said. "White security in Constantinople is worthless anyway. When I am dead, my successor will bring you proof all right, proof of a more convincing nature," he added.

"What do you mean?" I asked, seizing his scrawny neck.

But the scoundrel changed the subject, going back to his rant about how my troops and I should defect, how much easier life would be, how my wife and daughter would then be safe. How my mission was doomed to failure without reinforcements.

I stopped him right there. How did he know Charbonnet's news about reinforcements? He had been isolated—bound, gagged and blindfolded—until he was brought to me. Perhaps this was a lucky guess—he was a clever lad, after all. Perhaps I was a bit soft in deciding not to execute him back at the shtetl but rather to keep him alive. I suppose I wished to show that I was a better person than he, the cold-blooded executioner. However, the bigger issue now is why I cared to demonstrate such superiority. Was it because I still regarded him as redeemable away from the bolshevikii? Because I thought that I could reason with the son of a brother officer from the finest regiment in all the Russias to return to the path of rightness? Is it because some of his mannerisms remind me of his father? Was I attempting to become his surrogate father? I honestly do not know. My decision was probably based on all of these factors. He is now gagged and blindfolded again.

Saturday, 26 April 1919/ 1600 hrs. [4:00 pm]

Aishna has returned safely, but not alone. With her was a wagonload of people, who clambered out and crowded around as she greeted me. They were a gaggle of wretches—refugees from an insane asylum destroyed in a recent battle. Before Aishna could deliver any news, one of them came up to me and threw his arms around me. I confess I shrank back at first. He was a man of middle age with the smallest head I have ever seen on an adult. I have never been hugged by a man before, save for my father and brother—much less a crazy one. Then I realized the gentleness of his gesture. He did not wish me harm— rather, it was simply his way of greeting a fellow human being, I suppose. In a moment, I hugged him back. It was an amazing moment of clarity for me. No man outside my family has ever greeted me so warmly, dare I say, shown me so much love. What does that say about our world, where "normal" men plot murder and mayhem against their fellow humans and create this hell in which we find ourselves?

Aishna gently pulled Iusuf away (that is the wretch's name) and told him quietly that he had hugged me long enough. It shocked me that such an unfortunate even had a name. Aishna's compassion moved me greatly.

Not everyone in the group was as gentle as Iusef. One fellow looked normal enough in his ragged Russian uniform but was extremely agitated, moving from person to person, asking unintelligible questions, moving on before getting an answer. His name was Natan. When he came to me, he tried to muster a salute. Where Iusef was calm and peaceful, Natan was unsettled and restless. There is no peace in his world. He constantly strives for an answer without even being able to articulate the question. It dismays me to realize how similar I am to Natan. Like myself, he has a high energy level, and he seems to be driven by a force beyond himself, perhaps ambition. It is disturbing that I, too, am often agitated, unable to find peace or satisfaction. Yet he cannot regulate or even focus, whereas I am focused on my mission. But what shall I be like after this mission, after this war?

Leaving Vlad in temporary charge of Aishna's unfortunates and Shav in charge of the wagon and horses, I drew her into my tent. In private, she greeted me again with a very unsettling kiss. I asked for her news. She has been to the nunnery in Kiev. My aunt is awaiting my arrival with great anticipation. I was glad of this, yet also alarmed that she already knew we were coming. Spies must be everywhere. Aishna also reports that she did not locate the damnable Turk Tariq, but she did spot another group shadowing us—and it does not appear to have been Charbonnet's La Mort. Three groups are on our heels, it seems.

I told her we will not be getting reinforcements after all and asked if she had contacts with the Nationalist partisans.

"No one reliable," she said. "Partisans are not well disposed towards the Whites."

"But they hate the bolshevikii," I countered.

"Maybe there is a chance," she said doubtfully. "And we really need them now, do we not? I will go tomorrow to find someone we can trust."

"What about your people?" I asked. "The poor wretches you brought? What are we to do with them?"

I had seen enough to be certain that we could not take care of them. Some were agitated and wild-eyed, others were totally withdrawn, as though they were actually living in another world, with only their body in this one. Two of them—brothers, I believe—have that Mongolian appearance indicating mental defectiveness. None of them appeared to be able to take care of themselves.

"I am taking them to the nunnery. The Holy Sisters will take care of them until they can be moved to a new asylum," Aishna said. "And they have a caretaker from the old asylum coming soon."

I told Aishna about our prisoner, "Fyodor," confessing that I had been unable to extract any useful information from him.

"Send this little toy soldier to my tent, Lieutenant Colonel. I will break him and learn everything he knows. It will be my pleasure. Have Grisha, Vlad and Shav serve as witnesses. Grisha must keep a written record. You should not be there," she said, then gave a slow, knowing wink.

"You have my permission," I said, understanding that it was better if I did not know her methods.

Aishna took my shoulders and gave me another long, passionate kiss. It was all I could do to push her gently away. A day ago, I would not have pushed her away. But that was when I thought I might be a widower. Now that I know I am not, everything is different. I have never been unfaithful to Katarin, aside from a few prostitutes in the bordellos of Kiev, who do not count. (Katarin knows about these peccadillos and accepts them, as she knows they mean nothing to me.) Nor have I ever taken a mistress. Of course, Katarin is just as faithful. But this situation is different. I pray that when Aishna returns, I shall have the strength of character to resist her advances. I have been celibate so long on this mission that the mere thought of her is deeply arousing. I must find a way to resist yet not drive her away. She has become far too valuable to me and to the mission. It would be a calamity to lose her. But if I do not resist, I would certainly be guilty of adultery, perhaps more.

Saturday, 26 April 1919/ 1815 hrs. [6:15 pm]

In only two hours, Aishna broke little Fyodor and extracted much useful information, most notably Katarin's address in Constantinople and more precise information on Sabantsevski's whereabouts.

"How did you get him to talk?" I asked.

"My curved knife can be most persuasive," she said. "Grisha can give you the transcript of our interview."

I thanked her, hoping that I had hidden my embarrassment about failing to break the pompous little prisoner myself. I should have used similar physical inducements to talk the first day he arrived.

Aishna then departed on her search for the Nationalists and said she would be back in the morning. I expressed my hope that she would return in time for Sunday service at 0730 hrs. [7:30 am] She nodded, anarchist though she may be.

Sunday, 27 April 1919 / 0800 hrs. [8:00 am]

Shortly after Aishna's departure yesterday, a man entered my tent and, before being given permission, took a seat on a stool. There he sat, silent and erect. I was intrigued rather than annoyed, as I would expect. He was obviously one of the asylum inmates, but his clothing differed from the others. He wore a tatty tan military uniform that was completely unfamiliar to me. But it was his headgear that caught my attention—a broad-brimmed khaki hat, with one side pinned upright by a medallion of some kind and a feather, once white, stuck in its wide band. The hat was faded and worn, with obvious sweat stains. Despite his ragged appearance and unkempt brown beard, he had a soldier's bearing. I remembered seeing him earlier that day and thinking he might have shell shock. But he was sullen and withdrawn, not agitated like most of the shell shocked. As he sat there, seemingly lost in thought, I returned to my paperwork. He appeared harmless enough, and I wondered what strange circumstances had brought him to this point.

It may have been ten or fifteen minutes before he suddenly stood up and saluted, stamping a boot on the floor. I started at the sudden noise. He said something I did not understand and held his hand in rigid salute. I stood, returned the salute and told him to stand easy. He did not move. I tried other languages besides Russian, attempting French, my limited German, finally English. I asked his name and rank. He again spoke, but I could hardly understand him. It was some odd dialect of English.

"Where are you from?" I asked.

"Australia," he said.

I knew of Australia's existence as a far-off land, somewhere in the Southern Hemisphere, down with the sea monsters that still decorated some maps. I had read about the Australians' courageous exploits, along with the New Zealanders, at Gallipoli, but I had assumed they spoke the King's English, not this difficult dialect.

"Tell me your name and rank, very slowly," I said.

"Jack Christie Irvin. First lieutenant," he said, pronouncing his rank "lef-tenant."

"Unit?"

"Commander, Second Troop, B Squadron, Royal Australian Third Light Horse Brigade."

I told him to sit and tell me how he came to be here. I was beginning to understand his accent, although he would use a number of colloquial words I had never heard before.

Irvin had been part of the Gallipoli Cape Helles beach landings back in 1915 that were designed to seize the Dardanelles from the Turk and then steam on to Constantinople, compel the Ottomans to surrender and open up a supply line to the Eastern Front. It had all been planned by "Winston Bloody Churchill," as this Australian so memorably called him. He spoke with defiant informality.

From the reports that I have seen, this is what I know about the Gallipoli campaign, which began in February 1915. First Lord of the

Admiralty Winston Churchill ordered a British dreadnaught leading a flotilla to break the massive chain barrier that blocks passage in the Dardanelles and sail on to Constantinople. When this failed, Australian and New Zealand (ANZAC) forces were sent to other beaches on the Aegean side of the peninsula. Everyone expected the ANZAC troops to win easily, but the Ottomans were more formidable than expected. The ANZAC troops fought valiantly, although almost nothing about the plan went right. The campaign degenerated into trench warfare and a stalemate. The Turks repelled the attack, and their senior officers (mostly Germans) were brilliant tacticians. The ranking Ottoman commander, Mustafa Kemal, now leads the Turkish forces in their war against Greece.

Lieutenant Irvin and most of his men were captured by the Turks. His troops had landed on Y beach—the northernmost beach in the Aegean—to fight the battle in the Suir Bair Mountains. Their objective had been to finally capture Hill 971, the highest point in the range at 971 feet. However, on the night of 7 August, which was moonless, he and his men became lost in one of the many ravines in this area and cut off from their comrades. The next day, they were captured by the Turks, who sent them to a barbed wire encampment well behind the lines. It was hot and dry there, with very little water.

After a few days, the prisoners were divided into three groups—senior officers, junior officers and enlisted men. The non-commissioned officers were sent away with the enlisted, and the few senior officers were sent away next. Finally, the dozen or so junior officers were marched to a train, on which they rode for several days with minimal rations until they arrived in eastern Anatolia and a fortress at Sinop on a peninsula jutting into the Black Sea. There they were kept in a state of limbo—not actually prisoners in cells, but nevertheless confined to the fortress. They had nothing to do and had no news of the war or the outside world except what new prisoners brought in. It became difficult to separate fact from propaganda. The Turk captors did not feed the prisoners very much, nor did they seem to have much food themselves. The prisoners were hot in the summer and cold in the winter.

In the fall of 1918, there was a prisoner exchange. The lieutenant should have been sent to Mesopotamia with the other British Empire troops, but his name had been misspelled on the prison manifest as Jackvin. The prison was dealing with three vastly different alphabets—Turkish, Cyrillic and Western. Given that the average Turk troop was only semi-literate and officers seldom knew more than their own alphabet, such mistakes were common. Irvin tried to get his name corrected at the prison, but no one spoke English well enough to understand. Nor did they seem to care.

In the end, "Jackvin" was repatriated with the Russian prisoners. When the Russian ship arrived in Sevastopol, he was sent to processing, where he hoped to speak with someone who could recognize his identity as an Australian. After trying to communicate with several officials without success, Irvin finally reached Russian Major Kamaranski. Kamaranski understood him all right but demanded a bribe to correct the error. Irvin had no money at this point; as a consequence, Kamaranski had no interest in his case. When the lieutenant persisted in arguing his case, Kamaranski declared him "insane." The next day, he was put on a truck and taken to the asylum, where he had stayed until recently.

"If a person wasn't a bit off when he entered the asylum, he soon would be," Irvin said.

Irvin tried to maintain his standards in the asylum, and his sanity. But both became increasingly difficult as he realized what he needed to do to survive. He was not proud of what he did, but he survived. He bullied the weaker inmates and also stole their rations. That was all he was willing to confess, and I did not press the point. When the asylum was attacked and blown apart, he led the inmates into a nearby forest, where Aishna discovered them. He was uncomfortable being back in the world because he felt so "damned guilty" about the fate of his men. If he had not misread the map, he and his men would not have been lost. They probably would not have been captured. In his mind, he had let them down.

I told him he should not feel that way. He had carried out his orders to the best of his ability. His senior officers had not properly prepared the troops for the battles. I did not tell him of two things I had seen in a captured report for fear of causing him to permanently lose his grasp on sanity. First, most of the enlisted troops from Gallipoli were set to work building the railroad through the Tarsus Mountains in Southern Anatolia. Some 75 percent of those troops perished from the beastly treatment they received at the hands of the Turk. Second, the Turks at Gallipoli were ready to withdraw the day the ANZAC forces surrendered, 9 January 1916. One more day of resistance and the whole course of the war would have changed. Ah, the what-ifs of history.

One may reasonably ask why I believe this man. In part, because of details in his account that I know to be correct. Also, because of his soldier's bearing, which cannot be faked. He was no more insane than any other man consumed by guilt. Given what he had endured for nearly four years, if he were, as he put it, a bit off, it was certainly understandable. It would have killed a lesser man.

"How can I be of service to you?" I asked. He said he wished to get cleaned up and would like to borrow a uniform to replace his.

"Then," he said, "I will be responsible for the other inmates."

"After our mission, I shall do everything in my power to repatriate you back to Australia," I said.

He smiled for the first time. He also offered his services. As a light horseman, he knew how to ride, but he was used to fighting on foot. I told him I would consider his offer very carefully. I need an experienced second-in-command, and I believe Irvin would be suitable.

I called for Vlad to come and escort Irvin to his new tent. As they were leaving, Iusuf came in and hugged everyone until Irvin took him by the shoulder and led him away, saying they would presently go on a hike into the countryside.

I am disgusted at Irvin's account of Col. Kamaranski. Corruption of that kind was endemic in the Old Regime, but when we win this war, there can be no place for such rot. I am hopeful that our republic will breathe new life into Mother Russia. I shall take care of Col. Kamaranski at the earliest opportunity.

Grisha arrived to read his notes on Aishna's interrogation of Fyodor. What follows is his account. It is gruesome and not for the squeamish, but it must be known and remembered for this dark time to be understood. Shav brought Fyodor over his shoulder, naked and gagged, to Aishna's tent and dropped him hard on the ground. Shav pounded railroad spikes into the hard ground. She bound his hands and feet to the spikes so that he was in a spread-eagle position.

She laughed and said, "What cute little genitals. You will never miss them. Now, I will conduct this interrogation according to the ageless laws of my people. Since there is no way for you to return to the cheka, you are to begin the process of dying here. If you truthfully tell me everything I wish to know, your death will be fast and relatively unpainful. If you resist, your pain increases appropriately. I am Aishna, the Persian Assassin, an officer in the Legion of the Black Widow's Revenge on the Turk, which also used these laws. By 1917, I had earned the title "Mistress of Interrogation" by conducting one hundred interrogations, not one of which the Turk survived. In the process, I learned very well how to determine if someone was lying. Sergeant, please remove his gag.

"Are you ready now to answer my questions truthfully?"

"The only truth I know is that you are an ugly Muzhik whore," Fyodor foolishly replied.

Aishna laughed. "Such a brave little tin soldier you are. Very well. I will also punish you for being a coward. According to our laws, the coward is the most despicable person ever and is subject to our harshest penalties."

"Why do you call me a coward? I most am certainly not."

"Sergeant Kapolski reported that when you were captured, you were way behind your troops. A good commissar would have been in the first armored car or leading the cavalry. That way, he would have died an honorable death. But no, in my experience, chekist dogs are very good at posturing and imposing pain but easily collapse when they are receiving it. Now, as even you must know, cowards in any military formation must be executed before their disease spreads. That does not apply here, but I despise cowards, especially those who claim to be men. Since I already hold you in contempt for being a chekist, I am not interested in excuses for your cowardice. Are you ready to answer my questions?"

"Not a word, bitch."

What intrigued Grisha, he told me, was how she began using her curved knife like a surgeon with a scalpel. She did not slash wildly; rather she cut him just enough to draw vertical lines of blood from his breastbone down to the bottom of his stomach. Slowly she rubbed salt into the wounds, then sat cross-legged on the ground, speaking with Grisha and Vlad while licking the blood off her knife and smiling. After about ten minutes, she again asked Fyodor if he was ready. He shook his head. She then formed very neat horizontal lines of blood across the first cuts, forming numerous neat blood squares of 10 centimeters [4 in.] each. Again, she rubbed salt into the cuts, sat and waited about ten minutes, softly singing a song until she asked again if he were ready to talk. Although his eyes filled with tears, he remained silent.

"Very well, I suppose this is a pathetic attempt to prove your masculinity. But for you, there is no going back. Have no doubt of two things: you will slowly lose your physical manhood, and, before you die, you will tell me everything I demand."

"But this is against the Rules of War."

"A chekist demands Rules of War?" she said bitterly. "We obey no such rules. Now, I give you time to ponder how to answer my questions."

When he did not reply, she removed her boots and pantaloons, then stood over him so he could clearly see her black widow tattoo. Then, she slowly lowered herself until she was sitting on his face. She squeezed his nose shut, whispering something, and when she finally rose some three minutes later, he was choking, gasping for air and shaking with fear.

"Law declares that by kissing my spider you have so humiliated yourself that you must forever submit to my superior will." She raised her curved knife. "Last chance, maggot."

"You're bluffing."

Aishna shook her head and placed her knife against his genitals.

"All right. Stop. What do you want to know? I'll tell you anything. Just don't cut me anymore."

Aishna interrogated the sniveling Fyodor for the next forty minutes or so, pausing at points to ask Grisha and Shav if they thought he was telling the truth. When she finished, she asked the other two if they had any questions. Grisha found it unusual that she appeared very comfortable in their presence dressed only in her blouse, but it did not surprise me. What did shock me, however, was what she did next. She thanked Fyodor for his information, then slowly cut off his genitals, saying she had not a drop of mercy for chekists. His screams filled the room. The smell of blood permeated everything. His genitals now hung by a single bit of skin, which she called the "Abyssinian Flap."

"Your odds of surviving gelding are usually fairly good. But this flap will prevent healing. You will die slowly, and painfully."

Aishna then dressed and asked Grisha and Shav to help her get the screaming Fyodor outside.

As commander, I had a dilemma. Does Aishna deserve a medal

for honorable service, or should she be condemned for war crimes? Following the interrogation, Aishna had Fyodor strung up from a tree without breaking his neck so that he would continue to struggle. To see him dangling from the tree was a full magnitude of horror greater than hearing Grisha's description—my groin ached, shivers ran down my spine and my mouth went dry at the sight of his blood rows and his flap.

Troopers assembled to jeer and throw rocks at the dangling prisoner. As he slowly strangled, his screams became mere moans until, at last, he died. Shav hung a placard around his neck, "Chekist Bastard," and no one moved to cut him down, much less bury him. Then the troopers cheered Aishna and broke out in song—"Welcome to our Squadron," which is sung only when a new trooper is recognized as a true warrior. Aishna understood the honor and blew kisses to the men.

The troopers had solved my dilemma. What a quaint notion of the ethics of war I had retained from a time long gone! Seeing her work first-hand confirmed beyond doubt that she is a true Legionnaire. I realized I cared not a whit for Fyodor. There would be no punishment for the amazing, unpredictable Madame Aishna. She had extracted valuable information from the feckless Fyodor, and it has been carefully preserved by Grisha. He has left the document with me.

Monday, 28 April 1919 / 0900 hrs. [9:00 am]

Aishna returned to the encampment around 0630 hrs. [6:30 am] after a night in pursuit of Petluria's Ukrainian Nationalist Army. She brought a Captain Olganovski to speak with me. His Nationalist uniform consisted of the tan tunic, green trousers and black boots of the regular Russian army but with insignia of blue and gold, the Ukrainian national colors.

Piotr, as she called him, is the local area cavalry commander. He is formal and reserved in manner, yet our conversation was very revealing. I told him that General Deniken would not be sending re-inforcements, and he replied, "That seems typical."

He asked the nature of our mission. When I told him, he seemed to know all about Sabantsevski and even my own history with him.

"Why are you merely a Lieutenant Colonel after all your years of service?" he asked.

"The White forces are top-heavy with officers, and there are many more experienced officers ahead of me, so I accepted the lesser rank when I joined the Whites."

"That's the problem with the Whites," he said. "The Reds have the troops, the Whites have the leadership. Why should I help you? Deniken is on record stating that the Whites stand for a unitary Russia, just as the Old Regime did. Where does that leave Ukraine?"

"You are too weak to drive the Reds out by yourselves," I said frankly. "And you Nationalists do not have wide sympathy right now. You cooperated with the Germans during the Occupation."

"Wait, Colonel, Ukraine was never better off than during the Occupation."

"Well, if you had money. If not, it was a time of terror and starvation. Are you forgetting that the Germans confiscated most of the harvest from your Muzhiks?"

Aishna told him the story of the shtetl where we had stayed—how the Germans had starved and slaughtered the Zhidys.

"Why do you care about the fate of a bunch of stinking Zhidys?" he said, igniting a quick flash of anger in Aishna's eyes. "A Zhidy's life in Ukraine has never been easy," he went on, oblivious to her reaction. "Nor anywhere else, for that matter. Deniken has been encouraging pogroms as part of his strategy to reclaim Ukraine."

"General Deniken will succeed in driving the Reds out of Ukraine," I said. "But not because of pogroms. He shall succeed because the Reds are weak around Kiev. They are too far away from their central command in Moscow."

"That is why they sent Sabantsevski in that armored train," he said.

It *was* Sabantsevksi in the train.

"If anyone can win Ukraine for the Reds, it is Sabantsevski," I admitted. "If we fail in our mission, the Whites are doomed." I was overstating the case for effect.

"That might be for the best," the captain said.

I was appalled, and I argued vigorously. If the Nationalists thought they would receive a better proposition from the Reds than the Whites, they were tragically mistaken. The Reds would feel no need to cater to the wishes of the people in whose name they ruled. Their attitude toward the people was already apparent in the unitary dictatorship they had established in Moscow the previous March. The Whites, on the other hand, would not necessarily be willing to grant Ukraine outright independence, but they would certainly grant autonomy within the larger Russian context. Ukrainian prospects would be strong within the Russian republic. Once Deniken was triumphant, he would not forget those who had helped his cause. On the other hand, if the Nationalists refused to help the Whites defeat the Reds, he would probably ignore Ukraine. In fact, he might even hunt them down as enemies of the state, along with the Reds and the Green anarchist forces.

Captain Olganovski seemed unmoved, saying only that he will discuss my request with his colleagues. If they agree to join us, he will send word through Aishna, whom they trust. The implication that they do not trust me was not lost on me, but I said nothing.

"We need a timely response from you," I said. "We plan to move against Sabantsevski at the earliest possible date."

Olganovski smiled for the first time. "You'll have our answer within twenty-four hours," he said.

Aishna kissed my cheek, then rode away with the Nationalist officer. As I turned back to my tent, I saw Lieutenant Irvin in his Guard uniform, his beard trimmed, his boots cleaned of mud and a fresh feather in his peculiar hat. He was drilling the inmates gently but firmly and achieving some results. It was poignant to see poor Iusuf doing his best to understand and keep pace. Irvin stopped his charges and saluted me smartly, and I happily reciprocated. I am well pleased with his progress. I may, in time, award iberatn's insignia. I need a second-in-command with combat experience, and he would seem to fill the bill.

Addendum

I look forward to my return to the nunnery. A bit of history on this special place: in 1349, Abbess Olga founded a nunnery in a remote area for noble ladies, mostly from Kiev. Originally all the Holy Ladies were cloistered. Once they took their vows (not always voluntarily), their heads were shaved and they took the veil. They remained in the nunnery for life, dead to the world.

Around 1870, however, a new abbess, Ivana, rejected cloistering as medieval and decided that her nuns could decide at any point not to be cloistered, although the nunnery remains officially cloistered for complex bureaucratic reasons. Abbess Ivana further decided that her nuns could receive visitors on spiritual quests.

My aunt Katiya became abbess in 1910. Her official title is Pure and Virtuous and Most Holy Abbess Katiya Mother Superior of the Holy Ladies of Sainte Olga's Nunnery Retreat. Protocol required that I call her the Abbess. However, in my journal, I shall also refer to her as my aunt. Being a woman of enormous intellectual and spiritual curiosity, she arrived at the Roman [Catholic] idea of having her nuns "go out in the world to serve and spread the Gospel," serving the community during the day, returning at night. To my knowledge, hers is the only cloistered nunnery in Russian Orthodoxy where nuns enjoy such freedom of movement. As abbess, Aunt Katiya and the gatekeeper have even more freedom so that they can deal with visitors from the outside world.

Our family has always visited her regularly, especially on Holy Days. From the time I was a small boy, I have been impressed by her appearance: a small authoritative figure, yet with the humility essential to a nun, wearing her black habit with the tall, rounded klobuk and coif that hide all but her sharp, intelligent face. A rich gold scapular indicates her high rank. Over the years, I have developed as close a relationship with Aunt Katiya as circumstances allow.

A curious feature of the nunnery outside Kiev is that ten of the forty-five nuns have chosen to remain cloistered. I am particularly interested in one of them—Aunt Katiya alone knows which one—but in the past, my questions about these special ones have gone unanswered. Not this time, I hope.

Tomorrow, we break camp, and late in the morning will head for the nunnery. Aishna will rendezvous with us there.

PART TEN

Tuesday, 29 April 1919 / 2200 hrs. [10:00 pm]

After Kapolski's scouts left, our column departed for Sainte Olga's Nunnery at 1145 hrs. [11:45 am] with Lieutenant Irvin and the inmates bringing up the rear. The day had dawned as one of the most beautiful we had seen in some time. As we came over a hill, I saw the familiar domes of the convent with its robin's-egg blue cupolas on the bluffs over the Dnieper River.

The nunnery is a walled complex built like a fortress. Its substantial front door is guarded by Mother Alexa, who has been the gatekeeper for as long as I can remember. I pulled the bell cord several times but received no response. I pushed the door, which to my surprise, swung open. The courtyard was empty, which again was surprising because since about 1500 A.D., it has been open to the faithful each morning for prayers, reflections and gifts, and there are always people here. The courtyard is also the nunnery's cemetery, with the graves of its nuns and martyrs. A grand reliquary in the center holds the skull of Ste. Olga herself. Today there was a freshly dug grave marked with a simple wooden Orthodox cross inscribed with the name "M. Marina." Beyond the courtyard lay henhouses, a barn and the fields where the Holy Ladies raised their crops. No one was about.

With growing dread, I went to look for my aunt—no answer at her office or her room. Nor at the room shared with Mother Xenia, her second-in-command and likely successor, and Mother Alexa, the gatekeeper. Glasses of half drunk tea suggested they had been there recently.

I returned to the front door and motioned for my men to enter the courtyard, asking Grisha to come with me. We made our way to the chapel. I knew my way around the complex, having been given access to all parts since I was a boy, except for the dormitory and, of course, the cloistered section. But today, the place seemed eerily quiet. No one was in the chapel. I took a moment to kneel before the altar, something I have not done since this mission began, even though I have been in several churches. I was hoping to receive some divine inspiration and guidance, but I could not focus my mind. I was growing conscious of a faint sickly-sweet burning odor quite different from incense.

I rose and turned to see Mother Xenia, motionless in her black habit, a large silver cross hanging from her neck catching the reflection of the chapel's candles.

"Mother Xenia, where is my aunt?" I asked.

"She is gone, Misha."

"When will she return? It is important that I speak with her."

"Come with me, both of you," she said, leading us back to the abbess's office, seating us at the table where my aunt confers with official visitors.

"I must tell you a terrible story," she said with the calm, rational voice I had known for many years.

She then recounted how, two days before, she and Aunt Katiya had been sitting at this table, busy with ordinary convent business, when Mother Alexa entered to announce the arrival of soldiers. Mother Alexa could not identify them. They spoke Russian, but their uniforms were like nothing she had seen before—light brown, of cheap fabric. They were rude, and soon their commander barged into the room, demanding to see the abbess.

"Where is Colonel Mikhail Antonovich Markov?" he demanded. He knew that Abbess Katiya is my aunt.

She replied that my whereabouts were none of his business. He approached her, withdrew his pistol, and put it to her head.

"I am not intimidated," my aunt said quietly. "Pull the trigger if you must. I would rejoice in making my journey Home after more than fifty years of devoted service to the One I love."

The next moment seemed like an eternity, Mother Xenia said. Then Sabantsevski withdrew the pistol, saying an old lady like her was not worth a bullet. He asked her where I was a few more times—he seemed to think I was hiding somewhere in the convent—but Aunt Katiya was steadfast. He changed tack.

"Where is Galina, then? I must see Galina."

"I know no one named Galina," the abbess said.

He struck the abbess across the face and called her a disrespectful name.

"Who is 'Galina,' Mother Xenia?" I asked although I was reluctant to interrupt her story.

About eight years before, she told me, a young woman had come to the gate, disheveled and distraught. She appeared worldly in her makeup and furs, yet she said she wanted to join the order. In an interview with the Abbess and Mother Xenia, she identified herself as Galina, "a fallen woman and a sinner." She was not "in distress," which I infer means "not pregnant," but, as it emerged, she had fallen so far as to work as a prostitute. The nunnery was not for rescuing sinners, the abbess told Galina, nor was it a hiding place; it was a vocation. After several hours of investigation, however, Abbess Katiya saw fit to receive Galina as a novice.

"I did not approve of this decision," Xenia said. "The order has always been a distinguished order of noble ladies. Since when have we admitted prostitutes? But Abbess Katiya merely smiled at me and asked if I remembered the Magdalene. If such a woman was good enough for the Christ, surely Galina was good enough for the ladies of the community."

Mother Xenia allowed herself a small smile at the memory of her arrogance and how wrong she had been about Galina.

"Galina became known as Mother Marina, loved by everyone for her humility, generosity and hard work. She spent most of her time out in the fields, tending our crops."

Mother Xenia continued her story. Clearly, Sabantsevski meant Galina harm, and he declared he would now find her. The Abbess rose, telling him to leave God's house, but he pushed her back down. He summoned two of his men to guard the room—Mother Xenia described them as two giants with bayonets—and went in search of his prey.

My aunt behaved exactly as I would expect. She rose again to follow Sabantsevski, and one of the men prodded her chest with his bayonet. Mother Xenia was terrified that he would stab her superior.

"Never threaten a nun with death," Katiya told him. "That would be a welcome release. I am leaving this room. Mother Xenia is coming with me."

Mother Xenia hung her head when she said, "I was so frightened. I do not have Katiya's strength. I just sat there. The other man put his bayonet next to my nose and asked me how I would feel about having my eye gouged out. He could tell I was terrified. I think he would have done it if his comrade had not called him. He made me go with him. The soldiers had found all the ladies. Everyone was gathering in the chapel."

"Who were those two soldiers? Did you hear their names?" I asked, already planning special punishment for those monsters.

"No," she said, although I was not sure she was telling the truth.

When I confront Sabantsevski and his band, I shall treat all his men as if they are the ones who perpetrated this outrage against these two Holy Ladies. Yet Mother Xenia had far worse outrages to recount. I am enraged that these Red vermin should be so disrespectful to the Ladies of God. Do they hold nothing sacred?

I must take a respite from recording these events now to contain my anger.

It is now some thirty minutes later. To relieve my soul, I left my tent and walked around the perimeter of our encampment, speaking with my pickets and breathing deeply. I now know that to find relief in sleep, I must relate the following horrors.

With tears rolling down her lined face, Mother Xenia told us how Sabantsevski had assembled all the ladies in the chapel, including the cloistered. His men were there as well. Mother Marina was lying on the altar. She was completely disrobed, her wrists and ankles bound. Sabantsevski stood before her with a burning chapel torch, which he passed over her body again and again, coming closer each time to burning her.

At this point in her story, Xenia totally lost her composure and broke down sobbing. I instinctively reached across the table to comfort her without thinking that it was unthinkable to touch a nun.

A moment later, Xenia pulled away, seemingly as embarrassed as I. She began again in a flat monotone. As the commander's flame grew ever closer to Marina's body, he told the ladies that she could be spared terrible agony if the Abbess would simply reveal my whereabouts. My aunt Katiya calmly replied that she could not reveal that which she did not know. Mother Xenia said she began to wonder if the abbess knew more than she was saying, especially when the abbess went up to Marina and begged her forgiveness. Mother Marina told her there was nothing to forgive. Did this have to do with a long-running dispute between them?

I did not ask Xenia to explain. I needed to hear what happened.

Sabantsevski moved the flame ever closer to Marina's body as he pressed my aunt for information, and she continued to refuse to tell him anything. He grazed her breast with the flame.

Xenia again broke into sobs.

Grisha broke in, saying softly, "We saw the new grave in the cemetery for Mother Marina."

I took Xenia's hand now, without embarrassment.

In a few minutes, Xenia spoke again. "Mother Marina may not have lived an exemplary life before joining the order, but she died with more courage than anyone we had ever seen. Although clearly in agony, she would not even give Sabantsevski the satisfaction of screaming. At some point, she simply passed onto another plane, then left this world. May God grant me the courage to meet my end with even a portion of the courage Mother Marina displayed."

Furious at being thwarted, Sabantsevski demanded that all the nuns line up before the altar. It took bayonets to force some of the cloistered ones to obey. Sabantsevski went down the line, selected young and middle-aged nuns, twenty-five in all, whom the troops took away without explanation. He then chose ten older nuns, including the Abbess, saying they would be held as hostages. Mother Xenia had not been selected for either group, and Sabantsevski brought out a Red flag and presented it to her.

"When Mikhail comes to this convent, you must raise this special flag. If you do not, the hostages shall die. I wonder if they will meet their deaths with the stoicism of Galina here? I can assure you, those deaths shall be neither pleasant nor swift."

"Will you raise the flag now that I am here?" I asked.

Xenia produced a packet from a nearby cabinet. "This is the flag. I shall never raise it here. Before she was taken away, the Abbess told me there would be no cooperation with the Reds. She knew the fate of other priests and nuns in Petrograd and Moscow who had fallen under Bolshevik rule—torture and death. She knew this from eyewitness reports by the few who escaped to freedom."

"Is Evgania here?" I asked. My childhood sweetheart had been among the cloistered nuns.

"Forget her, Misha. 'Evgania' no longer exists. Besides, she went willingly with the twenty-five younger nuns."

Sabantsevski departed with thirty-five of the nuns—twenty-five "volunteers" and the ten hostages. The remaining nuns—only ten—huddled in the chapel to decide what to do. Some wanted to assist the bolshevikii who, after all, were the friends of the poor, the oppressed and the downtrodden. Yes, their tactics were brutal, but that was necessary at this point. After the Whites and other counter-revolutionaries were defeated, such cruelty would cease. Then God's work of spreading peace and justice to the world could begin in earnest. In their view, bolshevikii were not the enemy of the church. The real enemies of the church were the Whites, who resisted the bolshevik program of the kingdom of God on earth. The Whites sought to take away the people's newly won freedoms. Tales of repression of the Church in free Russia were simply White propaganda. When any Whites or others arrived, the Ladies would proudly raise the Red flag so that this present war could be brought to a rapid and just conclusion.

Mother Xenia had argued against these insidious bolshevik ideas. She admitted that the Ancien Régime, with its autocratic repression and occasional brutality, was hard to defend. Yet she also insisted that, as an integral part of that order, the Church had made the lives of the people better. Unlike the bolshevikii, the Church worked within the law and wished harm to no one. Besides, the Church is essential, for all are sinners in the eyes of God, especially women. Do you dare to pretend that you know God's will better than God Himself? Despite what had occurred, we are still members of the community and bound by its laws and our vows. God shall not forgive the breaking of holy and sacred vows. The Abbess had given orders that Xenia would never dream of disobeying, and she understands the fundamental evilness of the bolshevikii. Such terror tactics would not simply cease on some fine day in the future. A look at the French Revolution and its Reign of Terror illustrates that. Terror only begets more of the same until the revolution devours its own, as it did with Robespierre and his ilk.

I felt empty inside at the horrific death of Mother Marina. Perhaps my aunt was dead as well. I told Mother Xenia that my column would remain at the nunnery for a time to protect the Ladies, but she refused, declaring that the community was too badly divided. When I proposed that we go in search of the ten hostages, however, she readily agreed and urged me to leave as soon as possible.

But first, I had to settle the matter of the unfortunates from the asylum in our charge, whom we obviously could not take with us. Mother Xenia graciously said it would be the Holy Ladies' honor to care for them.

Back in the courtyard, we were greeted with a scene of confusion. Some of the nuns were demanding the immediate expulsion of my troops. Others argued strenuously that my troops should surrender to the Reds. I was approached by a nun who identified herself as Mother Anna. She seemed to be in her early thirties, and her face was comely. But she was haughty, and I quickly learned that she had an aristocratic sense of entitlement. She blocked my way and spoke with a raised voice.

"The community has suffered the loss of a pious and devoted sister because of you. You should be feeling shame for that."

"Why?" I asked.

She looked at me the way she might at a wayward child.

"Is it not obvious? Had you never embarked on your mission, Mother Marina would still be alive today. You were her murderer as surely as if you had executed her yourself. The Bolsheviks had left us in peace until that soldier came looking for you. The Ladies would have continued living in peace and harmony here indefinitely."

The naivete of her words shocked me. I replied, "The nunnery is balanced on the edge of a razor. Sabantsevski's feud with Mother Marina made her death inevitable. It had nothing to do with me or the war. The bolshevikii are atheists. It is only a matter of time before they move to close the nunnery. God is their mortal enemy. They promise a paradise on earth, not Heaven, so they have no use for churches, or nuns, or priests, or monks or any person of faith.

Mother Anna had listened, but her expression had not changed.

"This country could not possibly exist without religion and the Church. Do they mean to kill all true believers, as the ancient Romans tried to do? There are too many believers. If they kill us all, there will be no one left in the country except some intellectuals in the cities, who would soon starve to death." She paused.

"Has not the great poet Aleksandr Blok shown us that the true leader of the Bolsheviks was Christ Himself? The Bolsheviks are the friend of the downtrodden and the common man."

I tried to tell her of atrocities perpetrated by the Bolsheviks against priests.

She shook her head, her eyes suddenly soft and dreamy.

"Oh, no, Commander Sabantsevski would not, indeed *could* not do such horrid things. They must have been done by those horrible bands of muzhiks who roam the countryside."

Did you not see what Sabantsevski did to Marina? I wanted to shout, but I knew it would not do any good. Mother Anna was clearly a victim of Sabantsevski's great charm. She spat on me, then turned away and passed into the crowd. No doubt she will soon leave the order to join Sabantsevski's forces.

Mother Xenia tried to restore order, for, despite the bolshevik desecration, this place remains sacred ground. At the center of the courtyard, I raised my pistol and fired two shots. That momentarily stopped the roar of conversations and allowed me to order the men to fall into formation. The only one to ignore this order was Iusuf, who was still going about the yard seeking to hug anyone within reach. Xenia also told the ladies to move away from the door as the visitors must now depart. She was not wholly successful in this. Most of the ladies ignored her, and I fear she is incapable of full command of the nunnery, should it endure.

As the men assembled, I spoke with Lt. Irvin. He had heard from several of the nuns about Mother Marina and expressed his wish to join the mission against Sabantsevski. He now believes that the entire world went insane during his captivity.

"I agree," I told him. "Nonetheless, this particular part of the insanity is not your fight."

"I think it is," he said. His family and the girl he left behind had doubtless decided he was long dead and resumed their lives. He was a soldier by profession, and his skills are needed here to stop this disease before it spreads.

I nodded and shook his hand. I presented him with captain's insignia and announced he would be my second-in-command. The promotion was well received by my troopers.

Although I had not spoken with her, I felt braced by the spirit of my Aunt Katiya. I recalled an incident from my childhood when I was perhaps five or six. I was running around the cobblestones of the courtyard at the nunnery and fell, hurting my knees badly. I looked around for my mother to give me comfort, but only Aunt Katiya was nearby. She told me to get up and stop crying, as I was disturbing the serenity of this place. I still recall how badly it hurt when I tried to walk. My aunt put her hand on my shoulder and, with a kind voice, told me to remember the suffering of the Christ, who died horribly for our sins upon the cross. I looked deeply into her eyes, seeing not the hardness I had always seen before but a deep sense of peace and tranquility. It was at that moment that we began to draw closer. Mother Marina must have had that same peace and tranquility in the face of such pain. I long to know Mother Marina's history with Sabantsevski. What conflict led to that dreadful death?

I will stop at nothing to secure the safe release of my aunt and the Holy Ladies. While I fear especially for Aunt Katiya's safety, I know that Sabantsevski appreciates her supreme value as a hostage and will probably spare her to the last. I suspect he knows that witnessing the execution of her nuns would be its own form of torture for her. As abbess, she has always been conscientious in overseeing their health and welfare, a true Mère Superière [Mother Superior]. They, in turn, repay her concern with love and devotion.

When we left the nunnery, it began to rain. By the time we returned to our encampment, a thick fog had developed. I have prayed for the safety of the Holy Ladies. I pray, too, for better weather tomorrow as we begin our search quite early.

Although Mother Anna's accusation that I was Marina's executioner is unjust, I cannot help but wonder if it contains a kernel of truth. Would she have been spared if my aunt had known our whereabouts and revealed them? The inevitable confrontation between Sabantsevski and myself would simply have been advanced in time. I shall continue to ponder these events for a long time to come. As usual, the search for answers only leads to more questions.

Again I contemplate the cost of this mission, not only to my troops but also to those innocents who have been drawn into it. While I must believe in the rightness of what we are doing so as to inspire my men, it is becoming an increasingly heavy burden to bear. I pray for divine strength to carry on, as my men are enraged about the bolshevism of some of the nuns. I must address this immediately.

Before I retire, I must record a further reflection. There are no dead ends in life. I know this from Madame Daria, who taught that if you have the courage to take the detour, it will be there to lead you to where you need to be. She also taught that if you believe in the afterlife, it will be there for you. On the other hand, if you do not believe in it, it will not be. You will be correct—but miserable. God is on our side in this fight; I know we shall be successful against the Godless evil and its darkness. But at what price in terms of losses?

Wednesday, 30 April 1919 / 1400 hrs. [2:00 pm]

This morning I told the troopers that if any of them did not wish to join the search for the Holy Ladies, there were other duties they could perform. Our current complement is forty-one. I have divided them into six squads—one to protect our camp, three to conduct the search. I shall lead the main search party, with Vlad on my right and Shav on the left. The fifth squad, Sergeant Kapolski's scouts, looking for possible ambush sites, has already left. The sixth, under Captain Irvin, will search for Tariq's band of assassins, which lurks somewhere behind us. I had considered leading that squad myself, but Irvin insisted on doing it because of his hatred of the Turk. Allowing the men to choose their own assignments has worked out well.

I had been thinking of Tariq as merely a nuisance but recently decided he was more dangerous than that. Whereas I had thought that, as a Mohammedan, he would never cooperate with the Godless bolsheviks, I now see that their interests are parallel. Xenia told me that Sabantsevski has placed a third, even larger, bounty on my head. Tariq is probably following the ancient Mohammedan adage that "the enemy of my enemy is my friend," believing that killing me will give him the satisfaction of my head *and* the bounty.

Captain Irvin's orders are simple: capture Tariq or bring me his head. This is his first test of leadership. Ever since I lost my second-in-command at the outset of this mission, Vlad has filled this role. But while he is an excellent Sergeant Major, he does not have the background to be an excellent officer. Captain Irvin may be a special gift from God. We shall see how he handles himself today.

Aishna returned early this morning with more precise intelligence about Sabantsevski's location. She said that he was holding the hostages in a small hovel in a clearing, some two kilometers [1.2 miles] northeast of our position. Although she wants to be part of that pursuit, she has decided to join Captain Irvin in the search for Tariq. Her hatred of the Turk surpasses her love for the Holy Ladies. I would have liked to have her with me, but I am pleased of her choice, knowing as I do that she will deliver a death to Tariq that will surpass Fyodor's in its cruelty.

We also discussed the events at the nunnery yesterday. I saw that Aishna was deeply affected and was surprised to learn that she had known Mother Marina years ago as Galina. In fact, Aishna had been the one who suggested that Galina retire to the nunnery; she even took her as far as the front door. Aishna did not explain why Galina needed to retreat from the world. Nor would she enlighten me on Galina's dispute with Sabantsevski.

As we were talking, Aishna suddenly began to cry, something of which I had thought her incapable. When I moved to hold her, she pressed closely against me until she regained her composure. Then she gave me another passionate kiss—and pulled away, saluted and quickly left. While I understand Aishna as a warrior, as a woman, she remains a mystery. I expect she will play the woman of mystery as long as it is useful to her.

What kind of woman is she? Katarin, too, would have clung to me after such an intense and emotional conversation, and that is how it should be. But this womanly response is uncharacteristic of Aishna, who usually exhibits an air of manly freedom. She goes where she wishes, fights like a demon and recognizes no power greater than herself, save God. I would admire such an attitude in a man. However, I am ambivalent about it in a woman. Aishna is free, and freedom to her is anarchy, with all that it implies. In the same way, I fear that freedom in Russia would lead to anarchy. As an individual, Aishna poses little risk to our way of life. But what would the world come to if all women conducted themselves in such a radical manner? After all, women are supposed to be the conserving force in our society. When properly used, their power of the hearth curbs the savage instincts of men. Without it, our civilization would collapse.

Yet our civilization is collapsing, if it has not done so already.

Wednesday, 30 April 1919 / 1800 hrs. [6:00 pm]

Our patrols left mid-morning, but with the rain and the mud on the forest trails, our transit was slow. We headed northeast through the forest, searching for the Holy Ladies and signs of their captors. The two squads under Vlad and Shav moved more gradually on my flanks, with a plan to rendezvous at noon. We could hardly see with fog rolling in from the river, and I reduced our search interval from my standard fifty to twenty meters [65.6 ft.]. I felt pleasantly isolated from my men and the world as I rode along, wrapped in my rain gear.

Then a trooper shouted, "Sir! You must see. Prepare yourself."

Up ahead was a body hanging from a tree. It was one of the nuns. We cut her down and laid her gently on the ground, covering her with a blanket. Her eyes were wide open, and bulging—which suggested that her neck was not broken, that she had died while dangling there, slowly and horribly. I did not know her name or anything about her. I removed the rope and left her at peace on the forest floor. We had to move forward. There was no time to do more for her.

At the rendezvous point, Vlad and Shav had further horrors to report. Vlad's patrol had found a totally disrobed Lady impaled upon a long stake. She was still conscious and so received a quick mercy bullet to end her suffering. Shav's patrol found a disrobed Lady tied to a tree. She had been used for bayonet practice and was covered in deep wounds. She, too, was still conscious but beyond help, so she was also given a mercy bullet. We have issued far too many mercy bullets in our search for Sabantsevski.

That the Ladies were tortured in this manner and left in the open meant that Sabantsevski knew we would be coming this way—that he had meant for us to know his location or think we did. That they were still conscious meant that he and the other nuns were still close by. On high alert and rigid with outrage, we set out as a unified force towards the place where Aishna had said the Ladies were being held.

Suddenly we were under fire. The shots came from different directions, and it was sporadic, not sustained, like an attack. Perhaps it was someone after the bounties—Tariq? Makhno's Green anarchists? In the fog, we could not see who was shooting. All I could do was send a few men to charge toward the shots, but they found no one.

It looked like a trap. Sabantsevski was waiting for us, letting us enter a position only to find ourselves in a crossfire. Yet the gunfire was so random that no one had been hit. I ordered my troops to dismount, form a circle around the horses and fix bayonets. I drew my sabre and waited. The rain had stopped, and the forest became extraordinarily quiet for what seemed like a long time.

Then a tall figure emerged from the fog. He wore a Guardsman's greatcoat and high black boots. The Lee-Enfield rifle on his shoulder had a bayonet caked with blood. His head was shaved, and my first thought was that he was a deserter—not a good sign. Sabantsevski liked to provide his men with our uniforms.

"Hello, Misha," a woman said. Astounded, I looked more closely. This was indeed a woman. A woman I knew.

"Evgania," I said. "Can this possibly be you?" This was my sweetheart, who, until recently, was Mother Selania.

"I am Comrade Commissar Evgania, daughter of Lenin. I am a member of Sainte Olga's Free Revolutionary Women's Brigade," she said, raising her left arm to indicate a white armband with red letters painted on it. In her right hand was a machine pistol, pointed at me.

Questions raced through my mind. How long had this brigade existed within the convent? Many of the nuns were naïve about the ways of the world beyond the nunnery walls. Sabantsevski had preyed upon their beliefs and was now using them for his own ends. Had he moved on and left some of his "brigade" behind to delay us? As with the other nuns who shared bolshevik delusions, they made perfect martyrs. I remembered my aunt's words, "Never threaten a nun with death." These Ladies were fearless because they knew that a heavenly reward awaited them. How easy it must have been for Sabantsevski to trick them. Sabantsevski will use them too, framing them to other gullible souls as martyrs to the cause of freedom and justice, who died in his fight against the forces of injustice and tyranny to help the poor and oppressed.

My beloved Evgania was a bolshevik commissar? How could such a thing have happened? I asked her how she became one. There in the forest, she told me what I already knew about how conditions at the nunnery had relaxed after the Russian uprising of 1905. Some nuns were allowed to go out in the community, where they became friends with rebellious women who led them to revolutionary books and literature. Mother Anna was the chief of these. As Mother Selania, Evgania became a convert and slowly built a cell among the cloistered nuns.

"I was voted commissar," she said, standing defiantly before me. "We went about our business as usual and quietly gathered comrades. When Commander General Sabantsevski came, we were more than eager to follow him and his men."

I could not believe this militant figure was the same person as the girl who grew up with me on an adjoining estate. She had been an exquisitely beautiful little girl with flaxen hair, and something about her was irresistible. I would join her in the large playhouse on her father's estate, pretending to be her husband simply to be near her. In hindsight, I realized I had feelings for her before I was aware of what they meant.

Evgania was sent to the nunnery at ten; shortly afterwards, I went to the Pages School. One day I overheard her mother tell my mother that they had to send her to the nuns. Otherwise, she would cause trouble. At the time, I was mystified. To me, Evgania was an angel.

Now Evgania was forty. The years in the nunnery had taken their toll. Nonetheless, even with a shaved head, she remained a naturally handsome mature woman with a hint of the young girl. With a machine pistol, pointed at my heart.

"Drop your weapon, Evgania," I said calmly. When she did not, I heard Vlad and Shav raise their rifles.

"Stand down," I said. "I know this woman. I wish no harm to come to her, no matter what she says or does."

Evgania lowered her pistol but proceeded to denounce me as a devil, an instrument of the antichrist and a member of the oppressor class. She looked around and damned us all.

I was now close enough to smell the odor of sexual congress on her. Was her seducer Sabantsevski? Surely not—I believed her smarter than that. This encounter had to end—we had to rescue the hostages—but I could not resist a few more questions.

"What does your brigade have against me, against the Whites? Have I ever done you harm?"

"Why do you ask, you devil? We are revolutionaries."

"Who killed the poor nuns we found in the forest?"

"We did," she said proudly. "My brigade dispatched the counter-revolutionaries. The old world is dead. The old nunnery is gone. The property was confiscated by the Kiev Soviet. Yes, the Commander took ten hostages, but almost twenty-five of us left happily. The nuns who remained did so out of fear, and they will last only a few more days, a week at most."

"I do not believe so many were glad to leave that holy place," I said.

She laughed bitterly. "How ignorant you are, Misha. It was not a holy place at all, but a hell where those women with any spark of independence were completely cloistered." She spat on the ground before continuing. "Only the weak, harmless nuns were allowed any freedom. The strong remained cloistered against our will."

"Why were you sent to the nunnery so young?" I asked her.

"Do you remember Count Respain?"

"Yes, vaguely." His estate was located to the east of her father's.

Then Evgania told all assembled, without a trace of shame, that the Count had raped her when she was ten. For that, her own mother pronounced her a self-centered minx around older men and charged that she had been asking for what happened. Now that her marriage prospects were ruined, she was banished to the nunnery to avoid scandal. She never saw either of her parents again and had no idea if they were still alive. She had been punished for the mere fact of being a naïve and trusting girl.

My condolences for this injustice seemed so inadequate, and I wished that Aishna were present, or better still, my Katarin. They would know how to deal with such a woman.

"Evgania," I said, lacking anything else to say, "where is my aunt?"

"You can stop looking for the hostages, including your aunt. We stripped them naked and forced them to dig their own graves. Then we bound and gagged them, taking our individual revenge on them before throwing them in their graves, one at a time. They were buried alive. Be assured they are all dead.

"My special comrade, Major Nicholai, is nearby. How lovely to finally have a younger man. He has trained us in riflery, and the brigade has rifles trained on all of you right now. Go back to your camp. We are joining the supreme commander as his bodyguards. If you try to follow us, there are plenty of sharpshooters from other factions in this forest."

Evgania raised her pistol again. I raised mine. Looking into her eyes, I saw the Evgania I once knew. Despite everything, a spark of innocence, of goodness, remained, and I could not kill her. For a moment, everything seemed frozen again—Evgania, my troops, the forest itself, even the fog. Perhaps she, too, saw me as I once had been. She holstered her pistol.

Suddenly she unbuttoned her greatcoat, revealing her naked body. It was laced with long, thin scars that must have been the marks of a whip. I made an involuntary groan, as did other men.

"You have never see me *au naturel* as a grown woman. I wish you could have seen me as your wife, but that is no longer possible since you already have one, and children. I am exhibiting myself in this way so you can see what the so-called 'Holy Ladies' have done to me."

I went closer, holstering my pistol. She drew close to me and spoke softly in my ear.

"When I was young, I used to dream about being married to you, Misha, about being an officer's wife with many children."

"I had a similar idea about you. Nothing would have given me greater pleasure."

"Count Respain is still on his estate. One reason I have become a soldier is to kill that bastard myself."

"If you fail, Evgania, I swear I will kill him."

She was gripping my arms, and, at that, she squeezed tightly, then stepped back. She shouted an order, at which about thirty women slowly emerged from the trees, rifles trained on us.

"Retreat, Misha, before there is an accident. The brigade wants a fight."

"Draw back, men," I said, dispensing with military formalities.

"Farewell, Misha," I heard as we rode away.

I turned to wave, but Evgania and her brigade had already disappeared into the forest. Gradually my shock gave way to reflection. What we had seen from her was not exhibitionism but rather the repudiation of the life she had lived. I also knew that her farewell meant I would never see her again. In another time, I would have felt as though I had lost a part of me. No longer. I cannot reconcile that she is a bolshevik, a torturer, even a commissar. That is as bad as a chekist, and I shall not be fooled again as I was with Fyodor. No, she died to me today as surely as if I had killed her. Good riddance and goodbye to childish illusions! But I saw blood on my tunic where she had embraced me, evidence of her wounds. I shall not soon forget.

It has been about an hour since our return, and I write because I must record these events while they are fresh, not because I want to stop and reflect. Seeing Evgania has brought the past vividly to mind.

I was eighteen. I had just received a commission as an ensign [Second Lieutenant] and was awaiting regimental assignment when I visited my aunt. I told her that I wished to visit with the Novice Sister Selania and ask her to marry me. She smiled in a knowing way.

"You are free to ask her, my dear boy, but you must recognize certain facts. Our holy charter states that when a girl enters the convent, all her personal records from the outside are destroyed. If she ventures into the world again, she will be a ghost because she has no papers or identification. Secondly, virtually all the Ladies retain their noble titles, but only within these walls. Evgania keeps her titles here if her behavior has warranted it. Outside the walls, however, she loses not only her titles but also her patronymic and family names. Selania could have been a countess one day, but that was no longer possible. Should she renounce her vows and leave, she would be simply Evgania. If you took her to meet your mother, your mother would not receive her, regardless of her true feelings. You would be disinherited, and your slim chance of becoming a count would be gone.

"You have a brilliant military career ahead of you, very likely in an elite regiment. But not with a wife of such lowly station. Even in a lesser regiment, the ladies would not accept her. Your career would be effectively ended. You would probably be sent to Siberia.

"At the core of this situation is a rather delicate matter. If a young lady of the nobility is to enjoy the privileges of her station, there is something she must do. She was born with purity of body and soul. She must preserve it at all costs until her wedding night. Evgania failed this test of God-given purity. If she had not, you would now be seeking her father's permission for marriage."

I was thunderstruck by this absolutist view. "But Aunt Katiya, Count Respain forced himself on an innocent and trusting young girl. How can her purity possibly be compromised?"

"The count was driven from polite society and punished. It was Sister Selania's fate to be here, as it is for other nuns who are not here willingly. But with God's love, they shall see the error of their ways and earn a place in Heaven. Selania is a different person from the girl you knew. She has given her life to God, although she has not yet

fully realized it. If she suffered during this transition, it was as nothing compared to the agony of Christ upon the cross."

"Is Sister Selania suffering?" I asked.

"The life of a novice is full of pain and suffering as she decides
whether she will take the veil. Not a choice made lightly. But since
Evgania came to the nunnery as a sinner, she must take the veil when
appropriate. Then Sister Selania shall remain a nun forever. She is
earning her redemption through arduous work and prayer."

"Aunt Katya, I simply wish to greet an old friend."

My aunt looked deeply into my eyes as though examining my
very soul. "It would be best for all concerned that you forget you ever
knew the girl. Your visit to her would be too disruptive."

Every argument made by my aunt was compelling except one. Evgania was not responsible for her situation. If I could not marry her, I
could at least rescue her. In my view, she would suffer on the outside,
but she was likely suffering more inside. I wracked my brain to discover how to rescue her. The nunnery was built like a fortress, and I
knew the cloistered were behind locked doors. I had always thought
that was to protect the Ladies; now I saw that it was meant to im-
prison them. Even if I could rescue her, I realized that kidnapping a
nun, even if she wanted to escape, would cause a great scandal for my
family and lead to my ruin. I had never felt so impotent before, and it
was a harsh lesson.

The next time I returned home on leave, I told my mother that,
even after considering all the consequences, I wanted to marry Evgania. Reluctantly, she told me that Evgania had taken the veil and
become Mother Selania. She was now married to God. The matter
was closed, as far as my mother was concerned.

What my experience has taught me is this. Evgania had the curse
of beauty too soon. In the years since, I have seen it many times in
many countries. What happened to Evgania has happened to many
other girls like her. Another thing: it is always women who lock these

beauties away, as though they are diseased and a disgrace to their gender. This is the other, darker side of women's conserving power. It is left to the men to restore the honor of the family, in a duel, for instance. I dimly recall that Count Respain was shot in the leg in what was described as a hunting accident. Now that I know the facts, I think it was no accident. In any event, he survived but was severely crippled.

Evgania's blood has stained my tunic, but I will not have it removed. I have no further innocence to lose, but perhaps I still have a few illusions. What I have shed today is my illusion of the goodness of the "Holy Ladies" and Evgania, my youthful beloved. Today could have been very different had my aunt not been so dogmatic as to try to quash the nuns' independent spirits. Cloistering the troublemakers fostered their bolshevism and spread beyond them. To my aunt, it was immaterial whether the Ladies were in the nunnery voluntarily or not: it was God's will that they be there.

I can no longer place my faith in a god who would permit anyone like Evgania to lead such a cruel and wasted life. I hope my aunt, her jailer, will now suffer the torments of Hell, along with all the other Ladies who betrayed my poor darling. I shall now make it my personal mission to ensure that Count Respain joins the torment at the earliest possible moment.

Tonight, I must address the men at the campfire to explain that we are no longer riding to rescue innocent nuns. The nuns still alive are our enemies—bolshevik fanatics. I must speak of how we were betrayed by those we trusted, especially my aunt. It will not be easy for many of the troops to retain their faith in god. However, I have no choice. I must say what must be said.

I shall no longer seek my help from god but rather rely on myself alone, as I should have done now for a long time. I feel the power and strength of liberation now rising in me. However, I shall never forget Evgania as she was today and long ago.

PART ELEVEN

Thursday, 1 May 1919 / 0700 hrs. [7:00 am]

May Day. I have such happy memories from my youth of celebrations around the May Pole with Evgania and all the pretty girls in their spring frocks. Today, sadly, the holiday's blessed innocence has been swept away in favor of a political agenda—the declaration of solidarity among all the workers of the world. Socialist International ordered that workers would not fight in a capitalist war. They would join in solidarity with workers from enemy nations to sabotage capitalist war efforts and end the war. But how naïve that was. What rubbish to believe that the ties that bind workers to their class are stronger than their ties to their nation. The Great War proved this when workers (except for the bolshevikii and other radicals) fought for their own countries.

By birth, one is a Muzhik, a proletarian, a bourgeois or a noble, and there can be no negotiation of one's class. Yet the bolsheviks have succeeded in provoking class warfare, allowing the oppressed to seek their revenge against the oppressors. That accounts for the savagery and brutality.

I wager there are parades celebrating socialist solidarity in Moscow and Petrograd, along with interminable speeches. Not even the revolution has changed politicians, their venal nature is the only thing that has remained the same since my youth.

Thursday, 1 May 1919 / 1800 hrs. [6:00 pm]

I was about to leave my tent to address the men when Captain Irvin entered to report on his pursuit of Tariq Aziz. He looked exhausted, his blackened face streaked with dried sweat, his field uniform smeared with mud and blood. He spoke in good Russian, despite having told me he knew little of the language. "Oh, I picked it up in the asylum," he told me when I expressed surprise, but I let it pass for the moment, being too interested in his news to pursue the point.

Irvin told me that around midday today, he and the men emerged from the forest onto the steppe. They spotted Tariq Aziz and his forces out in the open. Our men attacked, pressing the advantage of surprise, and were on the verge of victory when another force suddenly appeared on their left flank. They carried a black anarchist flag and were "not very disciplined, but incredibly determined," as Jack put it. Aishna identified them as some of Nestor Makhno's Greens. As they were a larger force and clearly outnumbered us, Jack ordered a retreat to a more defensible position in the forest. They remained there for most of the afternoon, taking intense fire. Two of our men were killed, and many others wounded. Grisha is treating them now.

"And Aishna?" I asked.

"She is all right. I will get to that."

Jack went on to recount that he feared the two opposing forces would combine and slaughter us once night fell. He prepared those who could fight for an attack. Then in the distance, through the trees, they heard shots and shouting, all the dire sounds of battle. But the sounds did not draw nearer. Then they stopped.

To find out what had happened, Jack led the troops on a reconnaissance mission through the forest to a position approximately half a kilometer north from where they had entered. From there, the troopers rode until they saw the scene of the battle, a bloody engagement between the Greens and Tariq's forces.

About forty or so bodies littered the ground. Our troops searched for survivors, finding only one. He had been shot in the stomach and stabbed several times, but he was still conscious. He was an Azeeri named Jamal, whom Aishna proceeded to interrogate in Turkish on what had led up to the battle. The Greens, who are largely Muzhiks, loathe the Mohammedans and one had taken offense at something a Green said, "an insult to Allah and the Prophet," and such an insult must be immediately avenged. The Greens, in turn, loathe the Mohammedans. But not as much as they loathe our troops.

Was Tariq dead or wounded? Jamal pointed to a mass of mutilated bodies, in the midst of which was the dead Tariq. How large was the Green force? Perhaps as many as one hundred, Jamal said, adding that the Greens were not well armed; some were even fighting on foot. The Greens were after weapons and supplies, stripping the dead Mohammedans and taking their horses. Jamal thought the Greens were more interested in looting his knives and his gun than killing him. Where were they headed? West, he thought, back across the steppe.

I told Jack how grateful I was that he and his troops had been spared greater losses. But I was also concerned that the Greens were operating this far east, which was unusual. Jack and I agreed that they had probably been following us to win the bounty on my head. After all, Greens fight largely for booty and plunder. Perhaps when they encountered Tariq and his men, they decided to cooperate against their common enemy, but they had a falling out before they could find me. Here was another example of the changeable, sometimes irrational nature of this war. Allies today—antagonists tomorrow. Now the Greens, having plundered Tariq's forces, were probably off in search of more riches. Our forces are superior, and, with their own forces weakened, they should leave us alone for a time.

"Sorry about the Russian," Jack said, referring to his initial claim that his Russian was poor. He explained that he was suspicious of me as a White Russian officer after having been treated so badly by Major Kamaranski and considered it better to err on the side of caution before deciding to trust me. I was delighted rather than annoyed. My primary reservation about Jack as a second-in-command had been his lack of Russian. In fact, he knows several languages. He had studied Latin and French in school and learned the Egyptian dialect of Arabic in Alexandria and some contemporary Greek in Salonica.

"Is Jamal with you? And how is Aishna?" I asked.

"Aishna is a prisoner, sir. She is in the brig."

"What, Captain? Explain!" I shouted, jumping up from my chair.

"Jamal is dead, sir. At Aishna's hand. As she questioned Jamal, she grew more and more impatient. She disemboweled him, sir, right before the troops. She did it so quickly and fiercely I had no time to stop her. And I confess that for a moment, I was glad she had done it."

With Jamal lying there, gutted, Aishna had told Jack and the troops that this Azeeri was known to her. He was Tariq's deputy when the Turk raided her village seven years before. He had insulted her—she did not give details—and she could wait no longer to send him to Hell with the other Turk devils.

"I rebuked her strongly, of course, sir. I also rebuked her for torturing and killing Fyodor on Saturday and told her that this barbaric behavior had to stop. Then I arrested her and—for the sake of the men—said the only reason she would be spared court-martial for her offenses against the code of war was that she is a civilian. Aishna only laughed and called me a 'little tin soldier.' She mocked me for invoking military law and said, 'In this war, the only military law is killing as many of the bastards as you can before they kill you. Jamal was a Mohammedan, but he died as a warrior who understood this.'

"At that point, I lost my composure and seized her. With a little help from two troopers, I bound her hand and foot and threw her across her horse. She kept on mocking us about how weak we are as warriors until I shoved a rag in her mouth."

I could not help laughing at the picture of Aishna flung over her horse, bound and gagged.

"I wish to be relieved of my command, sir," Jack said seriously. "I cannot abide such lack of discipline and absolute barbarity."

"I understand your feelings, Jack, but this is a new kind of war. Just as the bolshevikii violated civilian rules after their coup, so the Red Army violates the rules of war. Had Aishna been captured by the cheka, her punishment would have been far worse than Fyodor's. The new rules are now simple, as in ancient times—kill or be killed. You are a fine officer. I want you to stay."

"I will think about it," he said. "But I have questions. First, what is Aishna's status in your command?"

"She is not my mistress if that is your meaning. She has no official role, but she has been invaluable because of her detailed knowledge of the land and her contacts with diverse groups. She simply desires to be seen as another warrior. As far as I am concerned, that is what she is. One day she will disappear and move on to her next cause. That is the type of woman she is—never in one place for long."

As Jack and I talked, it became clear to me that Jack was interested in Aishna as a woman, as who would not? I smiled at this but felt obliged to warn him that no man could ever truly possess her, except maybe temporarily.

Jack returned my smile and said he enjoys a challenge. Back in Australia, he once determined to capture a wild black mare—the fastest, sleekest creature he had ever beheld. It took him a year, but he finally captured her. Then he spent just as long trying to break her. In the end, he had the finest mount imaginable.

"What became of her?" I asked.

"When I was captured on Gallipoli, the mare escaped and led the other horses into the mountainous wilderness."

"Some things are not meant to last," I said, and the captain agreed. "If you want to try to tame Aishna, you have my permission."

He nodded, going on to praise her unconventional beauty, her extraordinary presence. He, too, was mesmerized by her blue eyes.

"And her spirit," I added, "the way she can get what she wants in a man's world."

We talked a moment about Aishna. I was surprised to learn that he knew her former name, Heghine Khachaturian, and that she had confided in him how she could be an avowed atheist yet wear an Orthodox cross.

"She said politics is her public side, but religion is her private side. That makes sense to me," he said.

In truth, she will continue to be a woman of mystery to both friend and foe, and that is much of her appeal. Even if she fully reveals her body to a man, as she has done to me, there will always be her secret self, which she jealously guards.

Another thing Jack wanted to know was my history with Tariq Aziz. I recounted Tariq's heinous deeds against Christian civilians, especially women and children, and his vow to kill me for the torments he suffered while in prison. I told Jack that I felt nothing for Tariq and would gladly see him shot. In my experience, Turks have not obeyed European codes of war any better than the Reds. When Jack seemed doubtful, I told him, in case he did not know, how the Turks had taken the ANZAC enlisted men captured at Gallipoli to the Tarsus mountains and worked them to death building a railroad. Jack was silent, but I could see the pain and anger in his eyes. I apologized for revealing something so horrendous, and he asked if my information was indisputable. But he knew, even as he asked, that it was. He had heard rumors for many years.

Jack began to pace, his mind and soul clearly in turmoil.

"Has the entire world gone mad?" he blurted out. "What has happened to civility, chivalry and honor? When did war degenerate into such barbarism? Were our standards mere illusions?" Jack was verbalizing many of the thoughts I had silently stored in my head these five long years of war.

"Perhaps we are like Roman legionnaires in the late days of the

Empire, fighting against barbarian hordes from all sides with little or no support," I said. "For many years, the emperors, senators and citizens luxuriated in too much prosperity. They lost the virtues of true Romans. In 476 when the King of the Vandals deposed Emperor Romulus Augustus, Rome had lost much of its territory. Romulus was just a feckless boy of sixteen, and the Empire no longer existed.

"Today we are not that paralyzed. We still have the ability, right here in our small part of the world, to strike a blow against the forces that would destroy us. Aishna is right, Jack. We must revert to that first rule of war—kill or be killed. The second rule of this war is also very simple. Give no quarter, expect no quarter."

Jack continued his pacing. "If we act in such a barbarous manner, how are we better than the barbarians? And let me ask you this. Do you consider yourself a European or an Asian?"

"That is easy," I said. "Kiev was always considered the easternmost city of Europe, not the westernmost city of Asia. As a Kievan, I am definitely European, unlike the crude Asian Boyars of Muscovy."

Jack laughed a little. "But I'm still asking, sir, doesn't disregarding the rules of war reduce us to barbarians?"

"This new barbarism, a thing called bolshevism, must be stopped here," I said. "It is a seductive ideology, promising heaven on earth to people who no longer believe in any other kind of heaven. If it is not stopped now, it could well sweep the world and usher in a new dark age. I have concluded, reluctantly, that we are fools to cling to our standards in the face of bolshevik brutality."

"If they are really so brutal as all that, sir, why did you volunteer for a mission so far behind Red lines?"

Clearly it was time to inform Jack Irvin about Sabantsevski. I told him how I had volunteered, or been chosen, rather, because of my personal vendetta against this scoundrel; then how the mission had grown into a sacred duty because of my conviction that Sabantsevski would become the Red Napoleon. The idea of the "Red Napoleon" had to be explained to Jack.

"He is definitely a bad egg, sir, but surely not all Bolsheviks are that bad," he said.

How naïve Jack is, but then he has been a prisoner for the last four years and still has a lot to learn about what has been going on in the world. He should know that the bolshevikii are using terror to grow and maintain their power, like the French Jacobins. But there was no time for another history lesson today.

Jack had one more question. Was it true that we had killed several nuns today? How could *that* be justified?

"Jack, we did not kill any nuns. Bolshevikii nuns killed their own. But you will learn more when I address the men. And you might want to ask the troopers what the Reds and the bolshevikii have done to their families. They will begin to open your eyes."

Jack is a quiet man. He does not boast, he acts. I sense a solitary strength about him to which the men will respond. As for Aishna, he is the right age to keep up with her, although I question whether he has enough experience with women to win her over permanently. I wonder whether arresting her like that enhanced his chances with her or destroyed them. We shall see.

Jack is also very much the orphan. Should he break away from us, he might yet find his way back to Australia. But I suspect that he is so changed by this war that he cannot simply return to his ranch, or station, as he calls it. He is a soldier to his core now, not a rancher. If he survives this mission, he will probably be adrift in the world and become a soldier of fortune, like many a stateless man. Perhaps he will be with Aishna, perhaps not. But whatever happens, his sense of honor and decency shall always remind me that outside of this hell, once known as Ukraine, such virtues still exist.

Before preparing myself for this all-important address to my men, I must visit the wounded from today's battle. And Aishna—I must talk with her. Jack and Aishna—two linchpins of this mission. God does indeed work in a most mysterious way, sending me just the people I need to help me see clearly when the mission seems darkest. I cannot reject God after all. I can no more reject God than I could reject Ukraine or my family.

Friday, 2 May 1919 / 0730 hrs. [7:30 am]

Just as I finished preparing my remarks for the troops and sat ruminating on the day's events last night, I became aware of two Muzhiks standing before me with pistols pointing at my heart.

"You come with us," one said in Russian.

"Where?" I said, nonplused.

"None of your concern."

"Going to an unknown destination with two strangers is certainly my concern," I said.

They raised their pistols as though to fire. I did not move.

"Here for the bounty, eh? From Sabantsevski?" I asked as I raised the Mauser I always keep at the ready on my desk. This twenty-shot machine pistol was unmistakably the superior firepower. They nodded.

"How much would you be paid to deliver me?"

The one who did the speaking named a sizeable sum in roubles.

"The rouble is virtually worthless," I said, "but Sabantsevski wouldn't pay you anyway and probably kill you for your trouble. I've known him a long time, and he has never kept a promise. You may now leave peaceably. You have ten seconds to decide."

Neither Muzhik lowered his pistol, and I fired two bursts. They were dead before they knew it.

By now I was hearing the sounds of an attack. After quickly reloading, I shot two more Muzhiks outside my tent. With sabre drawn, I joined battle with the attackers. I could only see shadows, being far from the light of our central fire, but I could tell who the enemy was by their ragtag garments. They were probably part of the same band of Makhno's Greens that had slaughtered Tariq and given Jack such a fight. Jack had worried that they would attack us tonight, but I had stupidly thought they would retreat westward after sating themselves on booty and plunder. It appeared they had no fear of dying, perhaps, like the nuns, even relishing their martyrdom. However, an anarchist Muzhik's bravery derives not from faith in God but from the conviction that they have nothing to lose and perhaps everything to gain. Aided by superior numbers and the element of surprise, they pressed their advantage.

It was a massive and concerted attack. No matter how many attackers I dispatched with pistol or sabre, there were always more. Yet I did not doubt the outcome, as my men were well drilled in night tactics. Such skills are essential for scouting and raiding. After a half-hour or so of fierce fighting, we regained the upper hand and swept the attackers from the field. They retreated as quickly as they had come, leaving their dead and wounded behind.

I stood on the field, torch in hand, offering a prayer of thanksgiving for our victory as I inhaled the odor of cordite, the nickel smell of blood and the stench of entrails ripped open. My troopers threaded their way through the fallen, looking for survivors and shooting the mortally wounded. Some were dragged away for interrogation, their cries and moans reverberating around the trees. The stench and sounds of the battlefield are so familiar to me that I find them almost comforting, like an old friend.

I took the time to examine the faces of the enemy with care—and respect—not possible in the midst of battle. These were indeed Muzhik Greens. Several bore whiplashes across their rough faces or deep scars. Their skin was leather-like and deeply wrinkled, testifying to years of work in the sun. Although it is difficult to calculate a Muzhik's exact age, I do not think any of them were older than I. What a contrast between these faces and those smooth, well-cared-for faces and glossy beards of men at the Imperial Court. It amazes me that

Muzhiks, surely a race apart, did not rebel long before now. *The Time Machine,* that fantastical novel by the English Fabian Socialist writer Mr. Herbert George Wells, predicted that, in the future, the human race would divide into the childlike Eloi and brutish Morlocks. By his lights, such a division was the inevitable result of capitalism. Yet here is Russian Ukraine today, with aristocratic Eloi and Muzhik Morlocks. Just as in *The Time Machine*, Morlocks dwell away from the Eloi, usually emerging to own the night.

Yet Russia is just newly—and only superficially—capitalist. But then, the British and their American cousins have never fully understood Russia, and it is likely they never will. The latest example is their confused and half-hearted attempt to intervene in our civil war in the far north. In theory, they fielded troops to Russia to help us, but they have been more hindrance than help (although not nearly the impediment those damnable French have been). I fear that once the Versailles Conference is over, the Americans will retreat behind their oceans again, leaving us to deal with this dreadful new world that has arisen from the calamity of the great War.

Five of my men died in this battle, even more are wounded, according to Vlad—a horrible outcome. Our numbers are reduced to thirty-six, and that includes Jack, Aishna and the wounded. I now know how King Pyrrhus felt when he said, after defeating a Roman legion, "One more such victory, and we are lost." I do not remember whether I said these words out loud or to myself.

Since evacuating Kiev for Odessa, we have lost more than three-quarters of our original complement, and we are in danger of having to abandon the mission altogether. My only hope now lies with the Nationalists. Without them, we will be outnumbered by Sabantsevski's force by a factor of at least two, based on what Kapolski has learned. And while many Red formations are unreliable, Sabantsevski's troops are steadfast fanatics. In a hard-fought engagement, we might still prevail, even though we would suffer terrible losses. Death and I are old adversaries, and I do not fear the Reaper as some do. I am confident that my troops, who fought with me in Poland, Galicia and Anatolia, feel the same. That fearlessness, along with our superior tactics, will be our advantage. May it prove decisive.

After the attack, I summoned the men to speak of the nuns as I had originally planned. Before I could begin, however, someone shouted, "The nuns were Bolshie scum!" (although his second word was several degrees stronger). The men applauded, and I realized I did not have to explain that particular aspect of the day. How long ago those events now seem—almost as if they happened in another year.

Then Jack told the troops the story of how he came to be here. He finished with a declaration that he wanted to join the search for the Red Napoleon. The troops cheered and welcomed him in song as they had Aishna.

Then I looked for Aishna. To my surprise, she was some distance beyond my tent, interrogating one of the wounded Muzhiks. She had him hanging from a tree by a noose. Despite the fact that her left arm was bandaged and bleeding, she was hoisting the wretch up and down, questioning him between yanks as he choked and gagged. Before I could reach her, she abruptly jerked him upwards and broke his neck. He was dead.

I ordered her to report back to Grisha to have her bloody dressing changed.

"A woman's life is blood," she said.

"I thought you were a prisoner," I said.

She scoffed at that. "You need my help getting information."

"Of course, but you gave this prisoner a quick death," I said, trying to hide a smile. "Quicker than some others I have witnessed."

"I was merciful because he was a Muzhik, not my enemy like the chekists. But first I acquainted him with my beautiful knife," she said, fingering the scabbard of her curved knife with the Legion's black widow insignia.

"Come with me to the medical tent," I said. "I need you in prime health for the future." That was a lie. She will not join the battle against Sabantsevski because she is, after all, a woman, and I do retain some shreds of chivalry.

"You know, Mikhail, if you were captured by the bolsheviks, you would envy Mother Marina the mildness of her death. You are such an important enemy that your death would be particularly long and gruesome."

I shrugged. "I have no intention of being taken alive by anyone. I have a poison pill, as do all my troops. Would you like to have one?"

She shook her head slowly. Perhaps the code of her League of the Spider forbade such an easy way out of pain. As we walked, she reported on her day's work. The Azeeri Jamal had told her that the Greens were trying to collect bounties on my head from both Sabantsevski and the chekists—something I already knew. But I played along, pretending to blame her for not warning me. She had not had a chance, she said, having been bound and gagged by that scoundrel Captain Irvin. She had not even had time to tell *him* before their argument. He was such a hothead, according to Aishna; maybe he was even crazy. She loathed the bastard, she said. She must really love him, I thought, to hate him so much. In any case, there is high emotion between those two, they are at odds, and that is a serious rift in my command at a time when I need everyone's attention focused on Sabantsevski. Another worry.

As Grisha attended to our wounds in the medical tent (I, too, had a slight graze on my shoulder), Aishna told me what she had just learned from that poor dangling Muzhik. Sabantsevski was headquartered in some estate near Chernobyl, due north of Kiev. She had also learned why the Greens had demolished Tariq and his men. They were expendable to the Greens. It was the Mohammedans' weapons the Greens wanted, not allies for their cause. The Greens just wanted to be left alone. They were fighting for land to farm for themselves rather than for the master. They had already seized many estates, killing the masters and their families, and they wanted a lot more.

I now know Sabantsevski's location—my father's estate. It was obvious. Where else? We will need allies to defeat him.

"Will the Nationalists join us?" I asked Aishna.

"Yes, they will," she said hesitantly, "but Olganov wants a hundred gold roubles for every man who joins us."

"We don't have that kind of money!"

"I told him that," she said, "but he said he would need it to induce his men to fight for 'that devil Deniken.' I also told him Sabantsevski was as much his enemy as ours. If the Nationalists don't help us defeat him, he will defeat us both separately. I think Olganov saw the truth in that. He will reconsider. That is how we left it.

"I don't like to fight alongside mercenaries, Mikhail. You cannot depend on them. They lack our passion."

Saturday, 3 May 1919 / 0430 hrs. [4:30 am]

Aishna left early to parlay with the Nationalists and said she would return mid-morning. I do not trust Olganov. He has a sterling record as a cavalry officer, but that was just against Austrians. How valuable would he and his troops actually be if they decide to join us?

Thus, I sit in my tent, knowing where my enemy is, but lacking the forces to defeat him. It is irony of the cruelest sort if, having come all this way, we should be stymied so near our goal. As so often, all our hopes rest with Aishna. I fervently hope for her speedy and safe return.

The battle to come will be the most difficult I have ever faced. Our attack must be a surprise. We must fight with no regard for honor. I am still struggling with how the Great War and this civil war that followed have swept all honorable notions away. Aishna's execution of Fyodor was more horrible than any I had ever witnessed. It shook me to the core. Now it bothers me not a whit. In fact, it seems only right.

Aishna has been essential to the mission, but her primal emotions and undisciplined actions trouble me. Should I release her as we come closer to my father's estate and rely on my own local knowledge, dated as it is? But who can say what our situation will be at that point? The only certainty is that God moves in the most mysterious of ways. As for Aishna and Jack, I recall one of Madame Daria's favorite axioms: "Should random fate discover something for you, hold it dear, for it shall become most valuable."

Friday, 2 May 1919 / 2230 hrs. [10:30 pm]

Before I sleep tonight, I want to record some thoughts I have had today before they fade. The thought of returning to my father's estate brings up thoughts of my childhood and how I came to be the man I am. I have been thinking about my mother, Milaslava, the Countess Markov. She was a remarkable woman. She ran the household alone since my father was often away in Kiev or St. Petersburg. Because she was deeply spiritual, even mystical, you might think she delegated domestic concerns to someone else. But she had exceptional organizational ability, and she functioned as supreme head of the household with a strict schedule. As for her children, she spent the most time with Sasha, my older brother, preparing him to succeed our father as count. She also instructed Tanya, my sister, on the airs and graces essential to making an appropriate marriage. As for me, I spent most of my time before Page School with my French governess Lilly, learning French, Russian, mathematics, philosophy and history. This was not a hardship, as she was very pretty in that distinctive way French women are.

To my mother I owe my disciplined and orderly mind (apart from the mysticism she and Madame Daria fostered). Lilly, on the other hand, encouraged my wild Cossack heart. This mix of traits that might seem unreconcilable enables me to see a situation from a number of angles. It also permits me to take risks, on this quixotic campaign, for instance, and on Aishna and Jack in particular. She is like a soldier of fortune, and he will soon be. I do not doubt they will, in time, come together.

PART TWELVE

Saturday, 3 May 1919 / 0700 hrs. [7:00 am]

Sabantsevski is toying with me by inciting other groups to attack us so that our manpower is continually depleted. If I am killed, that is his bonus. Therefore, my dilemma becomes ever more pressing. Is it wiser to retreat and regroup with reinforcements, then attempt another confrontation at a later date? Or do we stand and fight, facing certain death?

Although I know Sabantsevski's most likely location, we still do not have current intelligence about his force's numbers. We think there is no large Red force in Ukraine, but we may come across him leading a force of hundreds, even thousands. How many troops did his armored train bring? How many has he been able to recruit along the way? Nevertheless, we must attack and destroy him, and we shall. He is not the only one with a long-term strategy.

If I harbored any doubts about the brutality of the Reds, Sabantsevski in particular, the horrors we have seen on this mission—Mother Marina, the spike–studded barrel, the burned and tortured priests—have washed them away. Yet I have also seen such great courage and deep faith. I am no stranger to the horrors of war. I have seen the terrible results of modern technology on the battlefield. I still fear I may become part of the ghastly wounded, who God, in His mercy, would have been taken in an earlier age. These men must now eke out an existence in the shadows of society with wounds too ghastly to be seen. How could a man possibly survive with half his face blown off?

Saturday, 3 May 1919 / 1015 hrs. [10:15 am]

Jack is now completely recommitted to the mission. His doubts arose at the nunnery, where he had heard only fragments of conversations and been verbally accosted by a particularly fiery nun who disparaged the White cause in general and me in particular. I was able to give him a more accurate account of our role in this chaotic war.

I called in Vlad and Shav to ask their opinion of Jack. They endorsed him heartily and could not suppress another laugh at the memory of Jack with Aishna bound and gagged on her horse. They had received reports from men who served under him in the battle with Tariq that Jack possessed great courage and tactical skill.

I also sought their opinion of Aishna. Initially, they seemed reluctant to express one. I encouraged their candor. Vlad said although he felt uncomfortable with a woman in our formation, he did not doubt her courage and her valuable knowledge. Shav said it was nice to have an Armenian he could talk with. I asked if he desired her and told him to speak freely. Of course, he did, and he thought most of the troopers did so as well. Vlad, too, felt uncomfortable having her in the ranks in an unspecified position. I acknowledged his concern, which I share. However, I restated my opinion that the mission's success could now depend on her efforts. They agreed.

It hardly surprised me that Aishna was acting the coquette with all my troops. Does she do this consciously or not? In any case, it is a problem. I knew Shav's claim that their relationship was chaste was a false cover for their intimacy. Was I jealous? Certainly, but I must resist her. I cannot cheat on Katarin, even if she might be dead. I am in limbo in that regard.

Sunday, 4 May 1919 / 1400 hrs. [2:00 pm]

Aishna returned this afternoon from meeting with the Ukrainian Nationalists. Her bandage was still seeping blood, and I was concerned that her wound was becoming infected. She resisted my order to see Grisha after her report, citing more important matters to which she must attend. I told her that her health and well-being were vital to the success of our mission. She seemed pleased to have her importance acknowledged. In truth, I would be honored to lead a corps of women with her fire and drive. If I survive the battle to come, I will accept Mayr Lucine's offer of training her Legion to fight the Reds.

Aishna said that the Nationalists had fought amongst themselves over the issue of aiding us. Many of them, including the one she knew as Piotr, were now dead. The faction favoring cooperation had triumphed. A man known as Vladimir Palahniuk now led them. I could tell from the way she intoned his name that she did not care for him. I asked her what she knew about him. He had been a Sergeant Major in the Imperial Army for some twenty years. He was a good soldier, although so intensely conservative in his views that no power could change his mind once he had decided on a course of action. This reminded me of other Sergeants Major I have worked with over the years.

He will rendezvous with us tomorrow morning at a point ten kilometers [6.2 mi.] south of Chernobyl on the west bank of the Dnieper.

I almost informed Aishna of my decision that she should not be allowed to engage in the battle when it comes. She can observe with Grisha, but I cannot permit a woman to engage in combat. However, her eloquent eyes persuaded me to hold my tongue. I further recalled that she had been sung into the squadron by the whole company. She shall fight unless she voluntarily withdraws, which is unlikely.

I escorted her to Grisha, who applied salve to her wound and re-dressed it.

Monday, 5 May 1919 / 1400 hrs. [2:00 pm]

We broke camp early and headed northeast toward the rendezvous point. The tall grass of the steppe gave us some measure of protection. We were not far from my father's estate on the other bank, hence in country I knew well from my youth when I used to ride along the paths we now followed.

We saw no one on our way to the river, either military or civilian. I established our base camp on a bluff overlooking the river, which is bordered on the south by an inlet where my family used to swim.

I divided the force in two and sent the first group down to the inlet to bathe both themselves and their horses. My second group stood lookout over the flat lands around us. The same tall grass that had given us shelter could do the same for another force. Only the sound of the wind and the motion of the tall grasses repaid our vigilance. I surveyed the vista as far as I could, recalling that all this land was formerly under cultivation. That is surely a harbinger of regional famine next year.

Once the first group was done, they assumed the lookout, and our group began to wash. The water felt magnificent, although it stung my blisters, sores, cuts and scratches. I was not surprised to see Aishna, abandoning all feminine modesty, splashing in the water, naked like the men. She was bantering with the troops and telling bawdy tales of the Legion. Once they had recovered from seeing her naked, the men treated her as one of them, although I noticed that Shav was always close by. Her courage and skill in fighting have earned her such a status. Her wish, as expressed to me at another river, was to be recognized as a warrior. Indeed, she is. The numerous scars on her body are the marks of a warrior.

Once we were done washing ourselves, we washed our horses. And I now realize how appropriate it is for Aishna to have a gelding.

Monday, 5 May 1919 / 1830 hrs. [6:30 pm]

Vlad entered my tent, escorting a blindfolded man in an expertly tailored uniform without insignia or badge of rank. Beside him was a shorter man wearing a similar uniform, also blindfolded. Vlad explained that the men had come under a white flag of truce, requesting

an audience. He gave me his customary thumbs-up sign before removing the blindfolds to signify that he had thoroughly examined
them for weapons. I told him to wait outside.

The taller man blinked for a moment to restore his sight. I recognized him as Major Nicholai Igorevich Count Subtelni, a Ukrainian
from the Regiment. I had not seen him since 1916 and was about to
address him by his title when he said, "Comrade Major Nicholai pre-
senting the compliments of Comrade Commander General Sabantsevski to Colonel Mikhail Antonovich Count Markov. It is good to
see you again."

That he addressed me as "count" meant he knew my family was
dead. Another blow was that Count Nicholai was an aristocrat's aristocrat, a man of impeccable lineage. At thirty-five, he was old enough
to know better than to fall for the bolshevik line. If the Reds could
convert him, no one was immune. But then, no doubt he had his reasons. Perhaps some of his family were being held as hostages at the
time when he was caught up in the Tsarist Officers' Bolshevik Draft
and forced to serve in the Red Army. The previous year, Commissar
Trotski had realized the value of White officers to their cause. And
another reason: Evgania, the zealous bolshevik, was his paramour.
Surely her role had been to convince him to become a true bolshevik.
But I suspect that his Achilles heel had actually been his Ukrainian
heritage. He would hate General Deniken's insistence on a unitary
Russia. Of course, I, too, would love to see a truly independent
Ukraine, but not at such a high price. He must know that bolshevik
promises of an independent Ukraine are lies.

Nicholai introduced the other man as "Comrade Commissar
Koba, who has recently joined us." Captain Charbonnet had told me
about this Koba, and I scrutinized his pock-marked face and damaged left arm, which he attempted to conceal. His eyes were those of a
thief and a killer. He said nothing while seeming to take in everything.
They were certainly a strange pair, the Count and the thief—Nicholai

tall and elegant, Koba short and stocky. Perhaps he was there to ensure that Nicholai stayed "converted."

Merely to be polite, I asked how the Commander was.

"In prime health," Nicholai responded. "Could not be better."

After additional pleasantries, I asked Nicholai how I might be of service and was surprised by his response. He said that Sabantsevski knew I was meaning to engage him in battle and would like to propose a location for our armies to meet two days hence, one hour after daybreak. I immediately suspected a trap. This was not how Sabantsevski operated, nor any other Red leader I had encountered.

"You look skeptical, Count," Nicholai said. "But I assure you, the Commander's intentions are honorable. Even though you had your differences in the regiment before the Great War, he has always respected you as an excellent officer and an honorable man. He believes a contest between two gentlemen should be resolved in a gentlemanly and chivalrous manner."

"Just where does the commander want to meet?" I asked, irritated by Sabantsevski's posture as a "gentleman."

"The field in front of your family home," he replied. "That is our headquarters now. Perhaps you knew that. That large field is perfect for our armies to meet."

I struggled to disguise my outrage. "Who else is there now? Does the commander have any 'guests'"?

"Some volunteers from Ste. Olga's."

Evgania and her brigade, I assumed, although I did not care at this point if he held the entire damned nunnery.

"The Commander will guarantee you safe passage over the bridge two kilometers south of Chernobyl. It is the only bridge still spanning the river," Nicholai said. "But I must warn you—the Commander cannot be responsible for the actions of anyone not under his command, like the Greens or the Nationalists. Or bandits."

"Of course," I said. So that was Sabantsevski's game—if we let our guard down crossing that bridge, we would probably be ambushed by someone "not under his command."

"All right, tell your commander we shall meet him two days hence," I said, not seeing any other choice.

"Please tell me," I said, before ending the interview, "why did you join the Reds?"

"There is no mystery," he said proudly. "I have been re-educated and see the truth of things now."

I saw no point in arguing with him as he went on to regurgitate some bolshevik dogma. He appeared, at best, a true naïf in the political realm and, at worst, a dangerous fanatic. I asked conversationally whether the balance of Sabantsevski's forces felt the same. He assured me they did, some even more fervently. This was depressing: they would be formidable fighters, far harder to defeat than the Muzhiks had been. Especially since I knew that Commissar Koba would carry out the Red Army's policy of death for failure in this important confrontation.

Suddenly Comrade Koba spoke. "As a gentleman, you mustn't worry about a trap." He stepped closer to me. "I'll personally guarantee your safe passage to the field of battle. No exceptions."

Any reassurance these words were meant to convey was undercut by the way he spat out the word "gentleman." His face wore an ugly sneer. Why would he even say the words offering such a guarantee?

I summoned Vlad to put the blindfold back on Nicholai and told Vlad that these men had my personal guarantee of safe passage from our lines. I would personally hang any man who harmed them.

"Are you clear on this?" I asked Vlad. He saluted his understanding, and I detected a small smile briefly pass his lips as he placed the commissar's blindfold.

I now feel as if I have been restored to grace.

On further reflection, I believe Commissar Koba's "guarantee" was just bravado, nothing more. Being a short Muzhik with a pock-marked face and bad arm must be a terrible burden for any man.

Doubtless, he simply wanted to let me know what an important person he is. Yet I cannot underestimate this man for a moment. He is not physically impressive, but I suspect a keen intellect working in that peasant head.

Tuesday, 6 May 1919 / 1000 hrs. [10:00 am]

We have been joined by the Nationalists. Captain Vladimir Palahniuk has brought twenty-seven seasoned veterans with him. That brings our total complement to sixty-three.

Palahniuk is not the Muzhik I expected—short, stocky, physically unprepossessing like Koba—but tall and lean, with a shaved head and bushy red moustache speckled with gray. A long, angry scar runs by his left eye. There is a slight slant to his black eyes, which appear deep with experience. I particularly noticed his large and powerful hands, which looked as though they could break a man's neck as easily as a turkey bone.

Something about Palahniuk is wild and cruel, which is why Aishna disapproves of him. They obviously have some personal history. Yet it is always better to have such a man fighting with you than against you. I learned quickly that he does not like the Whites but hates the Reds even more, especially Sabantsevski. He joined us because he believed that my reduced force had no chance of defeating Sabantsevski, the worst of the Reds. I see that we have been joined by highly motivated and determined men, and that is encouraging.

In return, Palahniuk wants us to inform General Deniken that he and his men are now helping in the White cause, no doubt to help convince Deniken that a Tsarist Russia could always count on the loyalty of an independent Ukraine. I readily agreed but know that the general is not one given to change his mind on such basic issues as Ukrainian independence. It is the Breadbasket of Europe and too vital to the welfare of all the Russias not to be bound to the Russian state. However, the breadbasket has large holes in it, and to mend those holes, we require the goodwill of the people. Ukrainians might be satisfied with something less than complete independence, a looser relationship with Russia. God willing, I will meet with General Deniken after the battle. I am certain I shall be able to influence him on this issue, especially since I know something of vital importance that will definitely change his mind.

I inspected the men Palahniuk brought with him and interviewed each one. They are remarkably similar to their leader. Perhaps they are all from the same town. Afterward, in my tent, Palahniuk startled me by asking why I employ Zhidy whores in my command.

"Do you mean Aishna?" I asked.

He laughed. "Her actual name is Rachel."

According to Palahniuk, she is not Persian, as she led me to believe, but from a shtetl near Kiev. That is perhaps how she knew of the village where we found sanctuary.

"What about the Orthodox cross around her neck?" I said.

He spat. "Once a Zhidy, always a Zhidy."

I was shocked initially but then merely amused. "Aishna is a trusted and valued member of my command. She does what is expected of her and a great deal more."

"Watch your back, my friend. She is treacherous and dangerous."

"And how do you know these things?"

Palahniuk smiled, presumably at my naivete. "She is well-known in this part of Ukraine, and notorious."

"Do you have a personal grudge against her?"

He looked away.

"I do not care about your history with her," I told him. "After we defeat Sabantsevski, you may come to me to adjudicate your dispute. Until then, you are comrades-in-arms. Understood?"

Palahniuk nodded, saluted and left.

Almost immediately, Aishna flew in to denounce "all the lies Palahniuk has told you about me."

"What he told me is not of the slightest interest," I said soothingly, repeating what I had told Palahniuk about being comrades-in-arms. "That goes for you, too, Aishna."

With a sigh, she agreed, adding, "A woman without mystery might as well be dead."

"You have mystery in abundance," I told her. But my curiosity has been piqued, and when the time is right, I will relish hearing both of them tell their stories. Is she Heghine Khachaturian, or Rachel, or someone else? Armenian, Georgian, Persian or Ukrainian, Zhidy or Orthodox? I tend to think what she has told me is mostly true. But I quickly put such speculation aside. We have a battle to win.

Tuesday 6 May 1919 / 1400 hrs. [2:00 pm]

I have divided my force into three—a major gamble. But I have no choice. Palahniuk's force will head north and ford the river some ten kilometers [6.2 mi.] north of Chernobyl. Jack's force will cross the bridge two kilometers south of Chernobyl, where Nicholai promised us safe passage. My force will ford the river ten kilometers south of that.

Once on the west bank, we will reconnoiter the lands for troop strength and possible traps, then rendezvous at an abandoned estate not far from my father's. There we shall prepare for battle on the morrow.

Tuesday, 6 May 1919 / 2030 hrs. [8:30 pm]

We have rejoined forces at our meeting place. Jack reported that his contingent was attacked as they crossed the bridge. But the attackers were only rough brigands who were easily defeated with no loss of life to his troops. I am mystified by the presence of robbers in a land so barren of anything of value to steal. I despair for the desperate state of my homeland.

Shortly I will confer with my commanders—Jack, Palahniuk, Shav, Vlad, plus Aishna—about our strategy and tactics for the coming battle.

This is our situation at present. I chose this estate as my headquarters because it belonged to Count Respain, the bastard who seduced my beloved Evgania. I take some satisfaction from having found him hanging from a tree by his mansion. A sign around his neck identified him as a "capitalist bloodsucker and exploiter of the proletariat." I felt no need to bury his worthless remains. Since I could not otherwise avenge Evgania, I ordered him cut down, doused in gasoline and burned. May he rot eternally in Hell.

Evgania would have made a most splendid wife for me, despite what Katiya told me. I regret that I did not fight for her and rescue her from my aunt's prison. I would not have cared that she was not a pure woman when we married. For such was not her choice. I should have done all these things. Yet I did not do enough and feel a profound sense of sadness and shame. In those days, one simply could not oppose the Church.

Katarin has been an exemplary wife and mother. Even so, there is a part of her soul that she keeps locked away from me—not from malice but simply because we are different. In turn, there is a part of me she can never understand. I may lust after other women or remember fondly old loves, but no one will ever replace my darling wife. Katarin is my wife and my home. Where she is, my heart resides. She is far above all other women, and our bond is strong and unbreakable, even in Death, should it come to that. I pray that she and Marianne have continued to find safe refuge from this storm. I also beseech my God to watch over and protect my son, Vitali, as he does battle against the infidel.

All is ready. I have done all that I can humanly do. The success of our mission now rests in the hands of Almighty God. May He grant us victory on the morrow.

Tuesday, 6 May 1919 / 2200 hrs. [10:00 pm]

I am unable to sleep, although I need to be rested for the battle to come. My mind keeps returning to my conversation with Comrade Nicholai. I was reminded that I delighted in Sabantscvski's exile, thinking I would never see him again. Yet God, in His wisdom, has brought the two of us to this place for a final encounter. I had always felt that, unlike Mr. Herman Melville's Captain Ahab and his Moby Dick, I had control over my obsession about Sabantsevski. But in truth, Sabantsevski is my great white whale, and I never shall be rid of my obsession until one of us is dead. My feeling of control was only an illusion. We have been as isolated from our normal world on this mission as Ahab's Pequod was from port.

For all I know, Sabantsevski may feel obsessive about me, for I think I represent all that he was denied by the caprice of being born a Roman [Catholic] in an Orthodox State. We are complete opposites, fated to face one another in mortal combat from the time of our first meeting. It is the conflict created by these opposites that drives God's plan for us. Since the Fall at Eden, our natural state has been one of conflict and struggle, not peace. Peace is merely a brief interlude where we may happily dwell, a respite in our eternal struggle with the world. I hope we shall find a more lasting peace in the hereafter. This struggle, this restlessness, is as much a part of us as our breathing and as vital. Men such as Sabantsevski or Lenin obsess that a different, improved world is possible, but they are either deceiving themselves or those around them. The world is the way God created it, and there is no changing the basic nature of man. At least, not for long. Thus on the morrow, Sabantsevski and I will play out our roles in the eternal unfolding of life.

I now commit myself anew to the God I betrayed and seek His pardon for my acts. I am recommitted to upholding my heritage and my faith for those who come after me, just as my Cossack ancestors did for me.

PART THIRTEEN

Wednesday, 7 May 1919 / 1600 hrs. [4:00 pm]

I am in my father's house, which has been thoroughly ransacked by our tenants and Sabantsevski's troops. I am finding it hard to write, but I must record all the events of this climactic day. Sitting in the bed where I was born, wounded but determined to survive. May God give me strength.

At dawn, there was a light ground fog. The night had been quiet, although I had kept three patrols in staggered shifts all night to alert us to a last-minute attack. After a final prayer, we broke camp. Comrade Nicholai met us on the road to present a surprising proposal from his commander: the battle would not be a clash of our two armies but rather an old-fashioned saber duel, with seconds, between Sabantscvski and myself. That took me aback. Of course, a duel would keep my troops out of a close-fought battle, but if I won, would the Reds honor my victory? I did not trust them. His troops might mount a surprise attack. If it were a legitimate duel, I might lose. Sabantsevski might still be the better swordsman. But this fight was so very personal I could not think of a better solution. I accepted the challenge, and we rode with Nicholai to my father's estate.

After he rejoined the Reds, I told my senior staff that if Sabantsevski gained final advantage over me, they should shoot him immediately, also, if possible, Commissar Koba. If they were surprised, they did not show it. I think they know no honor is due to the dishonorable bolshevkii. I asked Aishna to be my second. That surprised Jack, who would be the natural choice, but she is the better swordsman. No bowing to rank or seniority at this point.

At 800 hrs. [8:00 am] we rode out from the ranks. My uniform was as crisp and polished as possible at the end of a campaign, and Aishna was at her most formidable in her Legion regalia of black pantaloons and a white blouse emblazoned with the fearsome black widow spider, her silhouette flattened by her leather combat binder. Sabantsevski, equally polished, rode toward us with his second, the Muzhik thief.

"Koba," I whispered to Aishna. "He is no swordsman. Kill that devil if I do not."

"My pleasure," she answered.

The duel began with the traditional courtesies. Sabantsevski addressed me by my patronym, and I responded in kind. He indulged in his usual gallantry toward Aishna, asking to be introduced to her, bowing, complimenting her on her brilliant garb. Aishna, for her part, acted the coquette, smiling, tilting her head, offering some flattery about his reputation.

Koba broke in, saying, "You'll soon meet revolutionary justice, Madame Khachaturian. You killed Fyodor, my best pupil."

It chilled me that this thug knew her name.

Aishna gave a scoffing laugh. "You'll both meet justice very soon," she said. "Galina was my aunt. Did you know that, commander?"

"No, Madame, I did not, but we are in a war. Let us spare many lives today by simply fighting each other. Mikhail, now we fight the duel we should have fought many years ago."

There followed a short discussion about terms. Sabantsevski wanted the vanquished army to return to their base. I could not accept that. The Reds would simply have to return to Kiev, but our band would have to travel much farther, facing all manner of risks. My counter-proposal was that the vanquished should leave Ukraine for the remainder of the conflict. He refused, saying that only People's

Commissar Trotski could make such an important decision, and he assumed the same was true for General Deniken. I had to agree. We sat there, at a stalemate, feeling the morning chill.

"You have come to kill me, and I have come to kill you. Let that be enough. Our armies will then withdraw from the field," Sabantsevski finally said.

We returned to our troops to inform them of the terms. But of course, I told my senior staff, plus Palahniuk, the same thing I had said earlier. If Sabantsevski prevails, they should attack the Reds without hesitation. Each of my men saluted, but Palahniuk, the dog, did not. But there was no time to deal with that bastard. All the more reason for me to prevail.

I dismounted, removed my tunic and walked back on the field with Aishna. We met Sabantsevki and Koba in the center, after which Aishna and Koba, as our seconds, turned and walked back the customary twenty-five paces. I had a moment to compare my saber to my opponent's. Mine is a straight sword called the 1913 Patton saber, good for thrusting and stabbing. His was the more conventional curved blade saber that could sever an arm or a leg. Perhaps I had the advantage.

"A word before we begin," Sabantsevski said. "I hear that you call me the "Red Napoleon." But do you really know what I stand for? I have been recruiting loyal followers, and within a few weeks should have a hundred thousand. Then I shall kill Comrade Koba and march on Moscow to overthrow Lenin's regime—they are all intellectuals and fools. I will end this idiotic war and unite all the Russians and punish the Germans."

"Have you not had enough war?" I asked in disbelief.

"We are soldiers. War is what we do. We have many wrongs to right. You and I are more alike than different, Markov. Actually, I would like you to join me as my second-in-command."

"Are you insane, man?" I said. "We are about to fight a duel to the death."

I began to circle him, my sword drawn. He, too, withdrew his sword, and as we began to thrust and probe for weakness, I said, "We have been following your trail of destruction and seen your cruelty over and over. We have many wrongs to avenge."

I attacked him, making full use of my speed. He parried back, and I thrust again. I lost track of time, my entire focus on his saber. I remember little except the continuous clash and ring of steel on steel. My eye was caught by a bright splash of blood on my chemise, but I felt nothing. He was bleeding too. Fatigue began to set in, but my efforts only intensified. Yet the attacks were slowing down. I had to keep going. I could not fail—the entire fate of Ukraine lay in my hand. If I could only kill Sabantsevski now, the Reds and the bolshevikii would fail in Ukraine for lack of a leader who was his equal.

I attacked one more time and landed a rising stab into his ribs, which caught him totally by surprise. My next thrust to his left thigh sent him to the ground. "Goodbye, Nicholai Janovich," I said as I raised my sabre and plunged it into his heart.

Turning to meet Commissar Koba, I was astonished when he took my hand and shook it.

"Thank you," he said.

"Good God, why?" I said, struggling to remain upright.

"You've created an important martyr. This guy is worth more dead than alive. You've helped me carry out my plan. You killed him before I could. I know he was planning to kill me and overthrow the Bolsheviks. But I would've liked to have you out of the way. But I don't want to make you a martyr."

Koba withdrew a pistol and shot me in the left shoulder. I fell to the ground. As he walked away, Aishna drew her pistol and aimed at his back. Her pistol jammed. She swore. Grisha and Shav picked me up and carried me off the field. I finally heard a gunshot. She must have wounded Koba.

"Your wound is not serious, Colonel. We'll have you back on your horse in no time," Grisha said.

Within minutes I was back on Elan. The Reds had taken Sabantsevski's body back to their lines, but they were not withdrawing from the field. Suddenly they issued a loud cheer and charged toward our troops with a rumble of hooves that shook the very ground. We responded by charging at full gallop. The two sides fell upon each other, fighting with sabers, rifles, pistols and bayonets. Aishna, committed to protecting me, successfully fought off several attacks. I saw blood spreading on her blouse, but she refused to leave the field for treatment.

The Red Army fought with super-human courage, with no apparent fear of death. I again charged with Aishna beside me, rallying the troops. Vlad took a nasty sabre slash to his right shoulder and fell from his horse. As he tried to rise, he was trampled in the melee. That rider fell and was trampled by another rider who was shot through the head. A severe blow to lose Vlad, a close comrade and my good right arm. Peace be upon his soul. He died an honorable soldier's death after an exemplary career. I am sure he is now in paradise and barking orders.

We began to gain ground, but the Reds rallied and pushed us back. We pushed them back. The battle was concentrated on the middle twenty meters of the field. The wounded continued to fight, many simply falling off their horses in death. No one left the field. I have never witnessed such commitment in battle, and I was lost in pride for my troops.

Commissar Koba remained in the background, as seemed to be his wont, protected by a dozen women under a banner that said, "Ukrainian Revolutionary Free Women's Brigade," carrying long rifles and bayonets. I could not see Evgania. Perhaps she had chosen not to witness the deaths of her friends and lovers.

Miraculous that anyone was still alive. Aishna was surrounded, fighting desperately. Captain Irvin and some of his troops came to her aid, and I saw them arguing. Obviously, he was trying to persuade her to leave the field; no doubt she was swearing back.

I turned to face Comrade Nicholai with his raised sabre. Too weak from loss of blood to fight, I fired my Mauser machine pistol and riddled him with bullets. Not very sporting, but a matter of necessity. I drove my saber into his heart for good measure. I was avenged, for Evgania.

At this, I heard a whistle from the Red side, probably Koba. The Reds began an orderly retreat. With the death of Nicholai, the Reds were without a commander. I ordered our troops to stand down. A shout arose. We would not pursue. We were in no condition for more fighting, and we might be riding into an ambush of Red Reserves. We had won.

But before our remaining troops could celebrate, we were attacked by Palahniuk's Nationalist troops, shouting such nonsense as "Death to our oppressors, death to the Zhidy-lovers who will not pursue the defeated Reds." As the troops struggled against each other, Aishna rode against Palahniuk and engaged him in single combat with maniacal intensity. When he fell to the ground, presumably dead, the Nationalists retreated.

But they had done their damage. No more than ten of our forces were standing as Grisha set to work.

Suddenly Charbonnet arrived with five La Morte men, apologizing for missing the battle but gratified to hear of the deaths of Sabantsevski and Nicholai—not to mention Palahniuk. "You have greatly reduced my workload," he said wryly. He and his men rode off in pursuit of the Reds, vowing to kill Koba.

Curiously, I take no pleasure in Sabantsevski's death even though it settles all the old scores. He was a brilliant commander and swordsman but a flawed man. Koba will never reveal Sabantsevski's plan to overthrow Lenin because his dead commander is now a legend, a martyr who will draw thousands to his cause. Had he lived,

Sabantsevski—the Red Napoleon—would have become the supreme warlord and killed millions. That was my belief, and that is why I took on this mission. Now I wonder who will try to take his place. There will be someone, as surely as the sun rises every morning.

I praise God for our victory, but I have no command left. I lost Vlad and Shav today—my right and left arms—and many a good trooper. Can we even continue? Our position has been compromised. The Reds will attack again with even greater numbers. I have assigned all able-bodied to bury only our dead and prepare to leave this place. Our only hope of survival is to evade the Reds and the cheka.

I have been wounded enough over the years to know how I should be feeling. Right now, I do not feel right. It is as if all my wounds over the years are weakening me. I have called for Kapolski. I never give a volume of this journal a title until it is finished. I am naming this Volume IX, Search For The Red Napoleon, for it is now almost complete.

1900 hrs. [7:00 pm]

Kapolski reported in. He and his scouts had been out scouting for the reserve forces I was certain Sabantsevski had hidden, as I would have done in his place. He found only a few small groups of Reds who were probably scouting us. I gave him a sealed letter for General Deniken in Tsaritsyn. He is now the ranking squadron trooper, as I am certain both Jack and Aishna will soon leave us. I thanked him for his valuable contributions to this campaign and directed him and his men to join the burial detail.

I have also spoken with both Jack and Aishna. Jack has several wounds but did not complain. "I shall soon die a soldier's death," I told him. "Do not mourn." I charged him with finding Katarin and Marianne to deliver a letter and escort them to Mayr Lucine's agency. He readily agreed. We said our goodbyes.

Aishna swept aside any formality and knelt by my bed. I tried to express my gratitude for her bravery and loyalty. Although I wanted to hear the story of her relationship with Palahniuk—I am curious to the last—she refused to say more than that he was a pig who detested strong, independent women. He had told me nothing but lies. Weeping, she said she would make speed to join Mayr in Tbilisi to keep Georgia, Armenia and Eastern Ukraine free from the Reds. I wished her good fortune. With a last kiss, she left, handing me a sealed letter, which I shall read in a few minutes.

Vive La Grande Victoire! C'EST FINI!

[Long Live The Great Victory! This Is Done!]

PART FOURTEEN
EPILOGUE

Captain J. C. Irvin

Thursday, 8 May 1919 / 1200 hrs. [Noon]

Colonel Markov died yesterday afternoon, sitting up in his own bed, pen in hand and journal open. He sat so tall and straight, I didn't know he was dead when I first entered his bedroom. Only when I asked him a question that he didn't answer did I realize he wasn't just sleeping. The last thing he had written—in shaky writing—was praise of our final victory. What a good thing that on his last day he killed two Red commanders and possibly wounded a commissar—a triumphant end for a great leader. But I will miss the colonel tremendously. He anchored me back into reality.

I will take this journal to his wife and daughter and add a few words of my own.

Before breaking camp, we buried the colonel in Saint Vladimir's Cemetery, his family's resting place. The rest of our troops we buried in the adjacent retainers' cemetery. We left the Bolshies and nationalists to the buzzards. Aishna and I spoke with each of the ten surviving troopers. We watched them ride off with Prime Scout Sergeant Kapolski leading. The sergeant's orders were to deliver the colonel's report to General Deniken's last known location at Rostov-on-Don. Medical Officer Grigori (the colonel's dear friend Grisha) brought up the rear, with four moderately wounded in his wagon. The terminally wounded had been given mercy bullets. I felt quite heavyhearted as they disappeared. My journey has been incredible, and it won't be even partially complete until I safely deliver the colonel's ladies to wherever they wish.

Aishna and I stood there for some time, looking awkwardly at each other. Finally, she said she needed to find Madame Daria and asked me to join her. We found Madame Daria's cottage in ruins. She was dead—sitting cross-legged on the floor—with no sign of struggle. A handwritten note on a table nearby said,

> With the murder of my sponsors, friends and clients, my time here is complete, and I shall soon flee my body and be free. My remains will decay and return to where they were before. I have a prodigious successor, my granddaughter, Mademoiselle Daria in Beirut. Please consult with her at 22 Street Zaki Allani.

We were stunned, but not sad. Like the colonel, Daria had left this world on her own terms. Somehow Aishna and I don't want to part just yet. I'm headed for Sevastopol, and Aishna has asked if she can ride there with me. After I changed back into my Australian horse guard's uniform, we began our long journey to Sevastopol. From there, I'll catch a boat to Constantinople to find Ekaterina and Marianne. Aishna is going to the port of Batumi, Georgia, to rejoin the Legion.

Friday, 9 May 1919 / 1000 hrs. [10:00am]

The main reason I agreed to take Aishna with me is that I had found a revealing letter she had written to the colonel. It was tucked in the back fold of this journal, unopened. He had not yet read it. It was in French, and this is my translation.

Commander, should I die in the upcoming battle for the soul of Ukraine, I want you to know the rest of my personal history. A dead woman requires no mystery.

I was born on 7 March 1896 in a mountain village in the Republic of Armenia (not terrible Western Armenia), about one hundred kilometers [60 mi.] from the Azerbaijan border. Our Christian Persian settlement had existed for over two thousand years. We are also descendants of Queen Thalestris, "the last Queen of the Amazons."

My father was a vigorous man who dealt in precious jewels and often traveled on business to the capital, Yerevan, and as far as the Balkans, Ukraine and Persia. He was called Davit, meaning "eager and dynamic," which he certainly was. My mother, Nazeli, "pretty girl," truly loved him, even though theirs had been the traditional arranged marriage. But then they had grown up together. I was the fifth of nine children she bore him over twenty years. I grew up wearing pretty, well-made hand-me-downs from my three elder sisters. We lived better than most in our village.

In 1909, I was thirteen. After first blood, I had an arranged marriage, as was customary. My husband, who was only fifteen, was an employee of my father, but the first time I saw him was on my wedding day. I disliked Boghos at first sight. His name meant "small, humble," but although he was small, he was not humble. Marriage ended my lessons at the local church school. Our marriage night was more like rape than lovemaking. He tried to beat me into obedience. I just hit him back, laughing, telling him he was weak and that my father never beat my mother.

I was quickly pregnant. Even so, he would come to me in the night and drunkenly molest me. I fought off his clumsy attempts. After a difficult pregnancy, I had a daughter he named Arbaha.

I spent as much time as I could with my aunt Galina, who was only eight years older than me—more big sister than aunt. She had publicly rejected the husband her family had chosen for her, and for this, they expelled her. She came to our village to ask my father for protection. He graciously gave her a small house. She was a skilled baker, which is how she made her living. Her house always smelled heavenly. I loved being with Galina. She taught me how to deal with Boghos with a curved knife, which I used on him the next time he tried to beat me. After that, he left me alone.

Everything changed on 7 July 1910. Before that, Boghos had been my biggest problem. But that day, a far greater problem arose. It was a scorching day, and I took Arbaha swimming in the mountain pool about a kilometer away—my secret place where no one could find us. No one but Galina, who was supposed to join us after she finished a batch of bread. But she never came, and I grew concerned. We returned to the village—and I was horrified that Tariq Aziz and his troops had captured it. One of those murderous savages tried to take Arbaha, but I whipped out my knife and sliced his neck. He bled to death. Tariq Aziz might have killed me on the spot, but he only laughed. No one came near me after that.

The villagers fought with all their strength but were outnumbered about three to one. My grandparents were slaughtered, along with the other elders. All the men under forty, including the worthless Boghos and all five of my brothers, were lined up and marched away, presumably to be sold into slavery. My mother, Galina and all the other women were confined in a single house.

Tariq, the beast, took the girls under thirteen, including two of my sisters, and gave them to his men to do whatever they wanted—marry, rape, even kill. Girls of the most desirable ages—fourteen to eighteen—were lined up and examined. He chose six of us for his "harem." I was not pretty like Galina, but I believe Tariq chose me because of how I cut that fool with my knife. Otherwise, I certainly would have joined the other homely girls who were sent away. I never found out where.

The six of us were kept under guard and "interviewed" privately by Tariq, one by one, each night. The first two girls refused his advances. He raped and killed them. I was number three. I wanted to live. I reasoned that Tariq couldn't be worse than Borghos, so I let him do what he wanted. The next morning, he decreed that I would join his harem in Baku. I pretended to be grateful and planned my escape.

That night, while he was occupied with girl four and his men were busy with their girls, I escaped. With only Arbaha and two loaves of Galina's bread, I raced to my swimming place and hid in the cave there.

About a week later, my father miraculously appeared, saying, "I figured you and Arbaha would be here when I couldn't find you among the dead." He did not ask how I had survived.

I had no idea he knew about my secret hideout, but he told me how he and my dear mother had come here before their marriage to swim. "Now we are safe," he told me. "Tariq and his men have left, taking our women with him."

The next day we boarded the train to Tbilisi with what we could carry in our cardboard valises. Father brought all his jewels. In Tbilisi, we went to the house of his old friend, Mayr Baroness Lucine, who took us in and provided a nursery for my daughter. She was also caring for a number of other children. My sole aim was vengeance for my family and friends. Father had his own mission: to find my mother. Then he left, and his parting gift to me was ten beautifully cut diamonds. I never saw him or my mother again.

I became an apprentice agent in Mayr's information-gathering operation, La Revanche. She had founded this secret organization in the spring of 1910, believing war to be inevitable, and it began with about fifty women. My work was a good return for the nursery. For a while, I was terrified that I might be pregnant by Tariq. I would kill myself rather than bear the shame of a Turk baby. But when I confided my fears to Mayr, she said she would take care of a pregnancy—she couldn't afford to lose me. I didn't know what she meant at the time, knowing nothing about abortion, but her words comforted me. The day my menstrual blood finally came was the happiest of my life, up to that point.

Mayr launched a search for the women Tariq had taken from our village. Our agent in Baku told her that survivors were most likely sold to brothels in Baku, Tbilisi, Odessa or Kiev. She decided to take me and two other girls to scour the best brothels. Our cover was that Mayr was a madam, and we were three of her "girls" recruiting other girls, the best to be had, for an anonymous rich man. We would inspect the girls in private and also gather interesting information about people and places to use for what Mayr called "persuasion."

In spring 1911, the four of us left for Kiev. At the first stop, La Maison Blanche, we found not only Galina but twenty-two of the abductees. They had been bought at the Baku Slave Market by a British syndicate of prominent industrialists whose mission was to save European women from exploitation by heathens. It was rumored that Queen Victoria had originally financed the group some forty years earlier. This was the best possible fate for these unfortunate women, who, because they had been raped, could never marry. They might have been bought as a lot by a sultan for his harem, in which case they would never be found. But La Maison Blanche was well known to a small, select group of Russian gentlemen. There they would have an elite clientele and the possibility of becoming financially secure in later life.

Galina told me that within a year, she was the favorite of several rich men. She enjoyed the elegant atmosphere of the Maison and soon realized that she was quite good at being a courtesan. After a life of hard work, she enjoyed the leisure and luxury. One day Sabantsevski appeared. Unlike her other gentlemen, who always treated her like a lady even though she wasn't one, he insulted her and treated her with unforgivable roughness. She told me about the incident in painful detail, how she ran out, semi-naked, screaming, "I don't ever want to see this beast again." Sabantsevski followed her, cursing. "I'll come back and kill you, you bitch!" His fellow officers came out to restrain him and tell him that his behavior was casting a bad light on the regiment. Two of them removed him, took him forcefully from the premises and warned him that he was now in jeopardy of being expelled from the regiment. In the meantime, Galina, fearing for her life, contacted me. After I heard her story, I remembered the perfect place of refuge, the last place Sabantsevski would ever look for her—Ste. Olga's Nunnery. I took her there the next day.

Mayr and I used two of my diamonds to buy the contracts of the other abductees from my village. They became agents in Mayr's organization.

We now focused our attention on full-time information gathering, intensifying our efforts after war began. We were in Tbilisi in 1915 when the Turks began their horrific slaughter of the Armenians. In response to this, fearless Mayr formed a new organization: the Legion of the Black Widow's Revenge on the Turk. The female spider is twice the size of the male, and after intercourse, she devours him. Our battle flags and uniform blouses with images of the black widow—her eight spindly legs and blazing red marking—struck fear into the superstitious infidels we fought. This was also when I changed my name from Heghine Khachaturian to Aishna, my *nom de guerre*. Initiation into the Legion was harrowing, almost unendurable. Even so, our ranks grew from one hundred to almost a thousand—a thousand independent women of all races from all over the Christian and Jewish world. My full title became Sister Aisha the Persian Assassin and Mistress of Interrogation.

What we went through to officially join the Legion will explain a lot about the kind of fighter I became. First, I had to kill ten infidels. Six of us were ready for initiation, which meant getting the spider tattoo. We had to strip naked and pin up our hair. We climbed into a tall wooden vat filled with thick white foamy liquid and stand there, without making a sound, for a full hour. This horrid liquid was to remove all our body hair, and it burned like fire. All we could do was grasp the hands next to us to avoid crying out.

As soon as we recovered from that pain, the three-day process of getting the spider tattoo began. We had to stay silent for this, too—it's part of how we learned to resist torture. I was amazed at how many women passed these gruesome tests that showed their commitment to the Legion. Once a woman becomes a Legionnaire, it is for life. I was now a black widow.

Next came advanced weapons and strategy training. I learned the arrow, lance, knife, scimitar and pistol. You know the rest. Except one key point. In a raid on an agha's castle, we liberated 103 mostly Armenian and Georgian women from his harem. These women joined us and solved the problem that most of us did not speak nor understand Turkish. They were also warriors seeking to avenge their captivity and so fought savagely.

I knew some good men too, Colonel Markov. I even had a covert affair with one of our male instructors, Hovan, "gift of God." Was he ever! By that time, I knew how to avoid pregnancy. We used his knotted-end lamb intestine for protection. We loved each other. He even asked me to marry him, but I refused because I loved my freedom even more than I loved him. Even so, we continued our affair. He taught me how to smoke and roll my own cigarette, along with many other useful tricks.

I kept my affair with Hovan going until he was killed in 1917. I deeply mourned him for a year with a white armband over my black Legion blouse. His death inspired me to fight the Turks much harder, as, in my mind, each one was Hovan's killer. They all died horribly, and when their blood splattered my armband, I wore it with even more pride. I loved being a Legionnaire. This was the happiest time in my life until I pursued the devils Tariq and Sabantsevski with you and your squadron.

I am a warrior. I live in the moment, knowing the dangers of my profession. I can never be an ordinary woman. Because of my flat nose, I was never beautiful like Galina. Being an ugly outsider has shaped my life, especially how I deal with men. I learned from experience that, at some point, they would leave me. So I left them before they could leave me. I would never marry again, and I became wholly self-contained.

Commander, I cannot begin to thank you enough for what you have done by punishing Tariq and Sabantsevski and, above all, for accepting me as a warrior under your command.

Bless you,

Sister Aishna, the Persian Assassin and Mistress of Interrogation

Friday, 16 May 1919, Morning

I have been riding with Aishna for a week now, and it has been awkward knowing her secrets as I do. She was mostly silent, as if she had a lot on her mind, until last night. We had just finished our meager meal, sitting together by the campfire. Suddenly she stood up and pulled her pantaloons down to reveal her spider tattoo. I have no words to describe how frightening that black widow tattoo with its tentacle-like legs and angry red marking looked in the firelight. Before I could recover from my shock, she removed her blouse to reveal the scars and wounds across her breasts and torso.

"You are the only man who ever beat me in a fight," she said, "the only man who ever rescued me. I want to have another child, and you are the only man who could be her father."

Then she undressed me and ran her fingers along my scars. She kissed me passionately. That kiss led to another, and another.

Thursday, 5 June 1919, 1030 hrs., Sevastopol, Crimea

Aishna and I made love many times on our journey to Sevastopol. It took us a month due to the many detours we had to take to avoid battles. We were also attacked by brigands several times, requiring us to kill several men.

This country was a wasteland, and finding shelter was difficult. We rationed the food we had carried away from the mansion, supplementing it whenever we could, as when we happened upon an orchard that was still intact and stocked up on ripe apples. The poor people we encountered were mostly kind—our uniforms were so tattered they couldn't tell which side we were fighting for. But sometimes, they recognized Aishna as a Legionnaire and, out of respect, gave her and her companion such help as they could.

In Sevastopol, we got the first news we had had in a month. Newspapers reported that General Deniken's counter-offensive had begun against Kiev, and it appeared he would go on to Moscow. We said goodbye at the port. Looking regal in her black shirt and pantaloons, Aishna declared her love for me. I blush to write it, but she said she could not help herself because I was so handsome. Before I could respond that I love her more than I have ever loved any woman, she went on to say that she loved Mayr more, even though she was now carrying my child. This came like a blow to me.

"Marry me," I said, taking her by the shoulders.

"No, Jack. Where I am going, you can never go," she said. "But my daughter will be beautiful, as beautiful as jasmine."

She pulled away, and—knowing what I did about her vow of independence—I was not surprised. Even if she did marry me, she would have to be free, unbound by convention. I knew she would leave me, sooner or later.

I sold my horse for a decent price and am now on a ship to Constantinople. I need to get there as soon as possible. Greek forces landed in Smyrna almost three weeks ago to protect the large Greek and Armenian populations there. However, they'll be tempted to move on to Constantinople and try to retake it from the Turks, a goal they've had since 1453. I must get the ladies out before that happens.

Tuesday, 10 June 1919, 1400 [2:00 pm], Constantinople

It was amazing to arrive in the city the Russian imperial troops had tried to capture for four years without success. My first task was to report to my embassy to recover my back pay. I am officially dead, so it was a struggle! In the end, it was my fingerprints that proved who I was.

My war service is now over since I had enlisted only for the duration of the war. I believed then that the war would be brief, and I could soon return to my sheep station. But here it is—four years later, and there is still more to do. So, I am a civilian, and I've bought some civilian clothes. I'm keeping my pistol, though. I may have to fend off an angry Turk or two.

When I went to meet Countess Ekaterina and Marianne, however, I wore my Guardsman uniform. (I decided the risk of meeting that angry Turk on the street was offset by making a better impression on the ladies.) A few Turks gave me dirty looks on the way, but nothing serious happened.

The ladies were not at the address I was given, and it took some investigating to find the new one. The house was part of a block-long row of colorful wooden Turkish houses protected by a tall stone wall. Each house had its own massive entrance door, and the knocker on the countess's was tarnished as if to disguise her status. I lifted it, and it banged, shattering the quiet of this rundown street. Someone opened the creaking door, and I saw a maid with black eyes and jet-black hair wearing a red uniform with black trim.

"I'm Captain Jack Irvin. I served with Colonel Markov," I said in Turkish, which I took to be her native language. "I'm here to see the countess and her daughter.

To my surprise, she led me through an exquisite courtyard with a bubbling fountain and palm fronds into a light and airy room. The countess, who was large with child, greeted me in French and introduced her daughter, Marianne. They were wearing black mourning gowns with white armbands. Both are very handsome women with golden hair, but they represent different generations. The countess is the epitome of femininity with her flowing hair, falling just below her shoulders, discreet makeup and a gown with décolletage partially disguised by gauzy white lace. Marianne is a copy of her mother but with her hair cut short and her high-necked gown without frills. Yet, with their secret language and signals, they act more like sisters than mother and daughter.

I produced the colonel's letter of introduction, but Ekaterina waved it away. "He spoke of you often in his letters," she said. "We feel as though we already know you."

The countess invited me for "luncheon," as she called it. The meal was the best I'd had in months. I tried not to eat too fast or too much, as Ekaterina and Marianne asked me about what life was like in Australia. And they updated me on the whereabouts of the princess and the ladies of the squadron. They were headed for Nice, on the French Riviera, which was the princess's ultimate destination. Our journey to Beirut to join Mayr and Revanche wouldn't be easy, I said, looking at the countess, who had to sit back from the table to accommodate her swollen belly.

"I don't need any special treatment," she said with a smile. I smiled back with a nod. I could tell that beneath their gentle manners, both she and Marianne were tough.

"Call me Katarin," she said over coffee, and from then on, we were all on a first-name basis. It was time to get down to business.

"What do you know about the colonel's mission?" I asked.

Marianne said they knew only the bare outlines of the campaign from short reports in Kiev newspapers. Two weeks earlier, they had learned of a major battle between Red and Nationalist armies at a deserted estate near Chernobyl. A few days later, it was revealed that a White force had been involved, and since all their dead were properly buried on the estate, they must have won. The next day, they learned that Lieutenant Colonel Mikhail Antonovich Markov, the White commander, had been buried in his ancestral family plot. The leaders of the other armies remained a mystery. Officials from the three armies were still not talking. That was all.

"What do you know?" Marianne asked me.

I debated whether I should hand over the colonel's private journal, with all its secrets, to these innocent women. Katarin seemed to read my mind, for she told me then that both she and Marianne were members of Mayr Lucine's organization, La Revanche. Besides, her husband had told her about the mission as far as Kiev—and about the Persian Assassin, Aishna. And she had told her daughter.

"Where is Aishna?" Katarin asked. "We were hoping she would come with you."

I was truly shocked. These women were far more than they appeared to be.

"Were you in the Legion?" I asked Katarin.

"No. During the war, raising Marianne and keeping our household going were more important. Besides, the Legion was a young woman's fight. But I'll always be loyal to Mayr. I've known her since we were girls, and I was one of the first to join La ReM when Mayr started it in 1910. My job was to gather intelligence in Ukraine and St. Petersburg. We saw a war with Germany coming. If Russia lost, and we thought she well might, it would be a disaster for Ukraine. The Turk devils would invade. Germany would help them. When Mikhail was assigned to Tbilisi, I became the liaison between La ReM and the Legion. I supplied intelligence, weapons, money and whatever else was needed."

Katarin shocked me again by revealing that Marianne was also intimately involved in Mayr's operations.

"She received her first training in St. Petersburg. I discovered that a pretty twelve-year-old could go anywhere. No one suspected her of anything. She was virtually invisible."

Marianne went to a Swiss school until the age of sixteen. At that point, she announced her intention to join the Legion. Her training took one year, after which she joined the campaigns of 1917 and 1918.

"I don't think the colonel knew about Marianne's secret life," I said.

"The Legion is a secret from *all* men, even a father," Marianne said. "Father would have disapproved."

"Did you tell your fiancé, Leonid?" I couldn't help asking.

"I told him I had fought for the Legion. I would have told him the rest on our wedding night."

Marianne's spider would certainly be a surprise for Leonid. There was no question at this point that the colonel's family should have his journal.

Katarin decided to read it aloud. After instructing Urthu, the Turkish maid, that we were not to be disturbed, she led us to a charming garden behind the house. Over the next few hours, she read the entries in her low, sweet voice. It impressed me that neither she nor Marianne even blushed at the sensational events. She stopped after the colonel's final entry, saying that my additions were private.

Katarin and Marianne were quiet for a time, clearly moved by the events leading up to the colonel's valiant end. They recounted their memories of L'Affaire Sandikoff and the princess that the colonel had not recorded. Then they had questions, many questions, especially about Aishna, who seemed to be as fascinating to these women as to me. They both knew a lot about the Persian Assassin, especially her less-than-sterling reputation with men.

Katarin expressed relief that her husband had resisted the temptation of sleeping with Aishna. But what about Mayr Lucine? Had she seduced him in Kiev? I couldn't tell her, as that was before I had joined the squadron as an officer, and the colonel had been unusually quiet about his meeting with her. Katarin gave a little laugh at that, saying that Mayr's job, in a sense, was seducing men, and occasionally women.

"Mayr seldom, if ever, sleeps with her husband. And they call him 'Jacques the Rogue' because he has so many women. Theirs is more a partnership than a marriage.

"Anyway," Katarin said with a quick change of subject, "I'm so pleased to know that Mikhail Antonovich died in his own bed and was buried in his family plot."

It was late afternoon by now. Katarin invited me not only to have dinner with them but also to spend the night. I promptly checked out of my hotel. Urthu was dispatched to buy our tickets for Beirut.

After dinner, Marianne left the house for a meeting, and Katarin and I settled into her salon with a bottle of fine French champagne. We sat near a fire, and I hoped to get some questions answered in that warm, intimate room. For instance, why had Marianne gone out alone? That seemed highly risky in this Turkish city, where Turkish women were never allowed to leave home without an escort. It was true, Katarin said, that a Christian woman out by herself was deemed to be a prostitute and fair game for rape. On the rare occasions when she went out at night with Marianne, a White Russian officer who was also a friend escorted them. When Marianne went out alone, however, that was a different proposition. She was a combat veteran, and underneath her modest cloak was her deadly curved spider knife. She would be quite safe. Nevertheless, Katarin and her daughter would be relieved to be out of this Turkish city and in Beirut with Mayr.

I wanted to know how she came to marry the colonel. She told me that she and the colonel came from north of Kiev, a vast area formerly known as the Circle. It was owned by six aristocratic families and—this is surely unique—was divided into six pieces, like wedges of pie. Closest to the center of each wedge was a family mansion, then as you moved outward, there were houses for retainers, then fields, and on the periphery, housing for the Muzhiks. In the very center of the circle were the community buildings—a church, a school, and several common buildings dating back to the fifteenth century.

The holdings in the Circle were kept together by an ironclad tradition: intermarriage among the families. So Katarin knew she was going to marry someone from the Circle; she just didn't know whom.

Her education, first at the estate school, then at the Ladies College in Kiev, was focused on molding her into a capable wife and administrator of a large household. A central principle was "always obey your husband." She graduated at eighteen. Lieutenant Mikhail Markov proposed to her at the graduation ball, having already received the consent of her father. They were married three weeks later in a gala ceremony at the estate church.

I asked Katarin whether she knew about Mikhail's love for Evgania, his childhood sweetheart. She considered this, finally saying everyone loved Evgania, one way or another. Katarin was two years younger than Mikhail and Evgania, and Evgania was the undisputed leader of the girls of their generation. Katarin had been allowed to join Evgania's crowd, which is where she first met Constanza (Mayr). Evgania would take the group to Mayr's cottage, where her mother, Mme Daria, taught them secrets about astrology and the zodiac, the meaning of dreams, even marital love. The cottage had a secret pool, hidden under a tent, where they could swim freely. Mme Daria also had a boys' group, but Katarin never learned what they were taught. Sometimes Mme Daria let the two groups mix to play and explore the countryside, freedom they would otherwise never know.

"It broke my heart that the magnificent Evgania became a nun— and then was taken away. But I'm glad she survived, even though she is a commissar," she said. She had a hard life from the beginning, Katarin went on to say. She was the daughter of a Count Vladimir and his wife, the Countess Ilsa. Ilsa was a plain woman whom Vladimir, a younger man, had married only for her title. She used to brag about "the beautiful daughter she had created," not seeming to realize that Evgania looked like her husband, not her. Ilsa was jealous of her daughter, though, so jealous that she hired Count Raspain to rape Evgania so that she would be hidden away in a nunnery. Vladimir, learning of her plot, vowed revenge. He forced his wife to swallow poison. He went after Count Respain and shot him in a "hunting accident." Respain didn't die, but he lost his right leg from the knee down. When Vladimir tried to liberate Evgania from the nunnery by offering Abbess Katiya a million roubles, she said no sum would be sufficient to interfere with God's work.

So Vladimir married his Armenian mistress, Hova ("breeze of wind"), and they had a second family. In 1914 he rejoined his regiment. He was killed soon thereafter, in August, when the Germans almost annihilated the entire Second Russian Army at Tannenberg [East Prussia]. The Muzhiks at the Circle had risen up in 1917, and Hova moved away with her children just before the rebels' pillage, rape and slaughter turned the Circle into a ruin.

Katarin cried as she told the story of Evgania and her cruel mother.

"Those of us who grew up with Evgania still remember her in our prayers. I hope we can meet her again. Of course Mikhail loved her, Jack. And I'm not jealous."

By this time, Katarin was sobbing, and—I blush to write it—I was holding her in my arms. With her face pressed against my chest, she opened her heart to me.

"I loved my husband deeply, even when he occasionally strayed. As for Evgania and Mayr, had I not learned about marital love from Mme Daria and our group, I would have gone into our marriage knowing nothing, perhaps dooming us from the start. On my wedding night, the reality was even better than I expected. Mikhail was gentle and creative. He was a strong, vital man to whom I joyfully surrendered as often as he wished. Our love had a strong base, and I believe his spirit lives on in this house."

Katarin's revelation was one of the most beautiful sentiments of love I've ever heard. We were both a little impaired by champagne, but I helped her upstairs to her chamber. Marianne was already there in their large bed. She rose and took over the task of getting Katarin to bed. Before I could leave, though, Marianne took my arm and told me to stay a moment. Once Katarin was undressed and under the silk coverlet, Marianne faced me squarely.

"You should know my *nom de guerre*. You may have heard of me. It's Deimos Arbah Wahid."

"My God," I said. "Indeed, I have." Deimos (Greek goddess of terror and dread) was the leader of the first platoon in the fifth company of the mighty Legion.

"So you know I'm for real," she said, stepping back and raising her white nightgown. What I saw on her hairless flesh was the black and red Black Widow tattoo. Even on this beautiful girl, it looked horrific.

I left hastily, shocked at her brazenness. But now I realize that in this world, where certain special women have been empowered by the Legion to fight great evil instead of simply suffering as its victims, that awful tattoo is a source of great pride. Marianne wasn't trying to be seductive, as I believe Aishna was when she bared her tattoo to both the colonel and me. Marianne was showing me she would be a powerful comrade. I believe Aishna did succeed in seducing the colonel—not that it matters anymore.

What I learned tonight from Katarin and Marianne has raised even more questions in my mind. What else did the colonel leave out of his journal? Aishna is still a mystery to me, and I need to meet this Mayr Lucine. I'm not sure I trust her.

12 June 1919, 1415, Sea of Marmara

Yesterday we boarded a French-flagged ship to Beirut, which should protect us from the warring Greek and Turkish Navies. I was extremely glad to get the ladies safely out of Constantinople, where, despite their denials, they were in danger. Our passage is five days if there are no incidents. We have passed through the Bosporus and the Sea of Marmara without trouble so far. The food and service are first-class, as are our two staterooms. There are no organized activities, but my two joyful ladies are full of amusing ideas. Most of the passengers are military or government, and our tablemates are wonderful company. Tomorrow we cross through the Dardanelles into the Aegean Sea. We will pass by the Gallipoli Peninsula. I'm uncertain whether I can bear to see it again.

13 June 1919, 1800 hrs. [6:00 pm], Cape Helles

Today we passed through the Dardanelles. It took all my strength and discipline to travel past Gallipoli, the scene of a battle so devastating to my country, without breaking down in front of my charges. They accompanied me onto the deck to pay our respects to my countrymen and the New Zealanders who lost their lives there. I wore my ANZAC uniform. Katarin and Marianne wore their finest dresses and the elegant hats the Colonel had seized from Sandikoff's warehouse.

The mountainous terrain seemed virtually unchanged. As the peak we called Hill 709 came into view, I stiffened. That's where my men and I were captured. Katarin and Marianne must have understood because they pressed against me on either side, and I felt their arms around me. Then I realized that we were not alone—the deck was packed with passengers and crew, paying silent homage. This is a day I'll never forget.

We cleared Cape Helles a moment ago and are now in the Aegean Sea. Time to put memories aside: this is a war zone.

14 June 1919, 1800 hrs. [6:00 pm], the Mediterranean

A Greek frigate had been shadowing us all day. Just before we left Greek territorial waters, we were boarded. Everyone had to line up with passports for inspection and questioning. Katarin, Marianne and I were all right, but several other passengers were removed, along with their luggage. None of them protested, as I certainly would have done had it been us. I believe this submissiveness is a result of the war. Most of the best men were killed off in the first year.

16 June 1919, 1800 hrs. [6:00 pm], Beirut

Beirut is nothing like I expected. I thought it would be devastated by the war, the famine, and occupation by the Ottomans and now the Allies. But it seems sane and largely peaceful. Katarin had the address of Baroness Mayr Lucine's agency, which we found in a nondescript building on Street Sheikh bin Said.

Mayr received us graciously. I had fulfilled my mission and was prepared to go, but Mayr held me back. She wanted to involve me in the Legion's work. The colonel had agreed to train the Legion for combat against the Reds. Would I do so in his place? She tried to entice me by promising a reunion with Aishna.

That night Mayr tried to seduce me. She is notorious for her adventurousness in bed, and I was seriously tempted. But I turned her down as diplomatically as I could. Why work with her to earn a reunion with Aishna? Aishna and I have no future. More importantly, I have had enough of Russia's wars—or anyone else's.

Yet Mayr Lucine did reward me for my efforts with an impressive diamond, which was probably courtesy of Aishna. She also said I could remain at her house for as long as I wish after she and the colonel's ladies depart for Tbilisi, Georgia.

The first thing I did was have my ANZAC uniform properly cleaned and repaired. For several days, I walked the streets of Beirut, just exploring the city and trading war stories with friendly soldiers and sailors. What to do next? Go back to Australia, join the British Army or just get far away from the madness? But to where? Perhaps stay in this peaceful place? That's tempting because there is talk from Versailles of a French Mandate over Syria and Lebanon. That would bring prosperity back to the city.

One day I remembered Mme Daria's note about her granddaughter in Beirut, Mademoiselle Daria. Perhaps if I talked my situation over with her, she would help me decide what to do. I found her at the address in Mme Daria's note, another colorful wooden house in a quiet, pleasant street. When I entered her room, I was struck by how much she looked like the colonel's description of Constanza, her mother—down to the intricate tattoo atop her left breast. She also seemed to know a great deal about me. I could tell that she had learned her mother's skills of divination and prophecy, and I began to visit her regularly as a client.

One afternoon she casually mentioned that she wished to have a daughter, and if I would oblige her, she would not charge me for our sessions. She was a beautiful and fascinating woman, so of course, I gladly obliged her for several days. I wonder if, in due time, there will be a new Amazon girl in the world.

23 June 1919, 1700 hrs. [5:00 pm]

I was right to go to the enchanting Daria, as she led me to an idea I had not even considered. Today, as she suggested, I began my voyage to the New World. I am bound for Marseilles and then to Southampton, England, to catch a ship.

14 July 1919, 1700 hrs. [5:00 pm]

Today I began my ocean voyage to New York City. From there, I'll go to Canada to "Return to the Empire." One thing still bothers me. The colonel had told me that he had specific intelligence that would change General Deniken's decision on Ukraine's status and that he would brief me further after the battle. I asked Grigori about this, and he knew nothing. He had probably told Aishna, but she claimed ignorance. I had been through his papers and effects at the Constantinople house and found nothing. I had also asked Katarin and Marianne but again, nothing. I fear the information died with him.

Wednesday, 21 July 1919, New York City

On board the RMS *Aquitania*, one of my tablemates was a Canadian nurse, a major in the York Rangers about my age. After a whirlwind courtship, I am now married to Grace Margaret Brownridge, and we are heading to Toronto to begin our life together. Real peace at last. Just as Mlle Daria foretold, my odyssey is now finished. But I'll never forget any of the persons mentioned in these pages whom I knew. I especially wish Aishna, Mayr Lucine, Katarin, Marianne and the various White Armies in all theaters the very best in their crusade against the Bolsheviks, which they must win. The alternative is too horrible to contemplate. No matter what happens, though, my family and I will always celebrate the anniversary of the colonel's great victory over the Red Army on May 7, 1919. It will never be forgotten.

PART FIFTEEN

Grace Margaret "Margie" Irvin

My father has given me this journal and with it, the responsibility of bringing this important story up to date.

My name is Margie Irvin, and I am nineteen years old. I was born and raised in Weston, Ontario, the only child of Jack and Grace Irvin. Weston is a small village near Toronto, where my father founded Irvin Lumber, the largest lumber company in Ontario.

After two years at the Ontario College of Art, I won a full scholarship to study design at the Paris Atelier of the New York School of Fine and Applied Art.

Monday, August 14, 1939, on board the SS *Normandie*

I am on my way to Paris! I left home on the seventh for New York City, and three days ago, we set sail. I am in first class and very comfortable. Everyone speaks English, but I'm eager to practice my French after four years of study. Not that I've been unhappy in Weston, but I'm thrilled at this chance to leave my hometown far behind. And of course, my friends. The crowd—six of us—have been close since kindergarten, but we're drifting apart. Two are married and one is pregnant. As I just turned nineteen, I'm much too young to think about marriage. This piece of good fortune is my chance for adventure—for *Liberation!*

The day before I left home, Father took me to our bank, Weston Trust, to get something from his safety deposit box. It wasn't jewelry or savings bonds, as I expected, but a dark blue leather-bound journal. The box also had some photographs in it. He left those in the box, but not before I saw one of an exotic-looking woman with very compelling eyes. I'll never forget that face. Father also bought a generous supply of traveler's checks for my journey.

I must be very careful with those checks. I'm on my own now for the first time in my life. Father also drummed into me that I have to be very careful with the journal. And I'm supposed to record all the people and places I see. Of course, I'll do anything my dear father asks.

Mother seems to understand better what my going to Paris is all about. Oh, I'm supposed to get the best training in the world—no matter what those New York art schools claim—but Paris is where I'll really become a woman. I've always been a good daughter, not only of my parents but of Weston as well—modest in dress, thought, and deportment—but Mother always gave me some latitude. When I turned sixteen, I was allowed lipstick and a bit of rouge. At eighteen, smoking and drinking in moderation. That's also when I bobbed my blonde hair. But everyone knows that French women are the most beautiful, polished and sophisticated women in the world—*soignée* is the word—and that's what I want to be. I want to be a fine artist, but even more, I want to be a desirable woman.

Mother surprised me—no, shocked me—when she presented me with an intimate protection device for the "inevitable romantic rendezvous in Paris." She is a nurse, but still, she's my mother! I felt very grown-up when she confided that during the Great War, she'd had such a rendezvous in Paris herself.

But back to the journal, which Father seems to think is central to my time in Paris. (He even loaned me his steamer trunk, which he had custom-made in Beirut with a special compartment for the journal.) I had time to read only about half of it before leaving. At first, I was disappointed. I thought I was finally going to learn about what my father did in the Great War. He would never talk about it. But he didn't even write it. It was by a Colonel Markov, a White Russian on a quest for some villain called the Red Napoleon. But I was soon intrigued by Colonel Markov and his lovely romantic family and his troops. And by the time I read about Aishna, I was hooked. What an incredible person! I had no idea such women existed anywhere. Could I ever be that strong and free?

I love being on board this ship. I feel drunk with the incredible sea air, champagne for breakfast and so many new people. I take frequent walks on the deck, and I study the women, whose style is so different from Weston. We have dances every night! I've even flirted with a handsome doctor from Munich, Herr Doktor Ludwig Franke. Last night we danced almost until dawn, fueled by champagne and kisses. Could this become the perfect shipboard romance I've always dreamed about? I'm meeting him for cocktails tonight.

Yesterday I sat in a steamer chair and read the journal all the way through father's entries. Frankly, I was shocked. How much do I really know about my dear parents, I wonder. I wonder, too, how many of those White Russians could still be alive after their ultimate defeat by the Bolsheviks and the passage of twenty years. Just how am I supposed to contact La ReM? Does it even still exist? If it does, they're likely not even in Paris but far away in some exotic locale. I'd love to know who that bold woman in the photograph was—I didn't have the nerve to ask Father about her. I'll bet she was either Aishna or Mayr.

Soon we will reach Le Havre, where I board a train for Paris.

Tuesday, August 29, 1939, Paris, France

I am staying on the famous Left Bank at the Pension St. Gabriele. It's on rue Dante, near the Seine and the Cathedral of Notre Dame. I've spent a week exploring and having lots of fun with other international students at the pension. One thing bothers me, though. I've noticed men in brown suits following us from time to time. I have no idea who they are or what, if anything, they want.

Yesterday I received a letter with a crest on the envelope. I almost tossed it away because I had been warned about impoverished Russian nobility (real or fake) here in Paris looking for a handout. They would certainly be asking the wrong girl. But I was curious, so I opened it. I was surprised to see that it was from Countess Ekaterina Markov and her daughter, Marianne—an invitation to a dinner party that very evening. Of course, I called to accept.

Dressed in my best frock and wearing a wonderful perfume my mother had given me as a parting gift, Chanel's *Bois des Isles*, I walked to the address on the Rue Saint-Germain, a grand old street only a few blocks from my *pension*. I took the lift, which looked like a big elegant birdcage, up to the third floor, called the second floor here. I was met at the door by a maid dressed in a black uniform with red trim. The room was stunning—a salon with a high ceiling, tall windows, and white walls with gold *boiserie*. It was crowded with beautifully dressed women, and they were all *soignée*.

An attractive blonde in a bright red gown with a low neckline came over and hugged me, saying, in French, "You then are the daughter of Jacque, Margee, yes? Good, I am Katarin." She kissed my cheeks three times, in the French way, then turned to everyone assembled, "This young lady is Margee Irvin, the daughter of Jacque." She told me that after my father had contacted her, she traveled here from their southern headquarters in the former Constantinople, now the Turkish Istanbul.

"We maintain an agency here because this is where most of our donors are," she said.

I gave Katarin an envelope with Father's cash donation. She thanked me profusely and gave me a warm hug. Then she introduced me to her daughter, Marianne, who looks a great deal like her, and drifted away toward other guests. Marianne, now in her late thirties and wearing a high-necked silver gown, introduced herself as "Deimos" and welcomed me to her home, saying, "My, but you are a pretty one, with such a divine scent." She, too, kissed my cheeks three times and asked me to thank Father for his kindness in accompanying her and her mother from Constantinople to Beirut, mentioning how considerate he was of her mother's pregnant condition. She told me that a healthy son, Alexei, was born several months later in Beirut.

"We will see you often in Paris, my dear," she said. "Let me get you something to drink. And may I offer you a cigarette? Please mingle. Everyone wants to meet you."

I lit up one of my beloved John Player's and began to pass among the beautiful guests. A tall blonde woman of middle age in a modest dark green gown with long sleeves introduced herself as the Princess Alexandra.

"I remember reading about you in Colonel Markov's diary," I said.

"I had the honor of evacuating his wife and daughter from Odessa to Constantinople in my yacht, also the ladies of the squadron. What a beautiful vessel that was! You know, the real purpose for that voyage was to smuggle artworks and other valuables out of Odessa to France. But during our voyage, Katarin and I talked often about La ReM. You know of La ReM, the intelligence operation that combined La Revanche and La Morte?"

I nodded.

"So after delivering my cargo to Monte Carlo, I secured weapons and other material from Marseilles and transported them to Mayr's headquarters in Beirut. I became La ReM's 'fixer,' and after Katarin became vice-commander of Revanche, I succeeded her as chief supplier. I have so many black-market contacts, after all. I'm still the chief supplier in Istanbul.

"We must talk further, Margie. Let's have breakfast with Katarin tomorrow morning. Come here at eight. There is a marvelous café near St. Sulpice that you will love."

Next, I met the Baroness Mayr Lucine. She is a tall, fair woman who wore an emerald gown with décolletage that revealed the intricate Amazon tattoo atop her left breast. Her red hair was pinned up in an elaborate style. As she gave me the customary three kisses, she called me "daughter." I responded by calling her "Mayr." She had come to meet me from her office in Bucharest, Romania, and told me she was their liaison to the Abwehr, the non-Nazi branch of the German Military Intelligence. Her contact is Herr Doktor Franke, known as der Löwe (lion), who had been protecting me on the ship.

"Why do I need protection?" I asked in surprise.

"You will learn," she said. "We have much to teach you."

I nodded and asked after Tomaz, her son with Colonel Markov.

"He is now a bodyguard in our organization for VIPs. As for my mother, Madame Daria, she died peacefully in 1919. My daughter, also named Daria, has been carrying on her work in Beirut. And she has a daughter. There is strong evidence that your father is her father as well."

"Yes, I read about that."

Father seems to have been very busy during this time. And I wonder how many half-sisters and brothers I actually have.

Then Mayr Lucine said, "Permit me to share Madame Daria's favorite axiom with you. 'Should random fate discover something for you, hold it dear, for it shall become most valuable.'

"You are very pretty," she told me, and I blushed. And I blush again as I record this compliment, as I was brought up to look at people for deeper qualities than their appearance.

Katarin returned with champagne and cognac in coupe glasses (the kind that are called Marie Antoinettes). As we sipped, I asked about a red and black banner suspended from the high vaulted ceiling of the paneled salon.

"It was the banner of La ReM," Katarin said. "We are now called Le Groupe. Do you recall a 'Major Nubtelni' briefly mentioned in the account of the meeting with General Deniken?"

I did not. She told me that he was a very fine officer in the regiment. He and his troops caught the Regimental Colonel Kamaranski at the Odessa quai trying to board a French cruiser in order to escape by himself. Nubtelni shot him dead, ordering that the traitor be left where he fell in the water. Nubtelni then boarded the cruiser and arranged for the remaining ladies to have safe passage to France. The next day he took charge of the defense of the city. I was glad to know of the death of that villain Kamaranski, who had betrayed both my father and Colonel Markov.

"What happened to the wives of the enlisted men?" I asked.

"Those brave women refused to be evacuated because they always did the cooking and nursing for their husbands, even fighting alongside them unless they were out on patrol. In Odessa, they were always by their husbands' sides," Katarin said. "I would have fought alongside Mikhail, I assure you, but he would never allow me to. He said I was doing my part as a nurse. And he believed I was too important to him as a wife and mother to risk my life."

Next, I met another Alexandra, a small figure not quite five feet tall with a doll's face. A lithe figure in a royal blue gown, she introduced herself as "Petite Alexandra."

"Colonel Markov rescued me from the black marketeer Boris Samsonovich Sandikoff. I was a pitiful creature then, known as 'Madame Alexandra,' a girl completely under his control. To my great joy, I have been a Markov for almost twenty years. Katerina adopted me, and when we arrived in Constantinople, she took me to a clinic where I was cured of my opium habit. Then I joined Mayr's group even though I was just a girl. Boris had trained me as a cat burglar and safecracker, and I still perform these functions for Le Groupe. Since I am so small, I can get into spaces no one else can. That was true even when I was pregnant."

I was intrigued that Le Groupe had a cat burglar and safecracker.

The biggest surprise of the evening was to meet Aishna's daughter,

Jazmyn, who kissed me on the lips, not my cheeks. Her father, she informed me, was Jack Irvin—*my* father. Jazmyn is my half-sister! Imagine! She looks like the fabulous woman I had glimpsed in the photo in the safety deposit box, with jet-black hair. And her eyes are the deepest blue I have ever seen, just like Colonel Markov's description of Aishna's. But she also has my father's nose and mouth, as do I. I could only stare at her and shake my head and, finally, embrace her warmly.

"You're so. . . exotic," I said, tearing up a little, surprised by the beautifully intricate spider tattoo on her left breast—the mark of the Amazon.

Jazmyn took me to a corner of the *salon* where we sat together on a spindly little eighteenth-century sofa.

"I want to tell you about my mother," she said. "After Colonel Markov's duel with Sabantsevski, her mission was to kill Commissar Koba. You know, don't you, that Koba is now Stalin?

It took me a moment to take that in, but she went on.

"My mother went in disguise on a number of missions behind enemy lines to kill commissars and search for Koba, even though he had put a large bounty on her head. He wanted her brought to him alive. Sometimes I went with her. Mama once told me that shortly after I was born, she took me with her far behind enemy lines, posing as a poor woman nursing her infant. When I was eleven, I was with her on a mission to Kiev. We were disguised as Armenian peasants. Someone—damn him or her to Hell—betrayed Mama to the Chekists. She told me to slip away so I wouldn't be arrested too."

Jazmyn went on to recount her mother's terrible fate. I was overcome with awe that she could have witnessed such events and survived to tell me about them now.

After Aishna's arrest, Jazmyn stayed in one of Mayr's safehouses, hoping her mother would escape and come find her. But on the fourth day, the Soviet government issued a directive for everyone in the city to assemble at the platform off the former Theater Street at a certain hour. Her guardian at the safehouse took Jazmyn to Theater Street, where they found a terrible spectacle unfolding. The platform was surrounded by a cadre of Chekists, rifles aimed at the crowd. And on the platform was a woman hanging naked from the scaffolding by her wrists. She was suspended from a hook, like a side of beef. Her body had been horribly beaten and burned, but Jazmyn recognized her as Aishna. Her own mother.

A giant brute of a man, wearing a mask and a blood-soaked Chekist leather apron, was whipping her with a cat o' nine tails with razor tips. A banner above her said, "By Order of Stalin, Revolutionary Justice for Comrade Fyodor." Punishment—terrible punishment for her own slow execution of the aristocrat turned Bolshevik Vasili Vasilievich Antonov, "Comrade Fyodor." As the torture proceeded, Aishna trembled but, like a true Legionnaire, never cried out from the pain. In the crowd, Jazmyn and the others stood helpless as the brute cut a horizontal gash across Aishna's abdomen and pulled out her female organs—and a dead fetus. Aishna let out a long moan and died.

The soldiers dispersed the crowd then, and Jazmyn's last sight of her mother was her once-beautiful body hanging from the hook, her organs splattered on the platform. Just as Aishna had castrated Fyodor, the Chekists had neutered her. Jazmyn, sobbing uncontrollably, was taken back to Mayr's safehouse and evacuated a few days later. She was told later that her mother was left to rot on the platform.

"The Chekists are now called the NKVD and are renowned for their brutality," Jazmyn said. "A leopard does not change its spots. They remain Chekists."

Jazmyn's story so closely echoed the dream Colonel Markov had about Aishna's death that I was overcome. I burst into tears, just as I had when reading his journal. Jazmyn held me close, crying too. That is when we really bonded as sisters. "My desire for revenge against Stalin runs very deep. It is the most important thing in my life," she whispered in my ear.

I learned a lot last night about what happened after Colonel Markov's death. Mayr told me that her husband, Major Jacques Charbonnet, was also killed while attempting the assassination of Koba/Stalin. After that, La ReM ceased to exist. The Legion ended, too—its tactics had proven outdated against the Soviets. Mayr and Katarin formed Le Groupe to gather information, commit sabotage and carry out revenge. Le Groupe includes both men and women. Most of the women agents are alumnae of the Legion and/or La Revanche. Most of the men were formerly with La Morte. The latter keeps tabs on Father and our family to make certain they are safe from the various iterations of the Cheka, and that's how they knew of my existence. The Cheka will continue its war until all of Stalin's adversaries are dead.

"Our agents were shadowing you in New York City. Doctor Franke protected you until you arrived in Paris. Once here, our agents posed as students to keep watch over your comings and goings. They reported you were being surveilled by some of Stalin's men—so, our timely invitation."

So, those men in brown suits were sent by Stalin. I'll just call them the Brown Suits.

According to Mayr, the Brown Suits are a shadowy group. Supposedly they are Stalin's murder, kidnapping and sabotage unit, reporting directly to him. He personally chose them for assignment outside the Soviet Union. But once they leave Russia, they can never return because in Stalin's paranoid mind, they've been corrupted by being in the Capitalist West. If they're recalled, it's because they failed in a mission, and they will be executed. That is all Mayr knows. But it's a good guess that Paris is their European headquarters.

"Where are all the men of Le Groupe?" I asked. I had been hoping to meet an interesting man.

"Our men and some of our younger female agents are on assignment, protecting our other VIP's."

I learned that most of the White Russians on Colonel Markov's mission were later killed in the war or sent to the Gulag. Colonel Markov never knew that his son Vasili was killed during the successful White Army siege of Tsaritsyn in June 1919. Major Orlov, the Colonel's friend "Grisha," was killed by a bomb in a room he was setting up for a clinic after the victory at Tsaritsyn. This is the city we now know as Stalingrad [Volgograd] due to Stalin's supposed leadership in retaking the city in January 1920. Prime Scout Sergeant Rupok Kapolski died of wounds from a scouting ambush during the same siege. I deeply regret the deaths of these three courageous men. As Jazmyn told me, our father, Jack, is the sole remaining survivor, and he is in danger as long as Stalin lives.

Virtually all of Sabantsevski's men who survived that battle with the Whites have also been purged, killed or imprisoned in the Gulag. Stalin's main rival, Leon Trotsky, the war commissar at that time, is in exile in Mexico. This year, on the twentieth anniversary of the battle, Stalin began writing installments of his history of the Russian Civil War. He omits any mention of Sabantsevski or his second-in-command, Nicholai Subtelni. He represents Colonel Markov as a villain and the battle at Chernobyl as a victory for his own outnumbered troops.

"In Stalin's account," Jazmyn said with a sneer on her lovely face, "he tracked Markov down for a month after the battle and heroically killed him."

"Disgusting that Stalin could turn a key victory for the Whites into a personal triumph," I said. But Jazmyn assured me that Stalin could indeed change history by controlling information, a nightmare come true.

But there was more. All the buildings of the Circle—the family estates of the Markovs and the others near Chernobyl—were completely destroyed. The cemeteries were destroyed too. Stalin ordered a highway to be built over the cemeteries for the Markovs and their retainers.

"It's a beautiful four-lane paved road that is exactly one kilometer in length and doesn't connect with any other road," Jazmyn said. "No one except Stalin is allowed to drive on it. That is the law in Chernobyl, and there are serious penalties for violating it."

I needed a few glasses of champagne and a good smoke to rid my mind of such horrible manipulation of history. The destruction of the Circle—and that insane highway to nowhere—sheer madness.

Our dinner was wonderfully lavish—like nothing I've ever seen. It was my introduction to true French cuisine, but I will not describe it here. My job is to record what I learned about the men and women in the journal. Now I understand why my contribution is so important.

After dinner, over cognac, Mayr Lucine told me more about Le Group. "In 1932, we joined with the Abwehr to supply arms and food to those fighting Stalin in Ukraine. He was starving the Ukrainian peasants by confiscating all their crops and seeds to sell overseas for hard currency. The Ukrainians called it 'Holodomor', the Terror Famine. It finally ended in the fall of 1933 after millions of peasants starved to death. But our agents continued sabotaging Stalin's regime. Anything that makes the Soviets bleed a bit is a good thing."

As the soirée ended, Katarin told me, "Princess Alex and I are a couple of stateless widows still living and working in the Stamboul White Russian Compound—the same house you read about. We are enchanted to meet you, Margee. I was not sure what to expect. You have grown up in a quiet, peaceful village—just the right place for your mother and father, who suffered so much in the war. I did not know whether you would be a timid and conservative girl or a bold, rebellious one. You are not quite either, I think, but I also think you are wide open to experience. This time in Paris will help you discern who you are. We will see you often. Perhaps we can even persuade you to stay and join our organization. But that is too much for you to think about tonight. Everything is much too new," she added. I felt overwhelmed, confused, even a little frightened at what might lie ahead, and she must have read all that in my expression.

"It is late," she said. "You will stay here tonight."

I was exhausted and more than a little drunk with all the champagne and cognac. Jazmyn took me to the bedroom she shared with Deimos. I sank into sleep immediately, but I remember two things before that. When Deimos removed her gown and underthings, I saw her spider tattoo. The journal described the Legion tattoo and the painful process of getting it, but it didn't convey just how horrifying and terrible it looks on a female's tenderest and most vulnerable place. The other, more superficial thing is how dowdy I felt in my white cotton Toronto nightie. Both Deimos and Jazmyn had silk nighties of unimaginable delicacy and glamour. I need to go shopping for lingerie in Paris. I want something along those lines for my wedding night. I also have to get rid of my Toronto party frock. That little dress with the puff sleeves and floral print just won't do in Paris.

Wednesday, August 30, 1939

All is changed. All is off. My Parisian adventure is to end before it really starts. This morning at breakfast, I expected to get some good shopping tips from my new friends so that I could be well dressed for the beginning of school. Instead, Katarin told me that war is about to break out.

"This wasn't supposed to happen," she said. "The Soviets and Germans signed a non-aggression pact a week ago. You read about that?"

I nodded gravely, although I had been aboard the SS *Normandie* on the twenty-third and more concerned about the novel I was reading and the dance that night than the news. "But why does this mean war? I don't understand."

"Last night our agents discovered that Hitler is set to invade Poland. Because of the non-aggression pact, the Soviets can't intervene. But Britain and France must come to the aid of the Poles—they have a separate treaty. The war will begin in a few days while the weather is still mild. The Atelier will close. We know that Stalin's agents are determined to kidnap you in Paris. You cannot stay here, *ma chère*."

I was shattered. "But I want to stay."

"But your parents would never allow that, nor would we. The Brown Suits are determined to kidnap you and trade you for your father. He is the last surviving witness to the battle near Chernobyl. You will be much safer in New York. We have found out that American students at the Paris Atelier will be transferred to the New York campus of the school. Jazmyn will go with you. She has a talent for art, and we are assured that she will also be admitted. I have already secured passage for both of you on the *Ile de France*. It will leave in a few days. You will have a lovely time in New York—as interesting a city as Paris, in its way. Your parents will also have protection. This is the only way, *ma chère*."

I was too shocked to speak. I could only nod my thanks. My Paris adventure was soon to end, but an adventure in New York was soon to begin. As my breakfast with Mayr and Katarin ended, Deimos and Jazmyn awaited me for a day of sightseeing and shopping. But it was hardly an ordinary outing—they both let me know they were carrying a pistol in their chic Parisian bags. I will cram in as much of Paris as I can in the next few days.

Friday, September 3, 1939, the *Ile de France* in transit to New York

Despite everything, we had several wonderful days in Paris—the Louvre, the Orangerie, Samaritaine, some exquisite boutiques—and my bags are bursting with marvelous Parisian clothes. Selfish of me to note this pleasure when the Germans have invaded Poland. France and Britain, among others, declared war today. So another European war has begun, just twenty-one years after the Great War. How terrible—no, catastrophic!

But we had some personal drama as well amidst the fun.

Yesterday—only yesterday, we were sightseeing in Paris!—we had just left Les Invalides and the tomb of Napoleon Bonaparte when we were attacked by a Brown Suit. Even though there were other people nearby. Deimos was shot, but Jazmyn killed the assassin. Jazmyn used some communication device in her bag to call an ambulance, which soon appeared. With klaxon blaring, it took us to a small private hospital where Jazmyn knew the doctor and his nurse. They took charge of Deimos and soon assured us she would be all right. The bullet had just grazed her shoulder.

We took a taxi back to Deimos's apartment, where Katarin said we must leave Paris immediately as the police would soon trace us and come looking for answers. We hastily packed, and Katarin, Mayr and both Alexandras saw us off at the Gare Saint Lazare. About two and a half hours later, we were in a safe house in Le Havre. We left this morning for New York. Word is this may be the last ship to leave France now that war has been declared. Although there might be German submarines in the Atlantic, it's still jammed with passengers. Katarin managed to buy us tickets for a nice cabin in first class.

I love being with Jazmyn. It is incredible that she will be with me in New York. Being with her is the fun part of my adventure.

Wednesday, September 20, 1939, New York City

Jazmyn and I arrived safely in New York City on the ninth in no small part because our ship ran at night without any lights, while other ships that kept their lights on as usual were sunk. My parents greeted us at the pier and seemed to know almost everything that occurred in Paris, Katarina having called them to fill them in.

I wondered how my mother was going to react to Jazmyn. It was a momentous event for her to meet another daughter of her husband—I gather she had just found out about her. But again, my mother showed her worldliness and generosity by embracing Jazmyn and saying, "You are a beautiful, brave girl. Welcome to the family,

Miss Jazmyn Khachaturian." My father embraced her in turn, and what could have been an awkward situation turned into a sweet and memorable occasion.

That weekend the four of us stayed at the Plaza Hotel overlooking Central Park. We had adjoining rooms and ate several meals at the exquisite Palm Court. With Father and Jazmyn on the alert, we did some sightseeing, including visits to the Metropolitan Museum and the Frick Collection. On Monday morning, Jazmyn and I registered at the school in Greenwich Village to begin classes the next day. We dressed in black, of course—very Bohemian.

Jazmyn and I have a small apartment in the Village. We have become even closer and feel like full sisters now. The studio classes are demanding but enjoyable, and we're meeting so many new people. Because the boys find Jazmyn irresistible, I also get a good amount of attention. Some of the boys are very attractive, but I'm determined not to get serious with any art student. I have no intention of marrying an artist.

In any case, it's hardly the time for marriage. There are rumors that President Roosevelt will soon draft young men—the first time this has been done in peacetime and surely the first step in our getting into the war—so these boys probably won't be here long. I'll just play the field and do my best in class. Even though Jazmyn has more talent than I do. There, I've said it.

Wednesday, May 8, 1940, New York

We have been so taken up with classes and parties that I've virtually forgotten about this journal. But today, Jazmyn received a letter from Katarin in her beautiful cursive.

Today, we find ourselves in an uncertain situation as the new European war has resumed after the Phony War this fall following the invasion of Poland. The Germans invaded Scandinavia last month, and Mayr's Abwehr contacts have informed me that an invasion of western Europe is imminent. My question for you is: whom do we trust besides the Abwehr? Both the British and French failed to honor their treaty obligations to come to the aid of Poland when the Germans invaded. True, they are now helping the Norwegians to resist the Germans, but I believe this is simply too little too late. Had the British and French attacked Germany from the west by land and air last September, the Poles might have survived. The British and French cannot be trusted, in my view.

What then of Hitler? After conquering Poland, he gave Stalin the eastern part, where many of you were born or lived. Our enemy remains the Soviet Union, which is one and the same with Stalin. Other than that, we have little interest in the war. We will maintain operations against the Soviets at the same level as before the war.

Today Mayr has received fresh intelligence that Hitler's ultimate goal, after conquering the West, is to destroy the Soviets. This could be good or bad news for us, and we are working to obtain further confirmation.

MISSION

Today is the twenty-first anniversary of the day my husband, Mikhail Antonovich, killed Nicholai Janovich Sabantsevski, whom he believed to be the Red Napoleon. Had Mikhail failed, this would have been a crushing defeat and perhaps the end of our civil war in Ukraine. But Mikhail confided in me at the time that he had some doubts about the Red Napoleon's true identity, although his public statements never betrayed them. And he has been proven correct.

Mikhail once told me that when he was young, Mayr's mother, Madame Daria, warned him that no matter how smart or tough he thought he was, there was always someone, somewhere, who could best him. And that is what happened to Nicholai Sabantsevski. The man who bested him was a peasant with cruel Tatar blood in his veins. He was not nearly as educated as Nicholai but rather was clever, calculating and ruthless. Of course, I speak of Joseph Stalin. Since achieving power in 1928, he has murdered, purged, or as in Trotsky's case, exiled, most of the Leninist Bolsheviks, along with millions of his class enemies. Those who remain are under his absolute power. He is the god of the atheist Communist World.

To honor the sacrifices of the men in Mikhail's squadron, plus Aishna and Jacque, our new prime mission is to destroy the true Red Napoleon. Only then will their mission be complete. However, the uncertainty of the new war makes this more complicated. The Germans may kill him first. It is true Stalin is one of the best guarded men in the world—but also one of the most despised. We have attempted to kill him in the past but failed, so now we are using new tactics. This will not be easy or fast, but we are laying the groundwork. None of us will be safe until this is accomplished, and I can only guess what madness he creates until he is terminated.

At this point, I am not at liberty to reveal any further details. Many of you will be called up to the team when appropriate. After he is killed, all will be revealed to you. In the meantime, remember, this is a level 4 briefing, not to be shown to anyone without a very good reason to know. I count on your continued discretion. Thank you for all your hard work. We shall prevail!

— C. Katarin.

Monday, December 22, 1941, New York, New York

After graduation from what is now called the Parsons School of Art, Jazmyn and I opened a successful interior design store on Madison Avenue between 56th and 57th Streets. The back room here is used by Mayr's agents. I am now an American citizen, and Pearl Harbor has brought my adopted country into the war. New York is not yet blacked out, but rumors say it is only a matter of time. Anyway, all the Christmas lights help to dim the gloomy news. We are losing badly to the Japs. German soldiers still occupy Paris. They are also in Kiev and very close to Moscow. The Luftwaffe continues to bomb Britain.

After handing out Christmas bonuses to our assistants today, I announced that Jazmyn and I are going to volunteer for the Army Nursing Corps. I suggested they follow our example because we've already canceled the store's lease, effective January 2. Of course, neither of us mentioned that we are getting out of New York because last week Brown Suits actually tried to kidnap me on 5th Avenue when I was in a throng of Christmas shoppers. Fortunately, Jazmyn scared them off by showing her pistol, and no one was harmed. How stupid do you have to be to get into the Brown Suits if you do such a brazen act in public? I had hoped they had left since my adopted country is now an ally of the Soviets. But that alliance hasn't changed Stalin's determination to kill my father.

Tuesday, May 5, 1942, Washington, D.C.

On January 2, 1942, Jazmyn and I, swept up in the flood of patriotic revenge following the Japanese attack on Pearl Harbor, volunteered to be nurses. We trained in Virginia and were then assigned to Bolling

Field, near Washington, D.C. It was there in the Officer's Club that I met Captain Edward Mitchell. Even though he was older than I was, I was captivated by his Southern charm. We began seeing each other on a regular basis and fell in love. Ed proposed, and I wanted to accept, but I dreaded the possibility of being a young widow. I countered that we could be engaged until the end of the war. When orders came for Jazmyn and me to report to Hickam Field, Hawaii, as nurses, Ed presented me with a beautiful engagement ring. We have corresponded as best we can under the circumstances.

June 10, 1944, The Pacific Theater

I've been far too busy nursing the wounded to keep up with this journal, but now we're in a lull. So we get a chance to work on our tans in a fenced-off private beach area. I've taken time to write today because something has happened that changed my life in a big way.

Two years ago to the day, we arrived at Hickam Field, near Pearl Harbor. By September 1942, Jazmyn and I were caring for the troops wounded on Guadalcanal. Since we were in a combat zone, we were trained and authorized to carry .38 caliber pistols. We could have had the heavier .45 the men carried, but I, for one, found it too heavy to lug around. And was I grateful to have it the day on Tarawa when a Jap tried to rape me, probably kill me too, and I shot him dead. When seconds counted, I would have been dead with the .45.

In May 1944, Jazmyn and I were sent to a very hot island in the Mariana Island chain, far to the east of the Philippines. On the north end of the little island was an emergency landing strip built by the Japs and expanded by our Seabees. Our hospital on the south end was for the constant stream of wounded bomber air crews and fighter pilots whose aircraft were too shot up to make it back to their own bases. Some of the flyboys were quite handsome, and, as they recovered, they got pretty fresh with us. My prominent engagement ring didn't stop them from trying.

A few nights ago, at about 0230 hrs., Jazmyn woke me. In the semi-darkness, I could see she was wearing her bathing suit and swim cap.

She said, "I must leave you now. Deimos has come for me. I must train. I must be ready. Stalin will revert to his old ways when the war is over. France will soon be liberated. Then the liberation of Russia begins. I'll always adore you, Margie. Wish me luck as I swim out to Deimos's submarine."

Before I could even respond, Jazmyn kissed me and slipped out into the night. I felt completely alone. I no longer needed a body-guard—between Jazmyn and the U.S. Army, I had been trained very well in self-defense—but I wanted my sister. I cried for a long time.

The next day, our head nurse asked me the whereabouts of First Lieutenant Allysiah Khachaturian. (Jazmyn was her *nom de guerre* and I liked that better than her Christian name.) I replied that she had gone for a midnight swim to ward off the intense heat, and I assume she came back, changed, then went to the hospital while I was still asleep. They mounted a search for her body but called it off after a few days. For me, things returned to a semblance of normal. I recalled that "Allysiah" meant "distinguished" and "kind," and she had been all that and more. I know in my heart that I'll never see Jazmyn again.

Thursday, April 4, 1946, New York, New York

When the war ended in early September 1945, I was sent to Manila to take care of the many wounded in the military hospital. I finally began my trip home in December.

On January 2, 1946, I arrived by train in New York's Grand Central Station. Still in my captain's uniform, I walked a short distance to meet Eddie under the clock at the Biltmore Hotel, the traditional place for lovers' rendezvous. He hadn't told me he was a full-bird colonel, and I was so proud of him. He looked so handsome in his US-AAF uniform.

Over lunch in the Palm Court, he proposed again. This time I accepted with all my heart, and we spent the night in the hotel. He warmly approved of my Parisian nightgown, which I had purchased with him and this night in mind. And I will always wear Parisian lingerie. Never again those government undies that were part of my uniform.

The next day we had a civil wedding with just us. This was followed by a car-trip honeymoon south to meet his family and have a church wedding, then up to Weston for another one. I know my days of adventure and experiment are over, and I am now ready to be a housewife to my Eddie and, eventually, a mother.

Other momentous news I have to record is heartbreaking. Katarin wired me yesterday that Mayr Lucine was hanged, along with Doktor Franke, sometime in 1945. Only now have the bodies been identified. It is believed that they were trying to escape from the German SS, which had intensified its search for Abwehr agents.

Some time afterward, Deimos was shot again. But she survived. There were reports that her would-be assassin was another woman, but she was never found. Katarin also wrote that her younger son, Alexei, a lieutenant in the German 6th Army at Stalingrad, had been killed in early 1943. How ironic, she observed, that both her sons were killed twenty-four years apart in virtually the same place, although serving in different armies.

With the execution of Mayr, Katarin is now leading Le Groupe from her house in Istanbul through a highly complicated and unstable post-war European environment.

Now that I know more about the people in this journal, it has become too painful to read again. I'm very disturbed by my father having been put in the asylum, a terrible mistake. If I am blessed with children, I never want them to read this journal either, for obvious reasons. And that goes for my Eddie as well. But, if I'm completely honest, my desire to keep it private is really about all that might have been for me as a Parisienne had not the war started when it did. I may ultimately send the journal back to Father or throw it away.

I can never pay my debt to Le Groupe, which saved my life on several occasions both in Paris and New York. They remain an important part of my extended family—dear Jazmyn, Marianne and especially Katarin, with whom I've continued to correspond.

New York City is almost as exciting as Paris. This is where we'll stay and build a family. Mayr's son, Tomaz, has arrived to serve as our bodyguard. We feel very safe in our Upper East Side apartment building on 96th Street, which has full-time doormen. We live on the fourteenth floor, with Tomaz on the seventh. We contact him only when we go out. So far, it's working out well.

Friday, March 6, 1953, New York City

I've been receiving secure calls from Katarin, so I wasn't surprised to hear from her. But what she had to say was stunning.

"Stalin was killed yesterday. We believe the new regime has no interest in pursuing his enemies, but for now, we remain vigilant."

"Was Jazmyn involved?" I asked. "When she left me in 1944, she was determined to join Deimos and kill him."

"Precisely. In 1948, after extensive training and minor plastic surgery to alter her appearance, Jazmyn contacted Colonel Evgania, who has been in the Kremlin since 1937 as a close advisor to Stalin. But she came to hate Stalin for terminating Leninism, in which she firmly believed, and has been our agent since 1945.

"Jazmyn flew to Moscow on a forged French passport and visa. My adopted daughter, Petite Alexandra, created these, as well as documents for Jazmyn's new life as Evgania's half-sister Nare, which means 'Fire.' She created a whole history for her as Count Vladimir's proletarian daughter with his mistress Hova before he married her. After chemically aging the documents, Alexandra broke into the correct offices to place them in the right files. Amazing.

"As 'Nare,' Jazmyn began attending cocktail parties so she could seduce important men, along with some wives and mistresses. By

1952, she had reached Stalin's inner circle. His latest purge, carried out to prepare for war, enraged that inner circle, as they could foresee that they would eventually be purged as well. They decided to kill him first. Over pillow talk with a Monsieur M., Jazmyn revealed that she had access to a new taste and odor-free French poison that would kill Stalin slowly, in utter agony, over several days."

I asked if she knew the identity of "Monsieur M."

"No. Jazmyn uses only a letter to identify someone, even Stalin. Stalin is famous for challenging men to marathon drinking bouts. He did that during World War II with foreigners such as Winston Churchill. He continued to do it with his own inner circle at the Kremlin. Sometimes at Kuntsevo, his dacha just outside Moscow, he had women for entertainment of a sexual nature.

"Jazmyn filed a detailed report on what happened. She went to the dacha as one of those women. Unlike the others, she was not scantily clad but dressed in an elegant gown with low décolletage. She found Evgania sitting beside Stalin on a couch, as usual. Evgania introduced her to Stalin. Now in his mid-seventies, he was clearly drunk and stood unsteadily. Jazmyn was almost 23 centimeters [9 ins.] taller than he, her low décolletage almost level with his face.

'How can you be here?' he shouted. 'I had you killed long ago.'

'I believe you are mistaken, Comrade Stalin, because here I am. I am Nare, Evgania's half-sister.'

"Evgania rose and put her arm around her 'sister.' Jazmyn slipped the vial of poison from her little evening bag to Evgania, who deftly poured it into his vodka. Then Evgania managed to pull Stalin back onto the couch, offering him his poisoned vodka cup, which he quickly emptied.

"Acting the complete innocent, Jazmyn moved away. But Stalin was still suspicious of her and yelled, *'You are mine, you bitch. Report to my apartments in the Kremlin tomorrow night for dinner.'*

"Jazmyn knew that his invitation was for much more than dinner.

If the poison did not work and she did not report to the Kremlin, his secret police would easily find her. Even worse, Evgania would turn on her if the poison did not work, for Jazmyn would no longer have any value to them.

"But she needn't have been afraid. About an hour later, Stalin complained of a bad headache. Evgania took him back to his apartments in the Kremlin and helped get him into bed.

"The next day, Lavrenty Beria, head of the Chekist MVD, arrived at Stalin's Kremlin apartments to check on his condition. Knowing in general about the poison, he was determined to seize power when Stalin died. He wasn't the only one—others in the inner circle had similar ambitions. He told the guards to keep everyone out because the Boss was unwell and would summon them when he felt better. The guards knew very well that entering the Boss's apartments without a summons would result in exile to the Gulag. His autopsy showed he died of hemorrhagic stroke, which was the desired result of the poison.

"It's a triumph. Jazmyn has avenged her mother and has great credibility with the Kremlin's inner circle, especially if they want someone dead. She and Evgania are relaying very useful information back to us. You know, I often wonder what if Aishna's gun hadn't jammed after the Sabantsevski duel and she had actually killed Commissar Koba rather than just wounding him, what a different world we would be living in."

"Yes, I've thought about that too."

"So, with Stalin's death, the search to destroy the true Red Napoleon is over. *Vive notre grande victoire finale sur Napoléon Rouge. Au revoir.* [Long live our great victory over Red Napoleon. Goodbye.]"

I am very happy that my father is finally free of this nightmare, as are we. Time for life to return to normal, and I can again breathe when I go outside.

I first called my Eddie at his office. He said he was delighted that he could now turn in the Luger he had brought back from Europe.

And although the gun—an eight-round 9 mm pistol—wasn't illegal, the City of New York was putting so much pressure on him to turn it in that it was disrupting his business.

My second call was to my parents. They had heard from Katarin. My father had shocking news of his own. Last night a Brown Suit tried to break into their house on John Street, but my father shot and killed him. Thank God they are all right, but this was disturbing news.

I called Eddie back.

"So Katarin was mistaken. The Brown Suits are still operational," Eddie said. "I'm going to hold on to that Luger. And call Tomaz to escort you to pick our son up from nursery school.

I agreed, knowing that I remained our family's most likely target. No. Wrong. It's our son, whose nickname is Laddie. If the Brown Suits captured Laddie, my father would trade his own life for his grandson in a heartbeat.

I called Tomaz to escort me to the Brick Presbyterian Church, which was several blocks away at 91st and Park Avenue. But he didn't answer when I called. Reliable Frank the doorman said he hadn't seen Tomaz leave. Where was he? Was he on some mission connected with the death of Stalin? It wasn't like him to leave without notifying Eddie and me. I had no choice but to go by myself to fetch Laddie. I would have to take the Luger.

It had been snowing earlier, but by now, the sun was out. It was very cold. Thank goodness I had on the fur coat Eddie gave me after Laddie was born, excellent cover for the Luger. It was holstered close to my heart. The matching fur hat and sunglasses helped disguise my identity.

Nothing happened on my walk of several blocks to the church, and I began to relax. Laddie and the other children were just inside the lobby, as usual. The mothers and governesses usually stopped to chat, but because of the cold, today they dispersed quickly in all directions. Our usual group—my best friends Roz and Lucy, their children, and a few others close behind—walked north on Park. As we went, the others dropped off at their apartment buildings as Roz and Lucy and I continued chatting. At one point, Lucy asked me if something was wrong. No, not a thing, I said. What would Lucy have thought if she knew I was armed?

By the time we reached 93rd Street, I knew we were being followed. A man in a brown coat was about fifty feet behind us. I knew he was a Brown Suit in winter gear. I had to think fast. We were a gaggle of six women and children now. Roz and Lucy lived at 1192 Park Avenue, on the corner of 94th. I had to get them to 94th Street to see them safely inside. As we walked that last block to 94th, I calculated. Did I want the help of a doorman? Ordinarily I considered the doormen along the way a guarantee of security in this quiet upper East Side neighborhood, but this was far from an ordinary time. With doormen come residents and visitors. How could I be sure a doorman would be alone? Would a doorman be armed? Too many uncertainties—too many chances for other people to get hurt. My plan was to get the others, including Laddie, inside 1192. The entire block to 95th was the back side of the Armory—no doormen, no other people. This is where I would confront the Brown Suit.

"Who is that man, Margie?" Lucy said as we reached her door. She had spotted the Brown Shirt behind us.

"Look, Margie, more men up ahead," Roz said. "They look like they're waiting for us. This is not good."

"Alfred," Roz said to her doorman, "call the police!"

"Look, girls, they're after me," I said, withdrawing my Luger. "Long story. Take Laddie inside with you. I'll tell you everything at our next cocktail party."

What happened next was swift and completely unexpected. The Brown Suit caught up with me, then pushed me and my Luger aside. He continued running toward the four men on 95th Street. He pulled a machine pistol from his coat and shot all four.

The next thing I remember was this man standing on the sidewalk, calling my name. "Madame Mitchell," he said, "I am Sweeper. After the death of Marshal Stalin, I was ordered to liquidate all our agents in New York City. That is what I have been doing since early morning, and now I am finished. You and your son are safe. I now begin my journey back to Russia. Good day."

When I returned to the lobby of 1192, Roz and Lucy began asking questions. Another gunshot, even louder this time, prevented further conversation, and soon I learned that "Sweeper" was also dead, with half his head blown off. I wondered if the sniper was Tomaz or a Soviet agent finishing the purge.

Roz and Lucy pressed me and Laddie to come upstairs for a stiff drink and to wait for the police, or Eddie, to take us home. The police arrived first, sirens blaring, and Eddie arrived shortly thereafter. Then a delayed reaction set in—panic, tears—but I had to pull myself together to calm Laddie. He had a thousand questions—he doesn't miss much—and as I tried to answer them and keep him calm, I began to realize that the nightmare was really and truly over. Soon my friends began calling, but I kept them in suspense. If they wanted answers, it would cost them some good liquor at a party for Eddie and me.

In all the excitement, I forgot to mention that Katarin also gave me big news about Deimos. She married the French doctor who attended her in Paris after she was shot in that terrifying incident at Les Invalides. They have a boy and a girl. She is being trained to succeed Katarin when she retires. Most think that will be soon because Katarin is finally a happy grandmother, knowing the Markovs will endure.

June 15, 1952

Today is Jazmyn's birthday, and I'm thinking about her, wherever she is. But she is beginning to seem like a dream I had long ago.

All the events in this journal are beginning to seem like a dream—a nightmare, in places—and now I've waked up. One day I intend to burn it, but I can't bring myself to do it quite yet.

October 25, 1956

I was listening to the news about the Hungarian revolt against the Soviets that began two days ago and sewing—a Halloween costume for Norman—when the phone rang. It was Katarin in Istanbul. She told me that Jazmyn was in Budapest, working for Le Groupe supporting the rebels. I was not surprised.

"We believe the Hungarians are rebelling because Stalin is dead and has been discredited. They don't think Khrushchev will respond as viciously as Stalin would have."

She went on to reveal a secret. Closely guarded by Party members. On Feb. 25, 1956, Soviet leader Nikita Khrushchev denounced his predecessor, Joseph Stalin, at a meeting of the Twentieth Party Congress of the Communist Party of the Soviet Union. Since Stalin's death, there had been a campaign of de-Stalinization. Khrushchev's denunciation accelerated that campaign.

"Part of that campaign is to collect and burn every copy of Stalin's history of the Civil War. Since that megalomanic version was sold only to Party members, it was easy to collect. Now it is gone. I am also pleased that his ridiculous road over our cemetery has at least been connected to other roads. Sadly our cemetery is beyond repair and the headstones are lost. But you are now well and truly safe."

Katarin then revealed the answer to a question that had always puzzled me. Who shot the Sweeper that day in 1953? She told me it was Mayr's son, Tomaz.

"After he shot the Sweeper, he returned to us."

But before she could say more, Katarin burst out, "Oh my God, Margee. This just came over the wires. Jazmyn has been killed. Others too. It was an explosion near the train station in Budapest. I must go. I have much to do. God bless you and goodbye."

At some point, I put the phone down. That part of my life was finally over. And I do not know whether to laugh or cry.

Norm's Final Note

I was four in 1953, and the events with Sweeper were my first encounter with death. He and the others implanted such a picture in my mind that I can still see it—especially Sweeper's blood on the fresh white snow. But my mother and I never talked about it after that day. In 1977 my parents moved to Pawling, seventy miles north of the City. In 1985 I moved to Minneapolis. She died 13 December, 2007 (outliving my father by sixteen years). I had only a few days to go through her effects, plan her funeral and prepare her house for sale.

During this time of intense work, I began to hope for more information. Surely the shootings on Park Avenue in 1953 were part of something larger that someone must have recorded. And then, I found this journal. I was retrieving her jewelry box from its hiding place in the wall and was astounded to find the journal in a leather bag beneath it. Did she want me to find it, or did she just forget it was there? It wasn't until the flight back that I even had time to begin reading it.

I believe it was my mother's love of history that prevented her from destroying the journal. She rounds out Colonel Markov's story. Who would have thought his search for the Red Napoleon would culminate in a fashionable New York neighborhood so many years later? And because I found it through random fate, as Madame Daria would say, this is most valuable.

Norm Mitchell
17 September 2022
Golden Valley, Minnesota

ACKNOWLEDGMENTS

I would like to thank my lovely wife, Julie L'Enfant, who was my first manuscript editor and Ellie Silver, who was both my copy and final editor. I would also like to thank Julie Scheife, Mike Corrao and Ryan Scheife at Mayfly Design for the cover, my logo and the interior of the book. And finally, Nick and Nata at Oakheart Scriptorium.

* 9 7 9 8 2 1 8 1 3 6 8 1 9 *